On A S

This edition first published 2016 by Fahrenheit Press

www.Fahrenheit-Press.com

Copyright © Grant Nicol 2016

The right of Grant Nicol to be identified as the author of this work has been asserted by him in accordance with the Copyright, Designs and Patents Act 1988.

All rights reserved. No part of this publication may be reproduced, stored in a retrieval system, or transmitted in any form, or by any means, electronic, mechanical, photocopying, recording or otherwise, without permission in writing from the publisher.

F 4 E

On A Small Island

By

Grant Nicol

Fahrenheit Press

For Simon

Whoever fights monsters should see to it that in the process he does not become a monster. And if you gaze long enough into the abyss, the abyss will gaze back into you. - Friedrich Nietzsche

CHAPTER 1

The first time I realised there was more to my oldest sister's life than the seamless facade she had led us all to believe was real, was when I found out she had been seeing a psychiatrist. Up until then, I had thought I was the only really crazy one in the family. I wasn't sure if I appreciated the competition. She had always been better than me at most things and I doubted this would be any different.

Elín was four years older than me, the eldest of the three of us girls and the living embodiment of an independently successful woman, or so she would have had us believe all those years she looked down her nose at us. So when I made the discovery that there was a flaw, no matter how small, in her well-defined armour I was keen to explore it whilst it remained visible. For I knew only too well that it would repair itself as soon as she realised she was treating me as an equal. A miscalculation she would not permit for long, but perhaps just long enough for me to imagine how it was going to end for us.

When she originally told me that she wanted to meet for a drink I assumed she had some new man in her life or a recently purchased toy she wanted to brag about. I would never have guessed the real reason was that she wanted out of our lives again. This time for good.

She chose a bar on the ground floor of a hotel at the top of Geirsgata right next to the dry docks where some of Reykjavík's most expensive fishing vessels were getting a facelift in preparation for the forthcoming winter. Old scars and barnacles were being sanded away and replaced with fresh layers of paint to protect them against the brutal conditions they would soon have to endure.

The hotel itself was new and classy and just out of the way enough so that the risk of her bumping into anyone she might know with her little sister in tow would be minimal. I had always been something of an embarrassment to her, a fact she had never spoken of but had never really made any effort to hide, either. It was one of her many ways of keeping me in my place.

She had outgrown the rest of our family at a surprisingly early age and now only very occasionally had any use for us at all. When our mother passed away ten years ago, the remainder of the family began to slowly but determinedly drift apart. Our father still lived on the same piece of land just outside Hafnarfjörður where we had all been raised but us three girls had moved away, as children will tend to do.

Elín had been the trailblazer amongst us, requiring no encouragement to leave the nest and find her own way in the world. And find her own way she had. The problem was that these days, her way involved doing things that were likely to get her killed. She just hadn't told me about them yet.

She stared across the table at me after giving me her 'What are you doing with your life?' speech for what would prove to be the very last time. She never seemed content until she had made me feel as inadequate as she possibly could, and only then would she relax and get around to what she really wanted to talk about, which was nearly always her and what was happening in her life.

'So, Ylfa, I invited you here to tell you that I've decided to move away, to leave Iceland. My time here is finished as far as I'm concerned and I'm ready to seek pastures new and green. This is why I asked you out tonight; you're the very first to know.'

There was no way my face could have hidden my disbelief at her statement. I wanted to ask her why she had decided this but the words stalled in my throat. As it turned out, she didn't need to be asked why – she had already decided to tell me. She had read the question in my face.

'Because I'm done here. Because I'm sick and tired of Reykjavík. Because my love life is a fucking disaster and my doctor says that it's time I made some changes in my life if I'm going to feel better about myself.'

'You're leaving on the advice of your doctor?'

'My psychiatrist. I've been talking to him about when I was younger and what I need to do to confront my past if I want to move on.'

'I don't understand. Move on from what?'

'I've been having these dreams for some time now about when I was a little girl. I've told the doctor all about them so there's no reason you shouldn't hear this too. For all I know it could have happened to you and Kristjana as well.'

'What could have happened to me and Kristjana?'

'I'm talking about what our father did to me when I was a little girl. When I was so young that he probably thought I'd never remember it. But I have, Ylfa. Sooner or later these things come back to haunt us, you see. You can't hide from them forever. There's no point in living your whole life in denial no matter how difficult or painful the results of facing up to the truth might be.'

'Whatever it is you've been dreaming don't you think that they might just be... you know, just dreams?'

She shook her head slowly at me as though that was the silliest thing she'd ever heard.

'I've been having them repeatedly for a while now and they obviously mean something, otherwise I wouldn't be having them. Any idiot could see that. We've gone over them again and again in my sessions and there's no doubt in my mind now that I was raped.'

'Raped? You're saying that... Dad... you know?'

Elín nodded slowly as if it would somehow help what she was telling me sink in.

'Our father had his foul way with me a long time ago and I've kept those memories locked away all this time because they were just too disgusting to deal with. They were too much for me to deal with back then and they're too much for me to deal with now. I've thought about this long and hard and it's finally time to move on, so that's exactly what I'm going to do.'

'So, that's that then? Don't you think Dad and Kristjana might want an explanation, or were you going to leave that to me to take care of? I'm amazed you even bothered summoning me here today to tell me. Why not just disappear without telling any of us you're even going?'

There was no reply forthcoming from the other side of the table. Just a cold stare that told me she didn't find me amusing at all. If I wasn't next to speak then it would have continued until I had withered under its frozen weight.

'So you're not going to try to work this out, you're just leaving?'

'I'm leaving.'

'Where are you going to go?'

'I won't tell you that until I've made up my mind one hundred per cent.'

I had heard her lie to me before and that was yet another one. She had a plan of some sort up her sleeve but obviously wasn't going to let me in on it just yet.

'If you're afraid we'll track you down and drag you back here kicking and screaming, you know that you've got nothing to worry about.'

Not amused in the slightest, Elín turned on her condescending lawyer's face that she usually saved for the courtroom or opponents she had already written off.

'There's no need to get cute, little sister.'

From behind those beautiful, ice blue eyes of hers I could see the very essence of what she had become. In spite of everything she had amassed around herself, her flat on Álagrandi and her expensive clothes, she was still completely joyless inside.

'It's not you I'm concerned about, Ylfa, far from it.'

'What then, Dad? You're not worried he's going to take off after you even though he hasn't left the house in the last ten years?'

'It's not him I'm worried about, either.'

'Then what is it?'

She let out a little frustrated sigh and stared out of the window as she decided how much to tell me.

'I'm not going to tell you where I'm going until I've got there. I'll be going to stay with a friend for a while.'

'Why all the secrecy? I don't see what the big deal is about telling us where you're going.'

'In order to make this work, really work as a clean break, I've got to secure my financial independence. In other words, I want to have enough money behind me so that I never need to come back, for anything.'

'Okay, but I still don't get it.'

'I've been having an affair with a married man for the better part of a year now and he's going to have to help me out a little if I'm going to pull it off.'

'And he's just going to give you all this money out of the goodness of his heart?'

'No, of course not. He doesn't have one of those.'

'Then what makes you think he'll do this for you?'

'I'm going to take it from him. I'm not going to bore you with the details now but rest assured he won't be able to say no.'

'Why do I need to know that? Why let me in on this part of your plan and not the rest?'

'Because if anything should go wrong and somehow something should happen to me I want at least one person to know. I want you to be able to point the finger at him if I'm no longer able to.'

'I don't suppose you're going to tell me the name of this lucky fellow?'

She shook her head very slowly.

'I didn't think so, Elín'.

'Not yet, anyway. Eventually you're going to have to know but even when you do you're to keep it to yourself, understand?'

'Unless something happens to you, right?'

'Right.'

'What makes you think something might happen to you?'

'Because, when he realises what I'm doing to him, he's definitely going to want to kill me.'

I studied her face for any sign that she was joking. She wasn't.

That night I dreamt I came across my sister's lifeless, naked body in a pool of water of some kind or other. I couldn't tell if it was in the sea that she was lying dead; maybe it was a river she was in or possibly even a bath. I held her head gently in my hands and waited for her to tell me what had happened. Her soulless eyes looked back at me, devoid of any explanation. I asked her who had done this to her over and over again but still she refused to tell me.

CHAPTER 2

The next day, try as I might to figure out Elín's motives, I just couldn't see where this sudden desire to flee had come from. It felt like an overreaction and that was not something she was known for. She had built her career as a lawyer specialising in divorces and family law by insisting on patience and making sure that people made considered and rational decisions. Although those were not her natural instincts when it came to her private life, this seemed impulsive, even by her standards.

On top of that, I couldn't get my dream of the night before out of my head. I had become obsessed with the notion that she was going to wind up dead, more than likely in a body of water, and that I would be the one to find her. The only thing left for me to ponder now was whether there was anything I could do to prevent it happening, or whether I was doomed to watch her destroy herself. Once she had an idea in her head it was impossible for her to shake it loose. Her determination to follow through with whichever scheme she was presently consumed by was what had made her the successful woman she was today but it would also undoubtedly be her downfall. Even as a little girl she had never been able to differentiate between a good idea and a poor one. She just had her ideas.

A text message arrived on my phone subtly reminding me that I was supposed to be seeing Baldvin tonight. Baldvin was my latest conquest of the male variety, ten years my senior but gorgeous. We had only just started seeing each other and I had made the all too frequent mistake of sleeping with him on the first date. Since then he had been pretty keen to see me again – no surprises there. I wish I could say I didn't generally make a habit of sleeping with men at the very first opportunity, but I did. It was the one habit I had that I had never been able to shake. We all have them, I guess.

If you were to compare my love life to a business, and plenty of my friends had over the years, you could say that we had a good turnover. A lot of the time I behaved like what most people would refer to as a slut but I wasn't at all happy with the negative connotations of that word. Most of my friends were sluts. That was a lie; they all were.

I was pretty good at telling within a very short period of time after first meeting someone whether we were going to wind up in bed together or not. If we were meant to, then I couldn't see the point in taking part in the commonly accepted social etiquette of drinking coffee or eating dinner together first. I had always felt that getting naked with someone was a pretty good way to get to know them. It was also, unfortunately, a pretty good way of ensuring that you never saw them again.

Either that or you would never be able to get rid of them. Generally speaking, whichever one you didn't want to happen would. But these are the chances we all take in life. I was confident that if someone were to write a review of my methodology it would show that it made me happy much more often than it made me sad. Anything that you can say that about had to have something going for it.

I sent Baldvin a message back saying that I hadn't forgotten about him but that I had promised my father I would visit him and that our rendezvous would have to wait until I had returned from Hafnarfjörður. He seemed to understand, or at least he didn't reply saying that he was going to make other arrangements for his night's entertainment. I took his silence as tacit agreement to wait for my call and left it at that.

The house we'd grown up in stood just outside the fishing village of Hafnarfjörður some five miles or so back from the sea in the heart of the lava fields. About a twenty-minute drive from my flat. Small trees dotted the barren landscape along with endless miles of moss-covered lava.

In summer it would be covered in beautiful purple lupins but at this time of year it had a more foreboding look. The heavy grey clouds that hung just above the hills didn't help that impression, either. Even though I had been living in Reykjavík for many years now I still thought of our childhood house and land as home, even if my sisters no longer did.

They never had a bad word to say about the place but never really talked about it any more, which was probably worse. They had both moved on with their lives, I guess. I was the only one of us who ever visited Dad now. It was a less than ideal situation but there was next to nothing I could do about it. No amount of bitching or guilt tripping or dropping subtle hints had ever worked so I had given up, too.

For some reason Kristjana had never learned to drive and whenever I offered to teach her she always had something else on. As for Elín, she made no secret of the fact that she simply could not be bothered with the old man any more. Recent events in her psychiatric care seemed unlikely to change that any time soon.

The first face I saw as I reached the top of the long driveway that led first to the stables and then our house was Jóhannes's. He looked up from whatever it was that he was sweeping and waved.

Even though my father thought of himself as tough and independent at the age of seventy-two he had finally succumbed to my nagging and taken on someone to help him look after the place. That someone was Jóhannes. He had chosen the 19-year-old from several candidates for reasons I had only ever been able to guess at. Jóhannes was as willing a worker as any who had applied but had never set foot on a farm before in his life.

He had been a very fast learner when it came to doing things the way Dad demanded they be done but I had always wondered why it was that he'd been chosen over the other applicants. Some of the other boys and girls who had applied had spent their whole lives in the country and would have been much easier to work with initially but Dad had been very particular about wanting Jóhannes. The ease with which he fitted in now suggested that Dad had been right all along.

It had only been in the last year that I had found out from Jóhannes himself what the reason behind their bond was. He had been brought up by foster parents and apparently when Dad had found that out it had sealed the deal for him. Dad had also been fostered when he was young and although he'd never elaborated much on those times it had obviously been the connection between the two of them that had made him think it would work out well. And it had.

'Hi, Ylfa. Your father's out with Leppatuska but he should be back soon. He was going to wait for you to show but decided it might be tomorrow before you did.'

I smiled briefly at his humorous comment and told him I'd be in the stables with the four-legged members of the family. Leppatuska, who was out with Dad, and Magga were the mares in the stables and Alvari and Farfús the stallions. They were all my little darlings and I loved coming to see them more than I enjoyed the rest of the family. Much more, in fact.

It would have been nearly impossible to pick a favourite amongst them but since Magga had been named after our mother, Margrét, she was perhaps a little more special than the others. After a quick hello and a nuzzle from each of them I heard what could only possibly have been Dad approaching the stables. He appeared to be demanding to know from Jóhannes where his typically unpunctual daughter was. As usual, when he thought that it was just the two of them speaking alone, he utilised some fairly colourful language. After being directed inside he mumbled something incoherent, dismounted and walked into the stables to see me.

'I was starting to think you'd only been joking when you said you were coming today. It's almost dinner-time. If I didn't know any better I would suggest you may have been entertaining a man last night and that's why I've been forgotten.'

He smiled slightly; he was very talented at amusing himself with imaginary tales of my personal life. I had never given him any reason to believe such things but he seemed to have figured it out all by himself. Maybe I took after my mother. Giving me a hard time was something he never seemed to tire of. A simple man of simple pleasures.

'Of course, there must be a much more palatable explanation than that,' he continued.

'I was out with Elín last night if you must know.'

Dad shook his head in disgust.

'You should know better than to spend too much time around that one,' as he liked to refer to his eldest child. 'She only ever has the best interests of one person on her mind.'

He certainly had a point there but I wasn't keen to linger on that particular subject.

'Which ones do you want us to take out now?' I said nodding in the general direction of the horses. He gestured rather dismissively at the two stallions so I quickly got to work saddling Alvari and Farfús for him.

As soon as I was done we set off out past Jóhannes and Leppatuska towards the trails that we used to exercise the horses. He already had her saddle off and was giving her a vigorous brushing, which she looked as though she was thoroughly enjoying. I let Dad take the lead and choose which path we were going to follow. The rain we had been getting over the last few days had left the ground soft and dotted with puddles.

Dad remained silent for the first half-mile or so, not an uncommon way for him to be. It made it difficult to tell if he was upset, tired or just enjoying the peace and quiet that the open spaces brought him. He had always preferred the fresh air of the countryside to the noise of city life.

The clusters of short trees and the small volcanic hills that dotted the region meant that within minutes of setting off neither the stables nor the house were visible any longer. A couple of twists and turns and they had simply disappeared. It was suddenly as if we had always been riding through the middle of a lush-looking wasteland comprised of moss-covered rocks and the loose black soil that those very rocks would eventually become. You would struggle to find a more beautiful-looking wasteland anywhere else in the world.

Finally, the silence was broken. Either Dad had determined that I had suffered sufficiently for my sins or his mind had been allowed to empty to the point where it now needed to be filled once more with conversation.

'So what did you and your sister have to talk about then?'

'Dad, I only met up with her to make sure that she's still coming to see Kristjana play on Thursday night.' That was something of a lie. I had been meaning to but had completely forgotten to mention it to her. What we had really talked about, however, wasn't going to be brought up during this conversation.

'I don't suppose you've changed your mind about coming along? She'd love to see you there.'

I had to try once more even though I already knew it to be a lost cause.

He waved his hand again as if by doing so he could swat the question away as if it were a fly.

'I haven't changed my mind. This is as close as I intend getting to that place.'

He was not a fan of Reykjavík or its denizens by any stretch of the imagination and even though he lived no more than a twenty-minute drive from the place, he no longer set foot there. He thought it had changed too much over the years and was no longer the way he had once liked it. Expecting him to accompany us to the sparkling glass-walled concert hall that now sat overlooking the harbour was always going to be a long shot. But as the sole remaining conduit between the two generations of the family it was one I was expected to attempt. At least I could tell Kristjana I had tried. She would be disappointed but I don't think she had ever realistically expected him to come. If she had been genuinely concerned about his attendance she would have come to see him herself. The only thing the two of them had in common any more was their lack of interest in each other.

'I thought I'd cook tonight. I bought some dinner for us on the way over,' I said, suddenly remembering the fish I had left in the back of the car. Luckily, it would still be the same temperature as when I had purchased it, such was the chill in the air. Winter had started to sink its claws into the land, slowly at first but its grip was tightening all the time.

Most of the standing water around the riding trails had either begun to freeze or had already done so. The streams we passed moved too freely to seal over even in the middle of winter. They would only gather lips of ice at their edges.

After about half an hour the wind began to pick up and I wished I'd remembered to put some gloves on. Tiny dots of ice had started to fall like tiny frozen beads from the sky, twisting and turning in an icy circular dance in front of us. I suggested we turn back to the stables. It was freezing cold and I was getting hungry.

'Maybe Jóhannes could join us for dinner.'

No reply.

'I'll ask him when we get back, then,' I added.

There was still no reply forthcoming so I took that as compliance. I had been looking forward to spending the evening alone with Dad but was starting to worry that we might struggle to find anything much to talk about. He seemed to be lost in thought, his mind otherwise occupied with one thing or another.

Once we had returned the horses to their stalls I told Jóhannes that I was cooking dinner and that he was more than welcome to join us. He said he would just as soon as he'd cleaned himself up so I rescued the fish from the car and headed into the house to start cooking.

Dad parked himself in his favourite chair in the living room and watched the news with the volume at a level that made me suspect he was losing his hearing. It was entirely possible that there were occasions when he could no longer hear me when I spoke to him. It was also possible that he simply chose when these moments occurred to suit his mood.

It wasn't long before the fish and boiled potatoes were almost ready and Jóhannes still hadn't made an appearance. I left Dad cursing the stupidity of various figures in Icelandic public office and headed around the back of the house to find Jóhannes. When Dad had taken him on as a stable hand he had built a small cabin-like flat just behind the stables for him to live in. Although a separate structure in its own right, it was no bigger than a tiny studio apartment but it gave him a completely self-contained room and ensured that the two of them didn't get under each other's feet any more than was necessary.

When I knocked I could hear music blaring from inside so I decided to stick my head in. I opened the door slightly, calling out as I did so. Through the gap I could see him standing next to his bed getting dressed. He had his back to me and was still oblivious to my presence. He was wearing his underwear and nothing else. He suddenly sensed me behind him and turned around but not before I had noticed the distinctive crisscross markings of old scars across his lower back.

I pretended I hadn't seen a thing and told him that his dinner was almost on the table. The marks certainly weren't recent and could have been remnants of his foster days or even earlier. Either way they were no business of mine and I tried to put them out of my mind as I scurried back to the kitchen.

I don't think that Dad had even noticed my absence but the smells from the pan were certainly starting to get his attention. Jóhannes timed his arrival perfectly, I handed him two plates as he walked through the front door into the kitchen and he dropped Dad's off at the dining table. The silence that enveloped the room was a sign I had done my job well.

'This fish is actually quite good, Ylfa. It makes me wonder why you've avoided getting married for so long. Jóhannes, don't you think she's ready to find herself a husband?'

Jóhannes smiled uncomfortably at me and kept eating. His blushes suggested that perhaps something of the sort had indeed crossed his mind.

Talk of marriage and grandchildren had become standard fare at my father's table. He probably thought that in old-fashioned Icelandic fashion all three of his girls would have given him grandchildren to play with by now but instead he hadn't even seen one. For someone of his generation the situation must have seemed quite unthinkable.

'No such luck, Dad. I'm still looking for the right one.'

'You've been doing nothing but look for as long as I can remember. It's about time you do what is expected of you and choose one that will give you as little trouble as possible.'

'Now that you put it like that, I can hardly wait to get started.'

Dad didn't appreciate the sarcasm and he scratched his beard as he looked at me.

'You could always move back here and stop throwing your money away in that city.'

Another of his favourite subjects was the wholly imaginary day when I finally came to my senses and moved back in with him. Once he had brought either of these subjects up it was hard to see any light at the end of the tunnel. He seemed to think that by simple repetition I would start seeing things his way. It was incomprehensible to him that I might just be happy the way I was.

'This is a great place to bring up kids. You know that already. You can have the place when I'm gone and raise a family here. You don't want to grow old on your own, do you?'

I wasn't sure how to respond to that one so I just let it go. We went back to eating in silence until everyone's plate was wiped clean.

'Does anyone want any coffee?' I chirped.

I got up and made my way back to the kitchen. Jóhannes signalled that he did and I knew that Dad would without him even having to reply.

Jóhannes pulled some crumpled envelopes out of one of his pockets and tried his best to straighten them out before putting them on the table for my father to look at.

'These came for you today. Sorry I forgot to give you them earlier,' Jóhannes said.

He collected the plates and joined me in the kitchen. From the living room I could hear the envelopes being opened and some indecipherable muttering taking place. As I ran some water for the coffee I looked over my shoulder to see what it was that had irked my father so. He was screwing a piece of paper up and stuffing it into one of his pockets.

The rest of the envelopes he simply threw across the room before returning to his chair and fixating on the television once again.

Jóhannes shrugged his shoulders and rinsed the plates off in the sink. It seemed he had got completely used to my father's moods. People could get used to all manner of things if they wanted to, no matter how disagreeable. It was just a matter of familiarity and repetition. I wasn't entirely sure if it was a good thing, though. Sometimes I just wanted to slap some sense into him.

CHAPTER 3

I had originally toyed with the idea of staying the night and driving home the next day but after dinner it became obvious that Dad would be happier if everyone just left him alone. So that's just what we did.

On my way back to Vesturgata I sent a text to Baldvin informing him that if he showed up in half an hour he could have his way with me. He hadn't so much as sent a cheeky message all day and I guessed that deep down I appreciated being given a little space. I quite liked being left alone; it was entirely possible that I wasn't that dissimilar to my father after all.

As I parked the car on Vesturgata in the pouring rain that had just rolled in off Faxaflói Bay, my phone rang. I answered it expecting that Baldvin had either finally succumbed and given me a call now he knew he was wanted, or worse still he was calling to tell me he couldn't make it after all. As it happened it was neither of those scenarios. It was my drunken hate-fuelled sister calling to vent her bitterness at someone. Somehow in the constant confusion that was her life she had mistaken me for someone who cared. I had hoped that after such a long period of ignoring me completely our recent meeting had been something of a one off. No such luck.

What I wanted to avoid was contact between the two of us becoming a habit again. I could still remember the days when Elín had been a constant part of my life and didn't want them revisited. I had a strong urge to hang up on her but knew that it would be better to hear her out. Trying to snub her would only vex her into a state of unbelievable determination.

'I'm just a toy he takes out of its box every now and then, but only when the other kids aren't looking. You know?'

If she'd made an attempt at a greeting I must have missed it. There was a noise that was caught somewhere between a laugh and a gurgle. She sounded as though she was drowning in a sea of vodka and still trying to see the funny side of it as the waves washed over her head.

'He buys me lots of stuff but it's not the same...'

I was tempted to ask her what exactly it wasn't the same as but she would only have told me.

'The car, this dress, even the fucking house is his.'

That urge to hang up and deal with the consequences later raised its head again in an attempt to get my attention. Perhaps foolishly, I ignored it once more.

'Do you know what they think about when they're fucking us?'

I told her that I didn't. It was the truth. I had no idea, nor did I really wish to.

'I bet the only time that he thinks about me is when he's screwing his wife,' she spouted triumphantly.

'What is it you want, Elín?'

'I want away from this awful place. Once you've made a mistake here it's just going to keep showing up over and over again.'

'I already know that. I mean, what do you want now? Why did you call?'

My question hung between us unanswered before she gurgled once more and then hung up. Maybe she just didn't know any more, either. As I stood there staring at my phone as if it was supposed to be able to explain calls such as that one to me, I saw Baldvin striding down the street in the rain.

I grabbed him and whisked him inside before we both got soaked.

I told him all about what Elín had said about leaving the country and what she suspected our father had done to her. Baldvin listened intently and didn't seem as shocked as I thought he might be. His advice was simple and practical, a lot like him.

'If she's serious then she has to take it up with him. Herself, though, not through you. Otherwise you'll end up caught in the middle. You could quite easily wind up saying something you might regret for the rest of your life.'

'I get the feeling I don't yet know the real reason she told me. It's like she wants me to know just enough to keep me worried about how it's all going to turn out. It could just be an excuse for her doing whatever it is that she's got planned next to rip off this lover of hers. Some sort of a deranged rationalisation.'

'And this married man that she's seeing, she won't tell you who it is?'

I shook my head; now that I was telling someone else about it, Elín's story sounded crazier than ever. I laughed at the whole idea but it was an awkward, uncomfortable laugh – even I could hear that.

'Maybe you should just try and forget about it. If she's going to do something stupid then there's not much you can do about it, is there?'

He was right there. Nothing I could do or say was going to stop her from screwing up her life if that was what she had decided to do. All I hoped was that she didn't take us all down with her.

Baldvin shrugged and smiled at me.

'Let her dig her own grave. There's no need to help.'

'You're right. I should just let her go ahead and hang herself if that's what she's intent on doing.'

I pulled him closer and kissed him. At least I wouldn't be going to bed with someone I secretly loathed. I wondered how many people you could honestly say that about on any given night, in any given town.

CHAPTER 4

When the phone rang I rolled over and embraced a cold pillow. Part of my brain wanted to find the location of the ringing while another part altogether wondered where Baldvin had got to. I rolled back towards my bedside clock and checked the time. He would have left for work an hour ago so there was nothing for it but to answer the phone. I checked the caller ID; it was Dad. I answered it anyway. He never called unless he wanted something and this was unlikely to be any different.

'I didn't wake you, did I?'

He could barely conceal his delight at my slightly befuddled greeting. I had never been very good first thing in the morning, even if first thing in the morning for me was actually nearer to first thing in the afternoon.

'No, Dad,' I lied, and rather poorly at that.

'Jóhannes dismounted badly off Leppatuska this morning and turned his ankle. It's no big deal but he can't drive anywhere the way he is and with him out of action I've just got too much to do. I wouldn't ask but I told the vet to call me as soon as she got the medication in and of course she's just called, hasn't she.'

'Slow down, Dad, what are you talking about?'

'I've got to give the horses their worming medication as soon as I can. There's been worms in their droppings and I've been meaning to do it for some time. I need you to pick up the de-wormer for me from the lady who gets that sort of thing for me.'

'Where is it you want me to go?'

'Mosfellsbær. Her name's Inga Björk.'

I grabbed a pen and took down the address as he rattled it off. There was little, if any, point in protesting. I had nothing else to do until I had to go to work later now that Baldvin had gone, with the possible exception of some painting. Unfortunately, the next subject I wanted to paint had already left for work himself so that idea was going to have to wait whether I liked it or not. Resigned to my fate as a delivery girl I assured Dad that I would get straight out there and pick up his worm medicine.

'There's no rush,' he said, meaning the exact opposite. 'You'll need to pay her too. It will be 10,000kr give or take. I'll reimburse you as soon as you come out to the farm.'

I cursed my bad luck and vowed to pay more attention to who was calling before answering my phone in the future. It seemed to be bringing me nothing but bad news. After a quick shower I filled my travel mug with fresh coffee and headed north out of the city towards Mosfellsbær.

Inga Björk's address turned out to be an unassuming little building that looked like it was part office space and part storage facility. If it had been a bit bigger you might have called it a warehouse but as things stood that would have been overstating it somewhat. The large car park outside had only two cars in it. One was feasibly Inga Björk's while the other had an overly serious-looking man leaning against it smoking a cigarette. As I made my way to the front door he briefly eyed me up and down before returning his attention to the cigarette.

As I entered the front office a slightly flustered yet very attractive woman signalled for me to take a seat. She was in the middle of a tense conversation on the phone so I sat down and waited for her to finish. She was having a heated discussion about her insurance policy with the people who had supplied her with it.

It seemed that whoever she was talking to didn't feel like giving her any assurances over the phone about when she might be getting her money. She eventually hung up without achieving what she had wanted and turned her attention to me.

'Sorry about that, bloody insurance companies. Are you here to look for fingerprints?'

As she waited impatiently for my reply her eyebrows lifted themselves as far up her forehead as they could without actually leaving her face.

'I'm not here for fingerprints. I'm just here to pick up an order for my father. He told me you rang him earlier about something he's been waiting on. All I know is that it has something to do with worming the horses.'

She seemed to be thinking furiously about something but I wasn't sure quite what it was. It could have been my father but no one thought about him that hard any more.

'Einar Dagsson? The Moxidectin, wasn't it? He normally sends his grandson to pick these things up.'

I had to smile at that. I wanted to correct her but didn't consider it necessary considering the day she seemed to be having. It did no harm at all for Jóhannes to be thought of as part of our family.

'Yes, Jóhannes. He fell off one of the horses and couldn't make it today.'

'Jóhannes, yes. That's no problem. There's nothing seriously wrong with him, I hope,' she said.

A smile worked its way onto her face and reinforced what a good-looking woman she was. I could picture Jóhannes really enjoying these trips to pick up Dad's bits and pieces from her.

'Nothing more than a twisted ankle, I believe. He should be up and about again in no time.'

She nodded as if this were a satisfactory outcome and disappeared through a door, which presumably led to her supplies. When she reappeared she was holding a plastic bag filled with syringes full of de-worming gel for the horses.

'This lot only arrived yesterday. Luckily it wasn't taken in the break-in. You might have seen the police officer outside. He's waiting for the forensic technician to show up. That's who I thought you were. Whoever it was got into the building and disabled the alarm somehow. I'm still very nervous.'

'I can understand that.'

'I only noticed something was wrong when I saw the note. Otherwise the theft might have gone unnoticed for days. When I arrived today I thought I must have forgotten to turn the alarm on last night but I've never done that before. Now the insurance company thinks that as well and doesn't want to pay up. The thieves left a note behind in place of the things they took. It's all a bit strange, really, slightly creepy, don't you think?'

'Definitely. What on earth did they steal and what did the note say?'

I couldn't imagine why anyone would want to break into a place that sold veterinary supplies. Maybe Icelandic farmers were harder up than I thought. As for leaving a note behind in place of the goods, that was just weird.

'Syringes, scalpels and most disturbingly a whole box of Ketamine vials. Enough to tranquilise a whale, almost. Everything you would need to operate on an animal except the sutures to stitch it back together again.'

'Ketamine? You mean the stuff they take as a party drug – Special K?'

'It's basically the same thing but when vets use it it's in a liquid form. It's a barbiturate; you inject it as a tranquiliser to sedate animals that are to be operated on. When it's used illegally as a party drug, they heat it up so that it becomes a powder so they can sniff it or whatever the hell it is they do with it.'

'And what about the note? They didn't say they'd be back later to pay for it, I imagine.'

'No, it's been a long time since I've read a Bible but it looked like a passage from it.'

'You don't remember what it said, do you?'

She smiled and pulled out her phone. I didn't understand what she was smiling about until she held the mobile's screen up for me to see.

'They told me not to touch anything but they didn't say anything about taking photos, did they?' she said as quietly as she could.

'Want a look?' she asked rather redundantly. My boring errand for my father had just taken on a much more interesting perspective. I leant in closer to the screen to get a better look at the photo of the message.

I had a dream that made me afraid.
As I was lying in my bed,
the images and visions that passed
through my mind terrified me.

'Is that supposed to be some sort of clue?' I asked laughing. 'Surely it has to be some sort of joke.'

Inga Björk just shrugged as if to suggest that my guess would be as good as any she could offer.

'To be honest, I don't know what the hell it's supposed to be. I just hope that whoever it was they don't come back any time soon. In the wrong hands that stuff could be deadly, and my guess is that it's now in the wrong hands.'

I paid her what Dad owed her and told her I hoped her day improved. She rolled her eyes at me and snorted as she handed me the change and the receipt, suggesting that she considered that possibility highly unlikely.

'A bad start can only be a sign of things to come, I fear, and as starts go they don't get much worse than this,' she said and got back to her work.

Outside the detective was still leaning against his car looking impatiently at his watch as he lit another cigarette. A fourth car pulled into the car park and a man hurriedly got out of the vehicle carrying a metallic briefcase.

'You took your time,' the detective said churlishly.

'I had to hunt around for that Bible you asked for. It wasn't as straightforward as you might think. I bet you don't have one just lying about the house,' the technician replied.

'The last time I had any use for a Bible was when I saw my ex-wife on my last birthday,' the detective offered without any sign of humour in his voice.

'When I told her what I wanted for a present she told me to pray for one instead. The owner's inside waiting on you. I told her you'd dust for prints and have a look around.

You never know what might show up, though. Even the clever ones make mistakes. They got into the place and past the security system no problem at all. If they'd bothered to reset it on the way out she may not have noticed anything was amiss at all, except for this.' He waved a plastic evidence bag with the note that had been left behind by the thieves in it.

'Maybe they had their own set of keys.'

'No, she's the only one with a set. She's never even had another set cut for another employee, apparently. It's a one-woman show. They took knives, needles and some sort of drug. What that all amounts to, your guess is as good as mine.'

The technician handed the detective a Bible and made his way inside to see Inga Björk.

I acted as if I wasn't paying any attention as I put Dad's bag in the back of the car and then pretended to check some non-existent messages on my phone. I typed the passage into my phone so I wouldn't forget it.

I had a dream that made me afraid.
As I was lying in my bed,
the images and visions that passed
through my mind terrified me.

Much later that night, after another dreary shift at the downtown bar I had studied art for five years at university to wind up working at, I finally got back to the passage.

As I lay exhausted in my bed I searched on my laptop to see if it was in fact as biblical as it sounded. It was.

It was from the Book of Daniel. Chapter 4, Verse 5, to be precise. King Nebuchadnezzar seemed to be having trouble sleeping and was having bad dreams about this and that.

Even though they were vivid and clear to him he was unable to comprehend their meaning, apart from an overwhelming sensation that they were a portent of evil. I knew how he felt.

It seemed a rather odd thing to leave behind at a crime scene. A riddle or some sort of clue to the thieves' real intentions, perhaps. If they had wanted to get away unnoticed it would have been remarkably easy for them to do so and yet they had chosen to leave a cryptic message in the one place that would cause their crime to be noticed. Perhaps they were trying to throw the police off their trail by giving the crime a religious overtone it didn't really have. Either that or they were doing just the opposite and pointing them in the right direction. Maybe even in a weird way they were hoping to get caught. Either way they were obviously not quite right in the head. Perhaps they had been having bad dreams as well. Eventually, I closed my eyes and waited for mine to come again.

CHAPTER 5

My night's sleep passed uneventfully, undisturbed by any visions of woe that were yet to befall our family and in the morning I decided to pick up where I had left off the night before. With the Book of Daniel.

King Nebuchadnezzar's dreams were indeed troubling him. Tortured by their constant presence his sleeping hours had become a source of great consternation. He sent for his wise men and told them to interpret the dream for him or face certain death. But as he would not share the contents of his dream with them, they were unable to do as he had demanded and were all sentenced to a fiery death. Daniel, on the other hand, rather than look within himself for the answer, prayed to God for help and the mystery was subsequently revealed to him in a vision. He then told the king what his dream was and explained to him that it signified things that were yet to come.

The next dream the king had was of a giant tree growing in the middle of the land. Once again he called Daniel to his side, this time asking him to explain the tree and its significance. The tree was able to shelter all the beasts, feed all the creatures and yet in the dream the king had been told to cut it down. To trim off its branches, strip its leaves and scatter its fruit on the ground.

I was contemplating the implications of what he had been told when my laptop informed me I had a new email waiting for me to read.

I opened my inbox to see what the rather timely distraction was. My anticipation faded to disappointment when I saw it was from Elín. Initially, I suspected it might be a spineless way of telling me she had changed her mind about Kristjana's concert.

The title of the email suggested otherwise. It was: Just in case. I had to wonder, just in case of what?

Hello Ylfa,

I thought that as a precautionary measure I would send you a copy of this. Just in case anything happens to me. This way you will have a record that only you will be able to access.

Just in case you thought that I might be reneging on our agreement to see our sister together, I am not. I will see you at Harpa as promised. I am in fact quite looking forward to what will be a rather special occasion.

Spoiler alert: If you don't want to watch me having sex then I strongly suggest you don't open the attachment on this email unless you really have to.

If that time comes, you will know it.

I have made a secret recording of lover-boy and me having sex in an attempt to convince him to do what I am about to ask of him. On the off chance that he doesn't acquiesce to my demands of his free will, I will use this recording as leverage to change his mind.

As much as my behaviour will cause him considerable distress, the thought of his lovely wife seeing firsthand what he has been doing with me will surely be sufficient to make him see things my way.

See you soon,
Elín

Blackmailing someone was a dangerous business at the best of times. I assumed that whoever this man was, he might just have enough money to give into Elín's demands without missing the cash too much. The problem was that if that was the case, then he also had the wherewithal to make life difficult for her. Possibly even very difficult. There was no way that he was going to take this sort of extortion attempt lying down. From what she had already told me, she knew she would have a fight on her hands. There was also a very real chance that she might end up in court. At least when the time came I assumed that she would know plenty of good criminal defence lawyers. Something told me she might just need one.

Without opening the attachment I cast my eyes back to the Old Testament text on my screen. I was starting to identify with the emotional turmoil of King Nebuchadnezzar. I was also having visions of terrible things coming my way. Even if they didn't come directly at me I was sure to be caught in the maelstrom that accompanied them and sucked down under their waves.

Possibly there was a Daniel somewhere in my life who would be able to explain my concerns to me. If not then I was going to have to learn to cope with my confusion and discontent in my own way. There wasn't a time in my life that I could remember, anyway, when I didn't have something to worry about that concerned Elín either directly or indirectly. Part of me wished she would make good on her threat to leave, and the sooner the better. She had to realise that with Reykjavík being such a small town she would hit black ice sooner or later with this little scheme of hers and wind up in a ditch. More than likely with her head in a puddle and her knickers around her ankles. Whatever the price of happiness was for Elín, it seemed inevitable that it would be too much for her to bear and she would end up miserable in any event. Whatever it was that she was so desperately trying to run away from, chances were that it was inside of her. Changing her location was unlikely to make her happy unless she could address the problems that raged within.

As I was re-immersing myself in the Book of Daniel another email arrived demanding my attention. This one was from a legal firm I hadn't heard of before informing me that my father had decided to sign the deed to his property over to me and that my signature was required on some legal documents. They wanted to know when would be a suitable time for me to sign them at their offices in Hafnarfjörður.

Before I could digest the fact that Dad had done this without so much as mentioning it to me, my phone rang. I picked it up, making a point of checking the caller ID as I did so. It wasn't a number from the phone's address book and as a general rule I don't normally take calls unless my phone recognises the incoming number. And then, only if I want to speak to the person. It was possible that this was from the solicitors in Hafnarfjörður so I took the call.

The man on the other end of the line identified himself as Detective Grímur Karlsson of the Reykjavík CID. He said he remembered seeing me in a car park in Mosfellsbær recently and that he had something to tell me. I could hear him sucking on a cigarette and could instantly picture the plain-clothes detective leaning against his car outside Inga Björk's office.

I couldn't for the life of me think what he might want. It was possible he was just routinely following up on Inga Björk's recent visitors or maybe she had told him about showing me the note and he wanted to have a quiet word about that.

I told him I remembered seeing him there also and asked him what he wanted. I hoped I hadn't broken any laws with my online research into King Nebuchadnezzar and his nightmares.

'There has been an incident at your father's farm in Hafnarfjörður, Ylfa. A very serious incident, I'm afraid.'

My heart sank in my chest as I found myself unable to breathe or form words properly.

I took a deep breath. 'Is he all right?'

'Your father is okay. More than a little shaken, it has to be said, but alive and as well as can be expected under the circumstances. I'm afraid I cannot say the same for the other resident of the property.'

I took another much needed breath and then absorbed what he had actually said.

'Jóhannes?' I mumbled to myself as much as to Grímur.

'We received a call from a man delivering feed for the horses to your father's property. When he arrived he made a rather disturbing discovery in the stables. It appears that there was a serious assault on the young man who worked there resulting in his death sometime in the early hours of this morning.'

'What do you mean?' I asked.

'Jóhannes was murdered, Ylfa.'

I had known exactly what he meant; I simply didn't want to believe it. There was nothing but silence on the other end of the line, which was eventually broken by the sound of Grímur taking another drag from his cigarette.

'It would be better if you came over, Ylfa. He's been through a hell of an ordeal but he's still refusing to go to hospital. The problem seems to be that he doesn't want to leave the horses on their own. One of them was killed along with the boy last night and I thought that if you came over he might finally agree to see a doctor. If you were here to see to the horses he might feel better about being more cooperative. He's had a nasty blow to the head but he's being rather pig-headed about letting anyone examine him. The paramedics have bandaged him up but at his age a full check up at the hospital would be a good idea.'

'I see what you mean. I'll come straight over.'

'Thanks, Ylfa. He may have a concussion – or worse.'

'Tell him I'm on my way.'

I hung up, rolled off the bed and threw on some clothes, all the time trying not to cry. I couldn't believe Jóhannes was dead. Grímur's words all made sense in my head but the reality of them was still some way off from sinking in. Who would attack such a sweet boy and kill one of the horses? What could they have possibly been after?

There was nothing of any value on the farm except the horses. Maybe it had been a case of mistaken identity and they thought they were on someone else's land. Maybe they had been out of their heads on drugs, looking for money to get their next fix.

The blood pounded in my head as I ran through all the possible scenarios over and over again as I drove. No matter what I came up with, though, it failed to make the slightest bit of sense.

By the time I saw the police car waiting at the entrance to the driveway I understood that it was all for real. Something had gone terribly wrong; there was no point in denying that now. The officer standing next to the car signalled that I should come to a halt and then stood directly in my way to make sure that I did as he wanted.

When he was convinced I was who I said I was he allowed me to complete my journey up the driveway. For the last hundred metres or so the car seemed to crawl along as if my world had fallen into slow motion. The sound of the gravel crunching beneath my tyres sounded louder than I would have ever thought possible. All my nerves were exposed and poised for the ensuing trauma. This was where dreams would shatter and those nightmares I had been having would become reality. The overwhelming feeling I had was that forces beyond my control had begun to pull me in opposing directions, waiting now for me to snap.

Grímur was leaning against his car smoking a cigarette. He was talking to the same technician I had seen walking into Inga Björk's workplace with his serious-looking metal briefcase. He had the very same briefcase with him now and latex gloves on and it looked like whatever they were talking about was making him uneasy.

He looked tense and I could tell he was talking faster than normal even though I couldn't hear what he was saying. Grímur, on the other hand, looked considerably more relaxed than his colleague. Solemn, perhaps, but not uptight. When he saw me approaching he said something under his breath and their conversation ended. They both turned to greet me, making me even more nervous than I already was.

I looked about for Dad but he was nowhere to be seen. Hopefully he had heeded their advice and got some himself some much needed medical attention. Grímur beckoned me to him and introduced me to his forensic technician, Björn Magnússon. He had seen something that hadn't agreed with him and it showed all over his face. He wanted to speak but instead just stared at me as if unable to bring himself to say anything in case it turned out to be the wrong thing. Grímur cleared his throat and stubbed out his current cigarette.

'He's inside the house, Ylfa. Remember what I said about getting that concussion checked out. He's not a young man any more.'

'Thanks, I'll go see him now.'

He simply nodded as if to tell me it was exactly what I should do.

'We sent the ambulance away when it became clear he wasn't going to play ball but we can get one back immediately if you can talk him around.'

'I'll see what I can do. What about Jóhannes?'

'His body's been removed. Björn's busy here with the forensic side of things and I will need to ask you some questions as soon as you're ready. You should talk to your father first, though. He was hit hard enough to knock him out for a short while so even if he won't go to hospital you will need to stay with him for now.'

I looked towards the entrance to the stables, which was cordoned off by yellow and black Lögreglan crime-scene tape.

'I have some questions for you, too,' I told Grímur. An understatement of enormous proportions.

He nodded again, 'Of course, there is a lot for you to catch up on. Just as soon as you've talked to your father. We're going to be here for a while so there's no hurry.'

I made my way into the house where I found Dad sitting in his favourite chair looking as white as a sheet with his head heavily bandaged. He had been shaken up badly all right.

His usual rock-like exterior was looking rather fragile to say the least. He was holding his head gingerly and there were still traces of dried blood down the side of his face. All in all he looked in a sorry state.

'I'm here now, Dad, are you all right?'

He looked up at me seemingly lost for words. For a moment I wasn't sure if he recognised me or not.

'I'm a little the worse for wear, my girl.' Another startling understatement if ever I'd heard one.

'I would imagine you are. What happened to Jóhannes?'

'Sometime in the middle of the night I heard the horses making a racket in their stalls. They never do that so I knew something was wrong. They were very agitated about something. While I was trying to calm them down I was hit from behind and knocked out for a little while. Not too long, mind you. When I came around I was sitting on the floor tied to a pole with something over my head. I could hear him moving around me but when I called out to him to untie me and face me like a man he just kept on doing what he was doing. A strange smell started to work its way inside the bag. I've spent enough time on farms to recognise what it was. Blood, and lots of it.'

'What did he do?' I asked, not at all sure that I wanted to hear the answer.

'He had been working with a knife. When he finally took the bag off my head and I was able to see what he'd been up to, he was gone. What I saw in front of me was something I wish I'd never ever had to see. He had taken a knife to Jóhannes and laid him out on top of Magga. On his back with his hands over his eyes. They had both had their throats cut and bled to death in front of me. They just lay there bleeding all over the place until they could bleed no more. Neither of them moved once, not even a little. There was nothing I could do to help, Ylfa.'

I tried to imagine what it must have felt like watching them die like that and being unable to do anything about it. There was no way it could have been a case of mistaken identity. Whoever had done this had wanted Dad to suffer as much as possible. The only question was whether he or Jóhannes had been the primary target of the criminals, and why? Had they wanted to scare my father half to death or had Jóhannes paid terribly for some mistake? I had trouble imagining that anyone could hold such a grudge against either of them.

'Who did this?'

He just shook his head, 'I've no idea.'

'The detective says you should go to hospital, Dad. Will you do that for me?'

He shook his head again, quite determinedly.

'Now that you're here, though, I will lie down for a bit. You're going to have to see to the horses. They'll need to see a familiar face. They know that something awful has happened just as you and I do.'

'Okay, but if there's any sign that you're not improving I'm driving you to the hospital myself.'

He put his free hand up in a sign of surrender. For once in his life he didn't look keen for a fight. If someone had wanted to hurt him, they sure knew what they were doing. Neither Jóhannes nor our favourite horse could ever be replaced. The way Dad looked now it was hard to imagine him recovering, but he was a resilient man and had surprised me before with his powers of recuperation. I helped him up from his chair and walked him to his bed. After he had lain down and closed his eyes I sat and watched him as he tried to rest. I was in no hurry to see whatever state the stables were in and chances were I wouldn't be allowed near them for a while.

Eventually, Dad's breathing settled and he looked slightly more comfortable. I held his hand until I could tell that he was asleep. Only then did I pull out my phone to call my sisters.

I called Elín first and thankfully the call went straight to voicemail so I left a concise message telling her the facts as I knew them and reassuring her that Dad was okay. She wouldn't be interested in any of the emotions surrounding what had happened, just the chain of events. Those she could digest in her own good time without the need to inject any unnecessary sentiment into the equation.

The next call was always going to be much more difficult. Kristjana was the emotional infant of the family and she was going to deal with this the same way she always dealt with stressful situations – poorly.

There would inevitably be a million questions from her regarding what had happened and I still didn't really know the full story myself. Even if Elín had answered her call, her indifference would have precluded her from asking too many questions. You could always depend on her to not to care too much about anything. She was good like that.

As I stood at the front door staring at my phone I saw Grímur waving at me. I took this to be a sign that Kristjana's call could wait for the time being and walked the short distance across to the stables. He pulled his jacket tightly around his chest as the wind began to pick up. The very strength of it had taken the temperature down well below what had been forecast and it didn't feel as if it was going to ease up anytime soon. Its icy fingers worked their way in under my jumper as I approached him. Grímur took me by the arm and pulled me close in a gesture that had conspiratorial overtones. The look on his face was serious even by his usually sincere standards.

'You will need to brace yourself for this. Both the boy and the horse were incapacitated before the attack with drugs of some sort. They both bled to death after they were cut and the amount of blood involved is significant. The poor lad who found them lost his breakfast all over the ground just here. It's not for the fainthearted. You don't have to look at this if you don't want to.'

Even as he was talking, the smell hit me for the first time. A nauseating, metallic odour that I instantly knew would linger in my senses for some time to come. The power of it made me want to pull away but I resolved to be stronger than that and forced myself to enter the stables.

I had readied myself for any eventuality but the truth was that there was no way I could ever have been prepared for the sight that confronted me when I saw what had once been Magga's stall.

Our beloved Magga still lay where she had died. Her beautiful brown face had lost all remnants of its kindness and sat awkwardly in a pool of her own blood. Grímur had been right about the amount of blood on the floor; it was indeed everywhere. A lake of crimson had settled across what looked like the entire floor. She had been cut along the length of her neck by what must have been an extremely sharp blade. The wound was enormous. It was a particularly sad way to say farewell to a dear friend.

'When we arrived your father was still tied up here. The delivery boy had been unable – or unwilling – to get the knots undone.'

He waved a hand at a pole close to Magga's stall. The rope used to fasten Dad to it was still attached, hanging limply as a haunting reminder of the morning's events. From his position he would have had a perfect view of the death of his two beloved companions.

'In there we not only found the horse exactly as it lies now but the young lad, Jóhannes as well. He had been positioned on top of the animal in what appeared to be a deliberate and thought-out pose. He and the horse both had their throats cut and bled to death where they lay.'

I looked at him for further explanation but none was forthcoming. Björn walked in on our conversation and joined the uncomfortable silence. He looked at Grímur and then back to me before speaking.

'It appears they were both incapacitated by the assailant. I found puncture wounds similar to those that would be left by a large bore needle on both the boy and the horse. I will need to wait for some blood tests but it is likely that they were both injected with a tranquiliser that paralysed them completely. Then the assailant went about cutting through some fairly large blood vessels so they would bleed to death.

'At that point they would still have been alive, although not still conscious. That's why there is such a large amount of blood. Their hearts would have just kept pumping until they were empty.'

'Would they have felt anything?' I had to ask.

'No,' Björn said. 'They would have both been completely anaesthetised.'

'I suppose that's something,' I said.

'Is there anyone you can think of who might have wanted to kill Jóhannes or scare your father like this? Do either of them have any enemies that you know of?' Grímur asked. 'Anyone they might have owed money to, for instance?'

I didn't have to think very hard about my reply. I couldn't think of anybody who would have any cause to do this to Jóhannes or my father and I told Grímur so. The two men looked at each other before Björn announced that he had work to be getting on with back at the lab. As he made his way to his car a freezing cold rain started to fall from the now leaden sky.

'Should I be worried about whoever did this coming back?'

'To be honest, I don't know. I've sent the K-9 Unit out through the surrounding countryside; they will be very thorough. If the criminals are still in the immediate area we'll find them but I imagine they're long gone by now.'

'But for how long?'

'Without knowing why this happened it's very difficult to predict what might happen next. Too much work went into this for it to be a random attack. My first thought is that your father might have been the target.'

'Then why kill Jóhannes?'

'Maybe someone wanted to teach him a lesson. One he would be unlikely to forget.'

There was a muffled snuffling from one of the horses. They had been keeping very quiet, almost as though they didn't want to draw any attention to themselves. I couldn't blame them.

'If anything comes to you once you've had a chance for this to all sink in, give me a ring straight away.' He handed me one of his cards.

'When I leave, the officer you met at the bottom of the drive will stay just outside the stables here with a clear view of the house. If you need a hand with anything, don't hesitate to ask him for help. The house will have someone stationed outside it twenty-four hours a day for as long as you think is necessary.'

And with that he turned away and forced his way through the driving rain. The presence of a police officer on the property was supposed to reassure me but it only served as a reminder of how close you can be to a thoroughly gruesome end.

As soon as he was gone I changed into my rubber boots and got to work. By the time I had hosed the last of the blood out of the stables I finally started to cry for real. The tears had been building up within me ever since I'd laid eyes on Magga's remains. I covered her with an old plastic tarpaulin. Since sundown the temperature had fallen even further and the arctic tempest outside was showing no signs of abating anytime soon.

As I made my way back to the house through what was quickly becoming a gale, I waved at our police sentinel through the dark. There was no way of knowing whether he had seen me or not. The inside of the car was as black as the night that surrounded us. It was probably just as cold too; the poor man was probably freezing in there. I had become chilled right through my clothes despite the work I'd been doing. Chilled not only by the freezing night air but also by the thought that out there somewhere was a man with visions more terrible than any I could ever have imagined.

CHAPTER 6

I could tell Dad had regained much of his personal conviction when I made my way through the kitchen the next morning to investigate the hubbub coming from outside the front door. Despite the furious wind and near horizontal rain, there he was standing outside the stables waving his arms furiously at the poor young man who had been commissioned to protect us all through the night. I couldn't hear what was being said but the conversation, such as it was, didn't seem to be going too well for the young officer.

He was probably as yet to experience anything in his short time with the police that could match the bitter determination of my father first thing in the morning. It could be a brutal part of the day at the best of times but when you found yourself on the wrong side of Einar Dagsson, it was sometimes hard to find the courage to carry on. The rest of the day suddenly lost much of its previous promise. This appeared to be the dilemma presently facing the young officer of the law. Instead of resolutely carrying out his duty to protect us from whatever danger lurked in the darkness of the surrounding countryside he was re-evaluating who he might be able to call upon to protect him while he performed a tactical withdrawal from our property. Dereliction of duty had never seemed so appealing.

As the standoff didn't appear to be reaching any sort of satisfactory conclusion on its own I grabbed my phone and called Kristjana. The night before I had been so tired that I had lost all interest in dealing with her. Now, though, she presented a speedy solution to the struggle unfolding before my eyes in the dim morning half-light. Her desperate need to talk to Dad as soon as I told her our awful news would be the perfect remedy to the skirmish unfolding before me.

She answered after a few rings, her voice heavy with sleep and confusion. I told her to take a minute to collect herself and then enlightened her as to what had happened to Jóhannes and Magga. She didn't interrupt once as I calmly recounted the events of just over twenty-four hours ago to her as best I could. Her listening in complete silence either meant she was having trouble believing me or was finding it too overwhelming to absorb. It was especially early in the day to be listening to such bad news but I found the absolute quiet on the other end of the line a little unsettling. It was almost a relief when she began sobbing quietly into the phone.

I told her I would be far too busy to drive back into town to pick her up but that she could talk to Dad if she wanted to. She did want to; at least I was pretty sure that's what she said. I wandered outside, waving the phone at my father. The beleaguered officer had retreated into his vehicle and was talking on his phone also.

I grabbed Dad and shoved the phone into his hand. It had the desired effect, as I knew it would. He wandered off into the stables berating his middle daughter for not being in complete control of her emotions at such a time. For a man who had been through such an ordeal he still didn't see any need for sentimentality.

I quickly took the opportunity to get into the car with the officer and apologise for Dad's gruff manner. He wanted to know what to do. He was prepared to stay as long as I wished but his face told a different story. I recalled Grímur telling me that he would be posted at the house for as long as I wanted him there so I told him he could go. The news was warmly received and he didn't waste any time pointing the car back towards Hafnarfjörður. As he was leaving he told me that if we had any trouble they would send someone back out straight away but that it might be someone else. I thanked him for his trouble but my words fell on deaf ears as he took off down the driveway.

Dad was now sitting inside the stables and seemed to have calmed down considerably. He had even adopted a more conciliatory tone with Kristjana and was answering her questions with patience and consideration. She was obviously demanding a thorough explanation of what had happened and so I took the opportunity to hurry back into the house.

As Dad's conversation with Kristjana finally came to an end, so did his patience and I overheard him telling her to focus her emotions on something more constructive. Not something she was well known for but he probably thought it to be good advice nonetheless. He had always struggled to understand the more sensitive of his three daughters just as Kristjana had struggled with his inability to take an interest in the many things she found so concerning.

With their conversation over Dad signalled through the kitchen window that I was needed outside again. It seemed that he was ready to put me to work. With very little in the way of conversation between us I helped him attach the old plough harnesses that hadn't been used in years to the two stallions. Once that was done I stepped back and let Dad get to work on attaching some ropes to the tarpaulin covering poor Magga. It was time to take her out of the stables for the very last time and find her a place to rest.

Once he was done I led the two horses very slowly through the rain following Dad as he walked ahead of us with his head hanging low. He seemed to already have a spot picked out in his mind where our solemn duty would be conducted. Magga's carcass made a horrible sound as her plastic shroud scraped its way across the property. Although it was cold to be out, I was glad of the rain for once; it would have loosened the ground for us, making the hole that much easier to dig. Even as the sun rose slowly in the sky, the gloom refused to budge in any way. It was if the day knew of the task we had been assigned and did not wish to intrude unnecessarily upon it.

Once Dad signalled where we were to stop I unfastened the stallions from their harnesses and let them graze where they wished. They had spent too long locked up since Jóhannes's death and so I retrieved Leppatuska from the stables as well and let the three of them stretch their legs.

By the time I returned, Dad had marked a rectangular line on the ground with a shovel so we silently went about our work. I had been right about the soil; the rain had relaxed it to the point where the black dirt parted relatively easily for us. Still, after a few feet of digging my arms and back ached. I was seriously unaccustomed to any sort of physical labour and regretted not keeping myself in better shape. If Dad was feeling the same way he certainly didn't let it show. If looks were anything to go by it was I who was feeling my age.

In order not to appear to be the weak link in the team I redoubled my efforts as best I could. It was easier said than done, though, and as I found that the digging was easier in some parts than in others, it was to the softer areas that my shovel slowly drifted. I thought nothing of it, figuring that a hole was a hole no matter where it was dug.

It wasn't until one of my thrusts hit something solid that I stopped to think about where I was digging. The ground all around us was full of small rocks but what I had hit with my spade looked different. It was old and discoloured but definitely looked like a piece of bone. The sudden cessation of activity on my part had drawn Dad's attention. The flash of anger that flashed across his face was short lived but I instantly knew that I should have paid more attention to what I was doing.

'That is exactly why I wanted you to keep to the lines I had drawn. Do you think I went to all that trouble just for fun?'

'What is it?' I still couldn't see that I had done too much wrong but obviously I had.

Dad took a deep, exasperated breath to calm himself and then slowly explained, 'Not long after you lot moved out of here when your mother died I had to bury a horse right where we are now. I had it here only a few weeks before it got sick and I eventually had to put it down. You've got to pay more attention to what you're doing. I want Magga to lie next to the poor thing not on top of it.'

Looking more closely at the horse's bone I could understand why he had been so particular about where we were to dig. I hoped I hadn't damaged the poor creature's remains too badly and apologised silently for what I had unwittingly done.

Under Dad's watchful eye I resumed digging, making sure that I kept the pit to the area that he'd originally intended.

'Tell me, Dad. Who would have wanted to do that to Jóhannes? I possibly didn't know him as well as you but I can't imagine him having any enemies. I can't believe that anyone would hate him so much that they would want to do that to him.'

'I don't know who would have wanted to do such a thing. As far as I know the lad didn't have any friends let alone enemies.'

I thought about who had put all those scars on his back and supposed that there was no way we could know everything about anyone's past.

'Why did they make you watch?' I continued, thinking out loud now more than anything else. 'If it was Jóhannes they wanted to kill then why go to all the trouble of tying you up like that? Why would they be so bothered about you watching what they'd done to him?'

'I don't know, Ylfa. I just don't know.'

'What did he look like, lying there?'

'He looked scared, I guess.'

'Scared?'

'Yes. With his hands over his eyes like that he looked like he had seen something terrible and couldn't look any more.'

'They put his hands over his eyes, though?'

'I think so. He had been positioned like that with his eyes covered and his mouth slightly open.'

'Like he had been trying to yell out for help, maybe?'

'His mouth was open because there was something stuck in it holding it open.'

'Like a gag?'

'I couldn't be absolutely sure but it looked like a piece of paper rolled up into a ball.'

We seemed to have got the hole to the depth that was required and Dad waved a hand over to where the two stallions had wandered.

'Fetch Alvari and Farfús and let's get Magga into the ground. I can't spend all day doing this; I'm tired enough as it is.'

I reattached the two stallions to their sad cargo and we dragged Magga the few remaining feet to her grave.

I found watching Magga drop into the sodden black ground quite upsetting. Nothing could ever make me understand why anyone would want to do that sort of thing to an animal. People you can learn to hate along the way for whatever reasons but animals are incapable of going out of their way to make you loathe them.

As if reading my mind, Dad put his hand on my shoulder and pulled me to him. Something he hadn't done since I was young. As he held me I sobbed whole-heartedly into his already sodden chest. I tried to rub the tears from my eyes but only succeeded in making it more difficult to see. I felt more vulnerable then as he held me to him than I had since I was a very small child.

'You've done more than enough today, my girl. Get back inside and get yourself dried off. I'll finish it from here. You've done all the hard work for me.'

The way he looked at me, I couldn't argue with him. I threw a ceremonial shovelful of earth over Magga, mouthed a silent farewell to her and headed back to the house. I threw one last glance back over my shoulder at Dad. He stood in the pouring rain over the grave with his head hung low in solemn prayer.

He wasn't a broken man but he had taken a big hit. He had lost two very good friends in one go and it was going to be some time before he realised just how much he was actually going to miss them. In the meantime it would fall to me to make sure he was able to carry on. Not as if nothing had happened, but in a manner that was as close to the way he had previously lived as possible. People are creatures of habit and it would take him time to find a new routine without them. Not only that but his head was still bandaged and he couldn't be left on his own until he had completely recovered.

As I approached the house I noticed the lights were still on in Jóhannes's flat. The police probably hadn't bothered switching them off when they'd finished searching the place. I pulled down the black and yellow tape from across the doorway and walked inside. His bed, which he should have been propped up on playing some violent video game or other, was covered in all sorts of belongings that had just been left strewn about the place. His room had always looked a mess but the way the police had left it was nothing short of a shambles.

Any of the surfaces that might once have been clean had been covered with dirty-looking fingerprint powder that made the place looked unloved and soiled.

It was going to take some getting used to not having him around any more. It was even harder struggling with the thought that someone had wanted to do him such harm. To make an enemy like that I'd imagine you would have to be a pretty nasty character yourself. It was hard to think of him keeping that sort of company. The odd thing was that I couldn't remember having ever seen him with anybody. He had been a loner in the true sense of the word.

I made a very half-hearted attempt to tidy up the place. There were books, clothes, pieces of paper and no end of assorted paraphernalia strewn throughout the small room. All I could do was stack things in piles of similar-looking objects.

The task of actually putting the place back as it used to be was not one I was ready to tackle yet. For the time being it was going to have to be enough to attempt to put his lodgings back in some semblance of order.

As I collected various pages of paper and notes that he had written to himself in one of the piles something in his handwriting caught my eye. On a page that contained some sort of computer-related jargon and lots of numbers in ascending order, scores from a game, perhaps, or computer code of some kind, I found carefully written:

Let him be drenched with the dew of heaven,
and let him live with the animals.

I was prepared to chance a guess at where that phrase had come from. In fact I was pretty sure I had seen it before. What I couldn't understand was what it was doing written down in his room. A quick search revealed what I already suspected: he didn't own a Bible and I had never known him to go to church.

Why, then, would he have a quote from the Book of Daniel lying around amongst some other fairly mundane facts and figures? Was it something he had read? Was it something that been said to him and he had needed to remember?

I folded the sheet of paper up and stuck it in a pocket. The urge to tidy his room had left me and I decided to leave the place in peace for the time being. There were things about Jóhannes I would probably never fully understand now that he was gone but in order to get to the bottom of what had happened to him, I was going to have to try.

CHAPTER 7

Jóhannes's death and our subsequent burial of Magga had left me fixating on the first loss that had really shaped my life, that of my dear mother. Margrét Ogmundsdóttir, the real Magga. The shock of listening to her tell us she was sick and then watching as the invisible enemy within tightened its grip on her was hard for us to take as teenagers.

In some ways the worst part was watching the reaction, or sometimes lack thereof, from each other. Until that time we had been three relatively straightforward sisters who played, argued and laughed as one. After her death, once the force that had held us together had gone from our lives, we began to see each other differently. We started to see faults with each other where before there had been none to see. Sisters were perceived to be too dramatic in their grief or conversely, not caring enough. It seemed that it was no longer in our powers to keep each other happy.

The toughest thing for Dad was that in his hour of need, due to our petty squabbles and selfish personalities, we decided that it was time for us to each go our own way. He was left alone at the very time when he probably needed us more than ever. He never said anything to any of us but it must have hurt like hell.

In my lifetime he had never appeared to need anybody else's help, so when the time came when he eventually did, none of us thought to even offer.

I could now see that we had been completely wrong. No one could go through what he had and not want someone around to depend on. I was going to make sure that it didn't happen again and I was going to do that by making sure I was there for him now.

In the days following our burial of Magga I did what had to be done to help him get through the shock of it all. I finished tidying up Jóhannes's flat, I cooked when he would let me, but mainly I looked after the horses. I exercised them, brushed them down, kept them fed and watered and cleaned the stalls out for them each day. Even with Magga gone and only three to look after I just couldn't see how he would manage on his own. It was simply too much for one person of his age but the time wasn't at all right for bringing that up. Another thing that had to be brought up at some point was why he had chosen now to sign the property over to me. He had never so much as mentioned it before and I hoped that there was some innocent explanation for the timing of it. I wasn't in any sort of mood for more bad news.

For the time being I was going to let things work themselves out at their own pace. Life has a knack of showing you the way if you'll just let it.

I called Grímur several times to see if there were any updates he could give me on the investigation. His concern about how Dad was coping seemed genuine enough but he wasn't interested in divulging any information pertaining to the case. When I asked him directly about the object that Dad had seen in Jóhannes's mouth I was met with a cold, non-responsive answer.

If he could have told me to just mind my own business I think he would have. It was possible that they had no idea who had killed Jóhannes and that was just the way it was. I certainly couldn't picture who it might have been and I don't think Dad could, either. Some people just do stupid things because they're stupid themselves.

One thing that Grímur did say was that crimes without motives were the hardest ones to solve. If they never found out who was responsible it would be impossible to understand why it had happened. The pain and the sadness would slowly fade in time, but if the reason for it happening remained a mystery, then that was a bad feeling that would never go away.

Like a stain you couldn't get rid of on something that was too precious to just throw away. You would always be reminded of something beautiful that you had once had and was now ruined.

I knew the time to leave had come when Dad could no longer hide his irritation at my continued presence. A sure sign that he was well on the way back to being his usual self. This realisation coincided with the day of Kristjana's maiden performance with the Icelandic Symphony Orchestra. I slipped away early that morning leaving Dad a note telling him that all he needed to do was call and I would be straight back but that I thought we could both probably do with a little space. I also made it clear that despite the fact that I hadn't mentioned it, I wouldn't be signing the title deed to the property until he had explained why he was doing it now. As far as I was concerned there was no hurry to do anything of the sort, and if there was, I wanted to know why first.

He wasn't the only one looking forward to some time to themselves. I had, for the meantime anyway, had enough of mucking out stalls and dodging my father's unpredictable mood swings. It was time to unwind and forget the traumas of the last few days and I knew just the way to do it. It would be all too easy convincing Baldvin to drop everything and meet me at Vesturgata, so that was just what I would do.

I gave myself half an hour to roughly tidy the place before calling him. The flat was beginning to get a rather overly lived-in look about it. There were definite signs that the canvases and painting paraphernalia were taking over the place. But rather than banish them completely we had to come to a compromise that involved a kind of land-sharing agreement. I couldn't let them take over the place altogether but on the other hand they were essential to my wellbeing.

I had in fact already planned to use them again as soon as I was done relieving the tension that had built up across my shoulders. I had mentioned it to Baldvin a few weeks earlier just after we'd first met when he'd come into the bar for a drink. He had been on his own and as it was a quiet night he had sat at the bar and we'd struck up a conversation as I'd polished glasses. Even though he had agreed to it, I still wasn't convinced that he'd taken me seriously.

After a few visits to my flat he had seen enough of my paintings and had still agreed to pose for me but probably thought that I would never actually get around to it. Well, if that was what he thought then he had been wrong. Very wrong.

During my tidying burst I had kept to hand the bits and pieces that I would need to start work on a new piece and as soon as we were done in the bedroom that was exactly what I did.

I didn't need to persuade him to get undressed; it was getting him to stand still that was the problem. His natural tendency was to keep moving about the place but once he realised that we weren't playing a game he made a better statue than I would have ever imagined.

In an effort to preserve his dignity when people viewed the finished product he insisted that he get to face away from me while I was drawing him. I had happily agreed to this one demand. As long as he was posing for me, I didn't really care.

If he'd been concerned about me making the experience a little uncomfortable then he really shouldn't have worried. As it turned out I don't think things could have been more uncomfortable for him if I'd been trying to make him nervous.

For as long as we'd been living away from home both Kristjana and I had always had a set of keys for each other's flats. I'm pretty sure that it had originally been her idea, just in case one of us locked ourselves out of our own flat.

This arrangement had come in handy on many occasions but as my sister had always been a bit more needy than me in the company department, she used hers a lot more than I used mine. I tended to revel in whatever time I had to myself whereas she found living on her own boring if she didn't have something to do.

Her cello took up plenty of her time when she wasn't selling t-shirts and woollen jumpers to tourists in a shop on Laugavegur, but as she only needed to walk down Stýrimannastígur and then turn right at the end of the street onto Vesturgata, I got more than my fair share of unexpected visits.

There had been occasions when I had been known to turn my phone to silent mode when I didn't feel like being disturbed, even though it would only make her all the more desperate to contact me. I'd figured that since she was performing later in the day she would have more than enough on her plate and might just leave me alone. That way Baldvin and I could be left alone until I had to meet up with Elín later on. Of course, as happens so often in life, I was quite wrong.

As the front door opened I could see Baldvin flinch as his instincts told him to cover himself with his hands. I had just about got my first outline done and wasn't about to redo it.

'Stay exactly as you are,' I ordered him in a no-nonsense tone.

On top of the fact that I didn't want him moving just yet, I knew that the only person it could be was Kristjana. For the life of me I couldn't think of a better way to put her off bursting in on me than having her confronted with Baldvin front on in his present state of undress.

She had never had much success dating men and was as awkward around them as anyone I'd ever met. I knew that her jaw would hit the floor as soon as she walked in and I wasn't at all disappointed with the reaction I got.

On her way down the street she had managed to get herself soaking wet. She was wearing her cello in its hard case like a backpack and her wet hair clung to her face as she struggled to figure out where she should be looking. Or not looking, as the case might be. Her surprise and shock slowly turned to something approaching amusement as she figured out what it was that she had stumbled upon.

'You can close your mouth now. You've got Baldvin at something of a disadvantage here. He can't shake your hand right now. I'm sure he'd like to, though.'

Kristjana took the cello case off her back and leant it up against the wall.

'I tried to call but you're not answering your phone and when I saw your car outside I just... I should have knocked, though, I can see that now. Nice to meet you, Baldvin, I'm Kristjana, Ylfa's sister. I'm sure she's told you all about me.'

She moved to offer him her hand but realised he had his fingers locked together behind his head for the pose. With no idea what to do with herself she just stood where she was, talking rapidly to calm her nerves or perhaps because of them.

Baldvin, on the other hand, had little or no choice but to stand there until she had finished saying her piece. I would have given pretty much anything to see the expression on his face as this imbecilic girl stood in front of him instead of making herself scarce.

'Baldvin, I'm playing tonight at Harpa. You should come along if you're not doing anything. In fact I need a lift there, that's why I came over. I need to find a towel, I'm soaked. I must look a real sight,' she said as much to herself as anyone else and finally headed off to the bathroom. She was smiling from ear to ear while trying very hard not to. I could hear Baldvin exhale heavily as she walked out of the room. I was hoping they had both found the experience as uncomfortable as I had found it amusing.

'You'll have to forgive her, she doesn't get out much. I'm so sorry about that,' I lied through my teeth. 'I had no idea she was coming over.' That was the truth at least.

'I hope she didn't let too much cold air in,' I said successfully resisting the urge to burst out laughing.

Baldvin cleared his throat hesitantly; he was obviously feeling a little awkward. I wasn't at all sure how men felt about being naked in front of a girl they'd never met before but I would have been in shock if it had been me. He still didn't know what to say.

'I won't be much longer if you can just hold that pose for me. Then I suppose I'll have to give her a lift down to Harpa.'

'No problem,' he finally said without turning around. 'I think she got a bigger shock than I did. I could give her a lift when we're done. I have to head back to Álftamýri soon so it would be on my way.'

'That'd suit me just fine, I hate being her taxi driver.'

By the time Kristjana had towelled herself off and made us all some coffee I had finished most of my painting and graciously allowed Baldvin to dress himself once again. If he had found meeting my sister uncomfortable he wasn't letting it show. If nothing else, it would give Kristjana something to talk about with her orchestra buddies later on.

Once we were all sitting around the kitchen table drinking our coffee I decided to bring up the recent events at the house. Kristjana had been terribly shocked at what had occurred but had been silent on the subject since her unexpected arrival. She had only met Jóhannes a few times but the thought of such violence so close to home had caused her great distress, as it had us all.

'It could have turned out even worse than it actually did,' she said alluding to the fact that Dad could quite easily have been killed as well.

'I think that if whoever was responsible had wanted him dead then he would be,' I said.

'What do you mean?' Kristjana asked.

'If they'd wanted him dead as well then he wouldn't be with us any more. He was meant to survive so he could observe it all. It's possible it was meant as some kind of warning. Dad seems to think there was a note left in Jóhannes's mouth but the police haven't said anything about it. He could have been mistaken, though; it must have all been pretty traumatic.'

'It sounds like something those biker types would do. Maybe Jóhannes owed them money for drugs. This could have been their way of settling the debt,' Kristjana suggested.

'It would have to have been a great deal of money. I'm not aware of him knowing anyone like that and I like to think that I knew him pretty well. He was a good boy, he wasn't mixed up in anything stupid like that,' I felt the need to defend poor Jóhannes since he was no longer around to do so himself.

The image of the scars down his back appeared to me as an unbidden reminder that there were probably plenty of things that I didn't know about him, no matter what I thought.

'I don't see any other explanation for it, though,' Kristjana continued. 'It's hard to see what an old man like our father could have done to make someone so angry. He's never done anything to anyone.'

'It's about time that Baldvin was heading off. He's going to drop you off on his way home. That way I can clean up here and I'll see you after the concert.'

'Make sure you sit down the front so I can see you both.'

She picked her cello case up off the floor and put it on her back again.

'It looks like we're off, then,' Baldvin said.

I gave him a peck on the cheek and told him I'd call him later. As they walked out the door together Kristjana smiled at him in a way that would have made me a little jealous if I hadn't known her better. Maybe it was just time that she got herself a man of her own.

CHAPTER 8

By the time I reached Harpa prior to my date with Elín, the rain had moved away but the wind was now strong enough to make walking into it something of a struggle. I had called Elín one last time to once again ensure her attendance and had been reassured that she would be there as soon as she was finished at the office. She worked in a modern building on Borgartún, which was no more than two or three minutes away if she drove or in the more unlikely scenario that she decided to walk, it would still only take her around ten minutes. I could almost begin to relax.

Still, my nerves dictated that I head straight for the restaurant bar on the ground floor as soon as I arrived. The open-plan dining and bar area was crowded with festival-goers from near and far. It was the second night of a major local festival that involved musical acts from all over Iceland but also incorporated bands from Europe and North America. The concert hall had been in operation for about three years now and served as one of the festival's main venues. The rest of the year it was home for the orchestra with whom Kristjana was to about to perform for the first time. The material they were to play was the work of a local artist, an up-and-coming composer who had made a name for himself both in Iceland and overseas.

I still hadn't seen the interior of Eldborg, the concert chamber in which she would be performing but by all accounts it was quite impressive. It was the largest of four performance spaces within the building and located up an imposing staircase on the first floor. As the minutes ticked by I became more and more aware of exactly how nervous I really was. About Elín, that was. Despite all her promises I knew all too well that for her, old habits die hard. I moved myself to the bar on the first floor balcony where I would be close to the Eldborg doors and was still in a good position to see anyone arriving below.

Two beers later my worst fears were realised as I heard the bell from within the hall heralding the imminent beginning of the performance. Still no sign of Elín. I cursed her solidly out loud without thinking where I was, drawing more than a few stares from other Icelandic concert goers. I joined the line filing into the hall and then looked around for somewhere to sit, alone. Despite Kristjana's suggestion that I sit as near to the stage as possible I decided to find somewhere nearer the back where my unaccompanied presence would not be noticed. I didn't want Kristjana to know that her horrible older sister hadn't made the effort to show up until after the performance. I was going to have harsh words with her as soon as I could. She had lied to the both of us repeatedly, and for the last time. I had reached my breaking point with her.

The blood-red velvet interior of the chamber gave the place a remarkably intimate atmosphere despite its 1,500-seat capacity. The low ceiling beneath the upper tiers added to the compact feeling and while I had a good line of sight to the stage I couldn't actually see any of the people above me. It felt cosy and grand all at the same time.

As the musicians filed out onto the large black stage I saw Kristjana take her seat on the right hand side with the rest of the cellists. She appeared calm and at ease, and was not looking about the room for us as I thought she might have done. I was genuinely happy for her; she was finally doing what she had always wanted to do.

Kristjana performed the first piece and didn't return for the second. I assumed she was backstage relaxing. Some people in the crowd seemed a little restless after the first piece. A lot of them left and the venue was filled again with new arrivals for the second recital. It was hard to tell if people had actually come to see the orchestra perform or if they were simply using their festival wristbands to their full advantage, taking in as many different venues as they possibly could in one night.

After the show was over I waited just outside the doors for her to appear. When she eventually did she gave me a huge hug as a greeting. Noticing the look on my face she asked straight away if Elín had come and I just shook my head. I wanted more than anything to wring Elín's neck like a chicken destined for the oven. She was really going to get it when I got hold of her.

Kristjana and her orchestra friends were heading out for a drink to celebrate their performance and wanted to know if I would join them. I briefly toyed with the idea but I knew that if I put off confronting Elín then my rage would dissipate and I would let her off the hook, again. I wasn't going to allow that to happen this time.

My mind was made up for me when one of the other girls wanted to know all about the murder at our farm. She had heard about it on the news and wanted to know if there was anything that had been left out in the broadcast.

'Left out?' I wasn't sure what she was talking about.

'Well,' she continued in a tone which inferred that I was expected to confirm or deny whatever rumour it was she had heard, 'I heard the killer is some kind of religious freak who left a quote from the Bible on the dead boy.'

Kristjana looked at me wondering if I was planning to make any kind of comment on the matter. I wasn't. I could tell she was dying to discuss what had happened but as far as I was concerned it was neither the time nor the place for it.

'We'll go see Dad together tomorrow,' I suggested. 'I'll call you in the morning but I've got to go.'

I squeezed her arm, ignoring the disappointed look on her face, and made my way back down the huge staircase as quickly as I could without seeming to hurry.

The rain had started again, sending dark sheets of water across the glass front of the building. Digging deep into my reservoir of loathing I pulled a woollen cap over my head and set off down Sæbraut towards Elín's office building. The clouds over Faxaflói Bay were dark and mischievous. The wind was sending spray up over the breakwater onto the road so I crossed over as I headed towards Snorrabraut and the back of the police station.

As I approached the police car park I wondered if Grímur was inside the building anywhere and if he was getting any closer to figuring out who killed Jóhannes. I turned onto Borgartún and headed for where I felt convinced my sister would still be. This time she was going to get to hear all about what the two of us really thought of her. If she was planning to leave the country then the sooner she did so the better as far as I was concerned. I had had enough of her self-centred ways and her broken promises. I couldn't have cared less if I never saw her again.

When I got to the corner of Borgartún and Noatún I looked across the car park that she and her fellow workers used to see if I could spot her car. It wasn't anywhere to be seen but it was possible that she had parked in the underground parking area. I wasn't going to let anything put me off looking for her now I'd made the effort and got myself soaking wet into the bargain.

While I was walking to the rear entrance of the building a motorcyclist appeared out of nowhere and almost bowled me over in his hurry to get back onto the street. As I turned to scream obscenities at him he was already heading east on Borgartún. My anger turned to concern when I saw that the back door of the building was open slightly. I had never seen it left open before during the day let alone at what had to be approaching ten o'clock in the evening. I began to wonder why it was that the man on the bike had been in such a hurry.

I looked up into the wild night sky and saw that the lights on Elín's floor were still burning bright. Only Elín could think that work was more important than her sisters. The woman's priorities were as skewed as her taste in men. It wasn't hard to imagine that life would easier without her around. I was starting to take a shine to her idea of leaving us behind for whatever it was she wanted to do elsewhere.

By the time I had made my way up to the third floor my feeling of concern had turned into something more serious. There wasn't a sound coming from anywhere in the building and no one answered my calls as I stepped out of the lift. The place was too quiet. Silent, except for the squishing sound my shoes made as I trudged along the carpet towards her office.

I wanted to hear her voice calling out to me to let me know that she was there but there was nothing, not a word. The door to her office was open and the lights were on but it was empty. As I looked around her desk, though, I could see signs that she was possibly still around. Her keys were lying next to her phone on the floor next to her seat. As I bent down to pick them up I noticed a strange chemical smell I hadn't come across before. It felt out of place in her office, medical almost.

I sat down in her chair staring at the keys and phone in my hand wondering what the hell was going on. There was a small business card holder on her desk. I reached out and took one of them: Elín Einarsdóttir, my sister and yet such a mystery to us all. I pocketed the card and looked about the office for some sort of clue as to where she might be. I was starting to think that maybe she had just gone to the toilet or popped out to the all-night 7-11 on the other side of the building. That was when I saw the piece of paper stuck to the wall like some sort of bizarre reminder on a fridge door. Something inside me twisted itself into a knot as I read the note. It was the familiarity of it that scared me. That and the certain knowledge that my sister was gone, and not the way she had planned.

Suddenly the fingers of a human hand appeared
and wrote on the plaster of the wall.

An old quote that I had heard years ago came back to me: once is happenstance, twice is coincidence but three times is the work of the enemy. I couldn't remember who it was who had said it but I knew one thing for sure: somewhere out there we all had a new enemy to contend with, whether we wanted to or not.

CHAPTER 9

Once I had fished Grímur's number out of my pocket, he arrived within about five minutes. At first I thought he might have been down the road in his office after all but when he arrived, for some reason I couldn't quite fathom, he had a dog with him. I was standing waiting for him at the back door as he and his black dog made their way across the car park. He must have noticed the slightly bemused look on my face as I greeted him.

'I only live up the street on Hátún and Bobbi was due his late night walk anyway. I like to take him out before bed each night.'

Bobbi was a Labrador from what I knew about dogs and he was slightly morose-looking, a little like his owner. When I offered my hand to Bobbi he seemed somewhat indifferent to the idea of meeting me. Grímur tied him to a post and took out his notebook. He asked me to go through everything for him once again so that this time he could make notes and then we would make our way up to the third floor for a look around. The fact that we were standing in a howling wind in the rain didn't seem to bother him. I suggested we move somewhere undercover as Bobbi stood sullenly in the downpour.

I started off my story with Elín not showing up to the performance and felt compelled to tell him that I hadn't been completely surprised that she hadn't appeared.

'So it's not that unusual for her to be unreliable, then?'

'No, it's not, but her keys and wallet are still here and she's nowhere to be seen. That's unusual.'

He wanted to know if I had touched anything while I'd been in her office. I told him that as far as I could remember I had only handled her keys and phone. I had left them on her desk but made sure that he knew they'd been on the floor when I found them. I told him about the note but not the fact that I'd photographed it on my phone. These religious quotations were no longer merely items of curiosity; they meant something and I was determined to discover exactly what that was.

'I'm going to have a look around on my own first and then I'll be back down. Björn will be here soon, you can send him up when he arrives,' Grímur said. 'If you'd keep an eye on Bobbi for me I'd really appreciate it.'

And so I was left standing alone looking out into the pouring rain with a wet Labrador for company while he disappeared inside. As soon as he was gone I untied the unfortunate dog and we both sheltered just inside the door on a rubber mat that had been purchased with exactly such weather in mind. True to Grímur's word it wasn't long before Björn arrived with his now familiar briefcase in tow. He hurried through the rain and into the building where he was greeted with much more enthusiasm than I'd received from my new friend Bobbi.

'Wet out there tonight, Ylfa.'

I was a little surprised that he had remembered my name but took it as something of a compliment.

'Grímur's up on the third floor having a look around. I'm not allowed back up until he says so, apparently.'

'He just doesn't want the scene disturbed.'

'Let me ask you something, Björn. My father says that there was something in Jóhannes's mouth when he was killed. Is that right or is he just making it up?'

Björn crouched down to scratch Bobbi's head for him and pretended not to hear me. Either that or he was trying to decide how he should answer. Eventually, he stood up again and looked me in the eye. He had been mulling over how much he should tell me and the fact that Grímur wasn't around might just have swung things in my favour.

'Look, sometimes there are details about cases like Jóhannes's that we like to keep to ourselves. A little something that only the killer would know. We don't want this becoming public knowledge, you must remember that.'

I nodded to indicate that I understood.

'There was a note left behind scrunched up in Jóhannes's mouth. It bore a striking resemblance to the one that we found at the scene of the Ketamine theft in Mosfellsbær.'

'And the one upstairs,' I added.

He nodded in a way that made me even more worried than I already was. I was just about to ask him what the note had said when Grímur reappeared. Björn threw me a quick look, which suggested I should keep our conversation to myself.

'Björn, good to see you. We should all head back up now, I think,' Grímur said. 'Just leave Bobbi where he is, he'll be fine. He can let us know if anyone else wants to use the door. Can you tell me what sort of car Elín drives, Ylfa?'

'It's an Audi: a new one; Sepang Blue is the colour I think.'

'Is it in the car park anywhere?'

'No, unless it's under the building.'

Grímur nodded and walked outside to make a call while having a look around the car park.

'Why's his dog called Bobbi? Isn't it an odd sort of name for a dog?' I asked Björn.

'He's named after the American chess player. Grímur met him when he was much younger.'

'What was in the note you found on Jóhannes?'

'You're not to tell anyone, remember?'

I nodded in agreement, wishing that he'd just get on with it.

'It was a quote from the Book of Daniel. Daniel 4:15: Let him be drenched with the dew of heaven, and let him live with the animals. I've no idea what it is supposed to mean in the context of his death but there is a connection to the other crime, as I said. And now this.'

A police car pulled up outside and one of the officers got out to talk to Grímur briefly before driving off again. When he had made his way back inside he signalled for us to follow him upstairs. I appreciated Björn's candour and wanted to see his reaction when he saw the note in Elín's office. The note in Jóhannes's mouth had been the same wording as what he'd written down in his flat. Somehow he had come across it before and I didn't think it had been in Bible class.

Upstairs, Björn stared long and hard at the letter before carefully putting it in an evidence bag. I had thought he would spend ages going over Elín's office with a fine-toothed comb but he only seemed interested in the note. Grímur noted that there was no sign of a struggle whatsoever and that there was no clear indication that any crime had actually been committed. His phone rang; the officers he had sent away thought they might have found her Audi. Leaving Björn to his work, Grímur and I walked the short distance down Borgartún with Bobbi to where they were waiting patiently for us.

As soon as I saw it I knew it was her car and told Grímur as much. It was parked behind an older office block that sat next to the hotel at the end of the street just before the intersection with Kringlumýrarbraut. It was certainly a strange place for her to have parked considering she only worked up the road. Hidden from view and yet close enough for her to walk to from her office. Grímur pulled her keys from one of his pockets and unlocked it. There didn't appear to be anything of interest in the front or back of the car, nothing that seemed out of place, anyway. Until he opened the boot. Two suitcases and a smaller shoulder bag sat next to each other.

Grímur opened the shoulder bag and found her laptop, passport and some airline tickets. She had planned to catch the first flight to London the next day and then on to Spain from Heathrow. Bilbao in the Basque country seemed to be her final destination. It appeared that her threat to leave us all behind hadn't been all bluster and noise after all. Except, of course, that she still hadn't made it away. If she was planning to catch these flights then she would struggle to do so without her car keys, wallet, tickets and passport.

'Did you know she was going away?' Grímur asked.

'She had mentioned it but I wasn't convinced she was serious. A lot of the things she says are just talk. She did say she was sick of Reykjavík and wanted to start over somewhere new.'

'Did she mention anything about Bilbao?'

I shook my head. As far as I knew she didn't even know where Bilbao was but obviously she did. I was suddenly very confused. Maybe she had decided to say goodbye at the concert but if that was the case, why hadn't she shown? Had she gone through with her crazy plan and that was why she had disappeared? Was that why Jóhannes had been killed? Grímur was watching me intently as if trying to read my mind.

'Is there something you want to tell me, Ylfa?'

I told him there was and that it was probably time to get out of the rain. The officers were told to watch the vehicle and her office just in case she reappeared. I felt like saying that there wasn't a hope in hell of that happening but at the same time I would have given anything for her to walk around the corner and ask us what we thought we were up to.

A little later as I sat on one side of an old wooden desk warming my hands on a cup of hot coffee, I was about to tell Grímur all about the ridiculous plan that Elín had dreamt up to fund her escape. Her escape from what, he was bound to want to know. I couldn't very well tell him until I knew myself. The best I would be able to come up with would be that she had decided to run away from herself. Hopefully the situation would make more sense to him than it did to me.

It dawned on me that I should have watched the stupid email attachment she had sent me after all. I desperately hoped that the last memory I would have of my rather irksome sister wouldn't be her writhing about naked with someone she obviously despised. Hope as I might, it was entirely possible that her video would indeed be my enduring memory of her if she didn't suddenly appear out of thin air. I was going to wind up hating her for that too. Somehow it just seemed to fit in annoyingly well with all her other selfish tricks. Grímur took his seat opposite me and asked me what was on my mind.

'I think someone's taken my sister.'

'Why do you think that, Ylfa?'

'She has been seeing someone. A married man. She told me that she'd had enough of her life here in Reykjavík and that she wanted to get away and start afresh. In order to do that she was going to need some money and she said that she was going to get it from this lover of hers.'

'He was going to give her the money?'

'Yes, but not willingly.'

'Can you clarify that answer a little for me?'

'She was going to extract it from him, unfairly.'

A stifled but nonetheless broad grin crept across Grímur's face. He obviously found my choice of words amusing.

'Extracting money from people unfairly is usually illegal in my experience, Ylfa. Was she planning to break the law?'

'I guess she was. She was planning to film them having sex and then persuade him to give her enough money to leave the country.'

'And did she go through with this plan? Did she manage to persuade him to do such a foolish thing?'

'I'm not sure. I know she made the movie and she obviously has tickets to leave tomorrow but I don't know if she managed to follow through with the rest of it.'

'By, the rest of it, I assume you mean the money.'

I nodded, unsure about how much more I should actually say.

'The reason I haven't said anything to anybody is that I didn't think she'd go through with it. I thought she was just fooling around and that she'd patch things up with him and he'd buy her something nice and she'd forget all about it.'

'Who is this man?'

'I don't know.'

He seemed to accept the answer even though I wouldn't have if I'd been him. He must have wondered why on earth I hadn't tried to talk her out of her stupidity. It was because chances were that she wouldn't have listened to me anyway.

'Do you think if we have a look at her laptop we might find out who he is? That isn't something I would normally do but under the circumstances I think it might be a good idea.'

I wanted to go home, open her email and satisfy my own curiosity before answering that question. Just In Case was the title she had given it. Just in case something happened was what I think she had said. Just in case what, Elín? Just in case my sister's too stupid to do this without getting hurt. Is that what you meant to say? Just in case you mess this up really badly and I have to pick up the pieces?

Grímur was staring at me, no doubt wondering what my next move would be and how he would counter it. He was going to have a look at the laptop sooner or later, whether I wanted him to or not. Something had happened to her and anything we could do to find out what that was had to be done. I found myself nodding the answer back across the table to him.

'Yes, I think we should have a look at her laptop,' I said.

'All right then, that's what we'll do.'

He made a call and asked someone to join us. When he was finished he looked at me again. More than likely he was silently calculating whether he was being told the truth or not. He was probably someone who only asked questions when he had to. The rest of the time he just let people tell him what he wanted to know in their own time.

'Ylfa, do you remember when she made this recording? Would you remember when it was in relation to what occurred at your father's farm? You see what I'm getting at here?'

'I do, see what you're getting at, that is,' I said. Until that moment I hadn't even contemplated there being a connection between the two events. I had a feeling that Grímur had learned to see connections where maybe others didn't quite yet. A character trait that his chess hero once had in abundance.

'The night she told me she was sending me a copy of it I had just left Dad and Jóhannes at the farm. I have no idea when she actually recorded it, though.'

'She sent you a copy of the tape?' Grímur was sounding slightly angry now. He must have still thought I wasn't telling him the whole story.

'She sent me an email but told me not to watch it unless I wanted to see her doing the business and frankly, I didn't.'

Grímur nodded as if he could understand that piece of logic if nothing else.

'So, it's possible she had already sent it to this man before she sent a copy to you and that could have happened before Jóhannes was killed?'

'Yes, but I really don't see the connection between the two.'

A man in his twenties walked into the room with Elín's laptop in his hands. He introduced himself as Eiríkur Matthíasson and pulled up a chair to the table. He was skinny and very fit looking, like an athlete or gym fanatic. He opened up the laptop and started typing on the keyboard. Fast and efficient, as though he already knew exactly what he was looking for.

'I'm not absolutely sure what it is you were hoping I'd find here,' he said, 'but the one thing of real interest is a file that was shot on the built-in webcam. The quality's not very good but the content's quite interesting, to say the least. Possibly not the sort of thing she'd want us looking at, though.'

He looked up and waited for Grímur to take over.

'Did she suspect something might go wrong, Ylfa?' Grímur wanted to know. 'Is that why you got a copy too? Or was it to make sure she got the money?'

He was getting angry again and I no longer knew what to say, so I said nothing at all.

CHAPTER 10

The pale legs pulled away from us, briefly revealing a pair of rather delicate, porcelain-like knees. Elín lay herself down on her bed in an overly theatrical manner. She was well aware that this was going to be viewed later and she wanted to make something of an impression. I doubted that the one it was presently having on me was what she'd had in mind but it was hard to know for sure. As she spoke, her words came out badly muffled by something covering the laptop's built-in microphone. She coyly beckoned someone toward the bed and then waited with an asinine smile on her face as another pair of legs appeared on screen.

The hairy thighs positioned themselves in front of us and with his hands on his hips, her suitor briefly attempted some levity before roughly slapping her leg to get her to move over on the bed. Knowing that this would ruin her close-up Elín refused to budge an inch and insisted that he climb on top of her where she was. The hairy backside on the screen duly obliged and before long my sister was putting on one of the worst shows of carnal enjoyment I could ever have wished to witness. Her enthusiastic partner didn't notice or just didn't care. Perhaps he considered her bedroom theatrics to be all part of the show and preferred them to whatever it was that he had grown tired of at home.

She had been right, much to my amazement. She was nothing more than a sole-use call girl for her presumably rich and hirsute lover. Occasionally, she made clumsy attempts to get him to face her hidden camera but they were brusquely brushed aside as he focused on the job at hand. He wasn't what I would have called a graceful lover but then I had never studied the act from such an objective perspective before. I was usually too busy staring at my ceiling wondering if they were going to want to stay the night or not.

If I had to be honest, Elín and I weren't as different as I sometimes liked to make out. We both used men, just for different things. She might like to pretend that she was the one constantly being taken advantage of but she took them for all they were worth. They were always rich and they always had plenty to give away. The problem she had was that the ones with money never had anything else to give her. She wanted them to love her but she never gave them any reason to. None I had ever seen, anyway.

She certainly didn't spare any effort trying to please this one, though. She had gone through what I assume was her whole repertoire of party tricks before we even got the briefest of looks at the man's face. At first it was nothing more than a fleeting glance but as soon as they were done he rolled off her and towards the camera, still blissfully unaware that he was being filmed.

For the briefest of moments he stared straight at the tiny camera in her laptop. All the day-to-day worries and problems had disappeared for a man who probably had plenty to concern himself with during the course of each and every business day. Aron Steingrímsson lit a cigarette and stared right at us through the lens.

Eiríkur pulled the piece of sticky tape that had been used to cover the ON light next to the tiny camera lens off the laptop and smiled. He looked at Grímur, who then looked at me, the three of us not really knowing what to say. Aron Steingrímsson stood up, exposing his full business credentials to the camera, and exited the shot. I hoped that that would be the last we would see of him.

Elín rolled over towards the laptop and gave the camera her best *What do you think of that, then?* smile before turning the thing off. The first image the two officers had of my sister was that of a smug, idiotic woman with no shame. If they had known her as long as I had they couldn't have got to know her any better. She was just that shallow and predictable.

Before the financial meltdown of 2008 Aron Steingrímsson had been one of the ten richest men in Iceland. Unlike many of his peers he had managed to avoid the embarrassing fall from grace that so many others had endured. He was now in the top three of that rich list. Grímur's gaze had become an intense stare. He was waiting for me to offer an explanation.

'You've got to keep in mind that I'm seeing this for the first time as well,' I said. It was supposed to placate him but it didn't work.

'Are you trying to tell me that your sister has been sleeping with Aron Steingrímsson and she's never told you about it?'

His tone said it all. If I'd been him I wouldn't have believed me no matter what I'd said next.

'She told me she'd been seeing someone, she didn't say who it was. She said he was rich and that she had become disillusioned with the way things were.'

An air of incredulity hung like a heavy cloud over the table. I could tell that Eiríkur was struggling to believe me too, although I sensed that he maybe wanted to a little bit more than his older colleague.

'So,' Grímur continued, 'she was unhappy with the way things were going. She wasn't merely content to be having an affair with one of the richest men in the country... ' he paused, waiting for me to say something but I kept my own counsel, ' ...but felt it necessary to make this foolish tape in order to blackmail him. My first impression of Elín is that she appears to be a uniquely stupid woman.'

Eiríkur had been working away on the computer, going through her files to see what else he could find. At last he took a break from his typing and looked across the table at me. His expression was more serious than it had been previously. He pushed the laptop over to Grímur to let him read something that he had found.

A wry smile spread across the old detective's face as if all his suspicions about my sister being a complete idiot had proved to be well founded after all. He struck me as a man who wasn't accustomed to being wrong all that often. He looked as if his years of seeing the worst possible sides of people had left him enjoying the times now when his misgivings about how rotten they all were inevitably proved to be correct. Without looking up from the screen he started reading what I assumed was an email my sister had written.

I thought that you might like to see what you look like while you're cheating on Róshildur. You should probably avoid her seeing this, though, don't you think? A divorce would be costly and embarrassing for you and your businesses and all I want in return for not showing her this proof of your infidelity is enough money to get out of your hair forever.

Ten million krónur or its equivalent in any major foreign currency, in cash (euros preferred) is all I require and you will never see me again. I think the figure is reasonable but if you consider it to be too steep then I will be happy to ask your wife what she considers your marriage to be worth when I meet up with her.

Grímur finally looked up at me and once more waited for a response. Again, I was not terribly forthcoming. All I wanted was some help finding my sister. It now looked as though she would be arrested as soon as they could get their hands on her. If they could get their hands on her. Her stupid plan had backfired after all. Just as she had predicted it would. And how.

'When was the email dated?' I asked hoping to throw the old dog off the scent a little. He dropped his eyes again and did some mental calculations.

'It's dated the day before the boy was killed,' he replied, realising instantly what I was getting at. 'Our main concern now, however, is the attempted extortion by your sister of ten million krónur. It goes without saying that we will need to speak to her as soon as possible.'

'But she's been kidnapped,' I protested.

'Ylfa, there is no proof whatsoever that this is the case but there is undeniable proof that she has broken the law. Do you have an address for her?'

I gave him her address on Álagrandi knowing full well that they wouldn't find her there. As far as I knew she hadn't lived in that flat for some time now. I thought hard about what she had told me about the house where she had been staying. Something on Grandavegur I think she had said, maybe with two storeys. I wish I had paid more attention to her ramblings in the bar now that I actually needed to know where she had been living. Grímur told me that I could go but that I needed to get in touch with him the minute I heard from Elín. If I heard from her.

'Don't do anything stupid before I see you again,' was his parting advice. Good advice it was too. If only I had planned on listening to him.

I knew that trying to get to sleep would be an absolute waste of time. I was convinced that the same people who had killed Jóhannes had Elín somewhere and yet the police were now looking at her as a criminal, not a victim. In a very short time she had somehow managed to become both.

Grímur was right in one respect, though; she was a spectacularly stupid woman. That she had got herself in trouble wasn't at all surprising, it was just how much trouble she had managed to land herself in that had me worried. I had to look for her. Whether I stood any chance of actually finding her was completely beside the point.

My first destination was Grandavegur, a small dead-end street that ran off Álagrandi virtually on the shore of Faxaflói Bay. If this was where she had been shacked up then she hadn't moved very far. The police would be visiting her flat any time now but they would be looking for her, not me.

There was only one house on the street that came anywhere near to the picture I had built up in my head. It was a two-storey timber house at the end of the street with a garage and a fence that ran along the front of it, affording it great privacy despite the block of flats directly opposite. It would have suited Aron perfectly for his purposes.

The rain hadn't abated and if anything, had increased a little since my walk along the harbour side. This time I had brought the car and there were now warnings on the radio that the approaching storm was imminent. It was hard to imagine the weather getting any worse but that was apparently to be the case.

Once I'd parked I sneaked over to the property's fence line, surreptitiously checking up and down the street for anyone else who might be lurking in the shadows. I was paranoid that the police might be keeping an eye on her old flat and taking down the numbers of any cars in the area. I hadn't seen anyone at all as I'd turned off Álagrandi onto Grandavegur but that didn't mean a thing. More importantly, I thought that Aron Steingrímsson might have someone watching his house for him. As I crouched down in the teeming rain I tried to see if any nosy neighbours were peeking out of their windows across the road. Everyone appeared to be in be in bed already or too busy glued to their televisions to be bothered watching the street, which was just the way I wanted it. I fumbled through the contents of the letterbox and pulled out two envelopes, both addressed to my sister. At least I had the right place. I virtually crawled along the driveway and went to turn around the fence and into the tiny front yard when my progress was impeded by a big black motorbike.

I couldn't be entirely sure but it did strongly resemble the one that had almost run me down outside her office on Borgartún. Staying down on all fours I made my way tentatively around the motorbike and towards the tall windows that made up the front of the house. The diminutive area in between them and the front fence contained among other things a barbeque that I had to negotiate my way around but at least I had a clear line of sight into the living room, where I could clearly see a man seated in front of the television. The lights inside the house were on, which I hoped would stop him from being able to see me from the other side of the glass doors. From where I was now, even if he looked directly at me all he should be able to see would be his own reflection in the glass.

Sitting on the sofa was a tall bearded gentleman probably somewhere in his forties. He had his feet up on the table next to a half-empty bottle of Brennivín. From my vantage point I couldn't see what he was watching but it seemed to have his undivided attention. When his mobile rang he answered it only after carefully checking the caller ID. I wasn't the only one who did that, then.

He listened intently to whoever it was on the other end, screwing his face up slightly at some comment and taking another drink of schnapps. When he spoke his voice seemed raised, presumably from all the booze in him. Whoever it was he was talking to, they'd pissed him off.

Barely two minutes later a car pulled into the driveway at such a speed that I doubted it would stop before ploughing through the garage doors. Aron Steingrímsson lurched out of the car and made his way straight through the front door. It was probably not one of his more discreet arrivals at the property but he seemed to be slightly preoccupied. A heated exchange followed in the living room, very little of which I could actually make out as the two of them were constantly talking over the top of one another.

Eventually, things cooled down and a black leather bag full of money appeared on the coffee table. Aron paid the hairy biker in cash from the bag and then when it looked as though he was set to leave, I decided to head back to the shelter of my car. It wasn't long before he pulled out of the driveway, this time around driving a little more conservatively.

As he headed down Grandavegur I started the car and followed him at a prudent distance. We headed onto the Hringbraut before turning on to Hofsvallagata and following it down to just outside the Catholic church on Túngata. He came to a halt outside a huge two-storey house and waited for the electronic gates to open for him. I pulled up outside a house further down the road and watched him disappear into the cavernous double garage. I didn't feel any closer to finding out where my sister was but I just knew that wherever it was, he held the key to unlocking that secret for me.

CHAPTER 11

Nine o'clock the next morning came and went and there was no Elín on the flight to London. That was hardly a surprise but Grímur seemed to think that she would still try to get on the plane and so dispatched officers to intercept her at Keflavík Airport. I tried telling him that she hadn't caught the flight because she had been kidnapped but again my pleas fell on deaf ears. It was possible he thought that whatever had happened to her was her own fault but he would have been foolish to admit as much to me.

From what I had seen and heard on Grandavegur I was convinced that some sort of handover had been arranged but somehow it had all gone wrong for Elín. How exactly I wasn't sure but it was clear that she'd never got her hands on the money, at least not for very long. Over the phone I told Grímur that I knew Aron had tried to pay the money to keep her quiet but that something had gone wrong and that was why she had disappeared. The silence on the other end of the line was thunderous, albeit brief.

'How exactly do you know this, Ylfa? Let me remind you that if you are in any way a part of these negotiations or are withholding information from us then I will have no hesitation in arresting you.'

'I know because last night I found out where she has been living these last few months and I saw two men exchange money. I'm pretty sure that it was the money she had been planning to take overseas with her.'

'If you knew where she has been living then why didn't you share that information with me yesterday when I asked you where she was?'

'I only found out where the house was last night. If I had known earlier, I would have told you. She mentioned a place on Grandavegur but all she gave me was a vague description. Last night I went looking for it and I found it.'

'Ylfa, this is not how this is supposed to work. If you have any sort of information that would help us find her then you are supposed to let us deal with it and not keep it to yourself. Do you understand?'

'I'm extremely worried about her but I just wanted to make sure she wasn't making it all up. I never know what to believe when it comes to her crazy tales. All I did was go looking for a house that looked like the one she mentioned and that was when I saw Aron Steingrímsson collect a bag of money from another man. It was nothing more than a lucky guess. I just want to find her in one piece.'

He didn't sound overly convinced but I told him exactly what I had seen at the house on Grandavegur and where to find it. I told him about the hairy man with the motorbike that could have been the one who almost ran me down. He told me that he would look into it and that I was to put a halt to all detective work. I promised him I would. He didn't believe me any more than I meant it. He observed that I was treading a very fine line and hung up on me.

My first stop was to be Aron's house on Túngata, where I eventually found myself a parking spot from where I could keep an eye on the house. The temperature outside had dropped again and the rain subsided for the time being but the wind seemed to be building in strength with every hour that passed. After about an hour of sitting impatiently in the car without any movement in or out of the house I decided to make my move. I wasn't sure if he'd be home or not or if he'd even talk to me if he was but I was convinced that he knew where my sister was and I was determined to get that information out of him. One way or another.

I turned the radio off and strode over to the waist-high white wooden fence that surrounded their beautifully kept lawn, put one hand on it and launched myself onto the other side. As casually as I could I straightened my clothes and made my way to the front door. I rang the doorbell and waited for an answer. Nothing. It was possible that no one was home but I wasn't convinced. Places like his always had somebody home. I rang it again and let it ring the second time. Eventually, I heard some signs of life from within so I rang it again and waited.

A short, heavy-set woman in her forties or fifties, it was hard to tell, finally opened the door after what seemed like far too long unless she'd had to walk from the other side of town. She asked what I wanted in faltering English with an Eastern European accent. I asked if Aron was home and she told me that he wasn't, that no one was home – except her, I presumed.

I tried to explain to her who I was and why I wanted to speak to him but I could tell I was wasting my time. I found Elín's business card in one of my pockets and scribbled my mobile number on it. I gave it to her with instructions to give it to Aron and no one else. She nodded several times and told me that it wouldn't be a problem or something to that effect even though she obviously didn't have a clue what I was talking about. I tried again in English but only managed to extract the exact same response from her.

I thanked her for her time and made my way back to the car, once again vaulting the fence, but this time the one at the end of the driveway. When I took one last look back at the house she was still standing in the doorway holding the business card and staring at the footprints I had left across the lawn. I felt a little guilty but I was sure that he had someone to take care of those for him as well. If he didn't, it wasn't because he couldn't afford one.

I decided to swing past Elín's work on the way home to see if I could chat with her bosses, Elias and Bjarki.

By the time I arrived they already had company in the form of a couple of uniformed police officers so I made do with asking the receptionist if she had heard any updates on Elín and left it at that. She didn't have anything new to tell me and I was mindful of the fact that I had already put Grímur's nose out of joint so I made myself scarce before my presence was noted.

I had been trying to piece together in my head just how things might have transpired once Aron had received my sister's ultimatum. His first reaction would have been easy to predict. One of sheer fury and disbelief. Once he had calmed down, though, he would have realised that she did have him at quite a disadvantage. No matter which angle you approached his predicament from, he had a lot to lose. People with a lot always stood to lose the most.

He would then have come up with a plan of his own to take care of this nasty business, almost definitely involving the man with the long hair and the beard. He had probably been plucked from any number of Reykjavík motorcycle gangs and commissioned with the task of retrieving the cash from Elín once the trade-off had been made. What I couldn't quite picture yet was how or even if the cash had actually changed hands in the first place. If the biker had taken the cash from Elín in her office then where was she while this was happening?

Surely he didn't just walk into an empty building and walk out again. I couldn't remember if he'd had a bag on his back or not when I'd seen him disappearing up Borgartún. It had been dark and I'd been too busy getting out of his way to get a good look. Too much of it failed to make any sense yet and that was the main reason I wanted to hear what Aron had to say for himself. He might just be tempted to find out who had dropped off one of her cards. It was a long shot but I didn't have any other options. I could just picture him questioning the housekeeper when he got home. I didn't expect he would have much more joy with her than I'd had.

He would have to be intrigued by the card though. As long as he actually got it, that was.

By the time I got back to the flat, I was exhausted. Possibly more from the nervous energy I had been expending than anything else. I hadn't planned on falling asleep on the sofa and got a real shock when my phone woke me up. I checked the caller ID and saw that the number was withheld. I answered it anyway.

'Hello,' I said as confidently as I could. I wasn't convincing myself so I doubted that I would have sounded any different to whoever was on the other end.

'Hello yourself. What the fuck do you think you're playing at, you stupid little girl?'

It was Aron; my visit to his house had had the desired effect. It had got a response out of him.

'I want my sister back. What do you think I want?'

'I don't know what you're talking about. I don't know where that stupid bitch is and if she's got any brains she'll keep it that way. You girls must have some sort of death wish.'

'I know all about what she was trying to do to you and I know you're the reason she's gone missing. If you just tell me where I can find her we can forget about all that other nonsense and get back to our lives the way they were before but if you've done anything to her I will go out of my way to see that you are ruined.'

He almost laughed when I said that but this time it was him that didn't sound too convincing.

'If you ever come anywhere near my house or my family again... '

He took a deep breath as he tried to compose himself. I kept silent and waited for him to continue.

'What the hell were you thinking? If you're looking for trouble you are most certainly going to find it. I know exactly who you are, Ylfa, and you had better remember that. If something has happened to Elín, it had nothing to do with me. She probably just got what was coming to her.'

'I have a copy of that tape myself, Aron, just you keep that in mind. If you don't tell me where she is I'm going to make sure that a lot more people get to see it. Your wife, just for starters. Does she have an email address, Aron?'

'Don't try to fuck with me on this, young lady. If you do, you will simply disappear.'

And with that finality, he hung up on me.

CHAPTER 12

I wasn't entirely sure what I was going to do next but I wasn't about to let that rich, arrogant man get away with treating me that way. In his business life he was probably very used to getting his own way but that was all about to change. I was convinced he and his hairy biker friend were the ones behind Elín vanishing off the face of the earth, and I had in my possession the proof necessary to make people believe me. Elín may not have known what she was doing when she embarked on her ill-advised foray into the world of extortion and blackmailing but she knew what she was doing when she sent me that email. There was no way I would be dismissed as easily as that again.

I spent the next few hours doing a bit of editing on my laptop with the footage that Elín had attached to her email. What I came up with was a very short film, which didn't show much more than Aron Steingrímsson rolling off my sister and walking out of the room once he had finished his business with her. I tried to edit it so that there was no unnecessary frontal nudity involved but in order to get a good shot of his face it was unavoidable. It was imperative that whoever watched my five-second creation would be able to pick out his face and easily identify him. Anyway, the whole idea was to make it as embarrassing as possible for him.

My next job was to write a cover letter and send it to my intended target, or targets. The threat I had hinted at about sending it to Aron's wife was probably my first choice but I had no idea what the poor lady's email address was. As such, I was forced to come up with another plan. One that would force Aron to answer some very tricky questions. Ones he couldn't simply brush aside and ignore.

I found the general enquiry email address for the country's biggest newspaper, Fréttablaðið, and attached my little masterpiece to it. I left the recipient in no doubt as to who the naked man in the film was just in case they thought it was some sort of hoax and explained that the woman he was with was my sister and that she was missing, presumed kidnapped.

I told them I was convinced that Aron was responsible for her disappearance because of their affair and the fact that she had attempted to blackmail him with the full-length version of what they were just about to watch. I also said that if they were interested in the rest of the story all they had to do was contact me and I would fill them in. I left my mobile as a contact number and signed off. Just before I sent it I felt a small pang of guilt that I might wind up helping a newspaper make its money but the need to expose Aron overrode it. I had no idea who read the incoming emails for the newspaper but I was confident that it would eventually find its way into the hands of the right person.

Once that was done, my next stop had to be Grandavegur again. I wanted to see if the hairy biker who had almost run me over outside Elín's offices on Borgartún was still around. If he was, I had some fairly pressing questions for him. As far as I could tell, he could quite easily have been the last person to see Elín before she disappeared and if that was the case, then I needed to talk to him. He could quite easily know exactly where she was also.

After checking the house on Grandavegur and finding that there was no one home, I parked at the end of the street nearest Álagrandi and waited. The end I was sitting at was the only entrance to the street, the other being a dead end, so I would have a good view of everyone coming or going. I had stocked up on coffee and a couple of sandwiches on the way and settled in to wait for any signs of the motorbike man or any other visitors to the house. Eventually, though, boredom started to take its toll and I reclined the seat to make things more comfortable for myself.

Unless he arrived on foot I would still hear anybody approaching and even if he was walking I was sure that I would see anyone passing the car. There were few people out and about on the footpaths and only the occasional car passed either into or out of the street. At one point I got out and went for a walk back down the end of the street, just to stretch my legs more than anything else. I peered through the big glass doors at the front of the house once more.

The place looked completely uninhabited; even the bottles and ashtrays that had been visible the other night had been tidied up. It was possible that whoever I had seen talking to Aron in there had only been a temporary visitor and had cleared out as soon as he had been paid for his dirty work.

About five and a half hours later I decided I was wasting my time and decided to head back to Vesturgata. My legs were getting stiff and I badly needed to use the toilet after my large coffee. It hadn't occurred to me that I might not be the only one doing a bit of covert detective work but it probably should have. If I was so interested in Aron and his henchman then it would make sense that they had taken something of an interest in me and what I was up to. I had taken Aron's bluster and rhetoric with a pinch of salt and had thought that he had just been trying to scare me off. But, if he was responsible for kidnapping Elín then it made sense that he would go to pretty much any lengths to protect his own interests.

As soon as I walked into my flat it was obvious that I should have taken him much more seriously. Someone had broken into it while I had been staking out the house on Grandavegur and their investigations within my home had been somewhat thorough. My living room had been turned upside down, my canvasses tossed about the place like playing cards strewn across a table top. I checked the rest of the flat to see if anything was missing or if they had just decided to mess the place up a bit. They had emptied every drawer and every cupboard but the only thing I couldn't find was my laptop. That was definitely gone.

If anything else had been taken, its absence would only become clear a little further down the line. I didn't have the energy to do anything more than a rather perfunctory clean-up. To get the place right again would have taken me all night and it was more important that I got some sleep. It didn't take a genius to figure out who was responsible for my flat being invaded and I wanted some rest before I made my point to him early the next morning in a way he would never forget.

I rang work and blew off my shifts for the rest of the week. My supervisor Kristrún wasn't at all happy about my late notice; she was already struggling to cope with the extra demand that the festival brought with it every year. On top of that, most of the staff had already taken the week off to go see the bands rather than working but when I explained everything that had been going on she relented.

I was up again before most of the city would have risen from their beds but that was the whole idea. I showered and fixed myself a coffee before once again ignoring the state of the living room and heading back out of the front door. I was used to the place looking like a dump anyway. I had a destiny with an address halfway up Túngata and the mess in my flat would once again just have to wait. Getting even was the only thing on my mind and it just couldn't wait.

Once again I sat in my little car and waited for something to happen. As I had no idea what time Aron and his household rose in the morning I thought it would be a good idea to arrive as early as I could and just wait. The only problem with that logic was that I once again found myself waiting, and waiting, and waiting for something to happen. The first sign of movement I saw was the automatic garage doors opening and Aron driving out in his Mercedes. I noted the time – 6.45 a.m. – for future reference, and let him get on his way to work. It wasn't him that I wanted to talk to, anyway.

I was going to take a more indirect approach this time around. If I really wanted to hurt him, it was his family that I was going to have to go after. Eventually, the rest of them showed. At around 8.30 a.m. the garage doors opened once again and the two kids and his wife got into a Volvo and headed off to school. I thought about following them but I didn't really want to know where the little ones went to school. What I wanted was to speak to his wife, Róshildur. So I waited patiently for her to return, hoping that she didn't have anything too important to do on the way home. About twenty minutes later she reappeared and waited for the automatic gates at the end of the driveway to open.

It was the opportunity I had been waiting for so I launched myself out of the car and made my way hurriedly across the street to her. She saw me approaching and had a slightly puzzled look on her face as I waved at her. She pulled the car into the driveway but then got out to see what it was that I wanted. I made my way through the gate onto the driveway and tried my best to give her a convincing smile. She did not, however, look at all convinced.

'Hello, I was wondering if I could have a word with you.'

My greeting elicited no noticeable response from her so I simply continued.

'My name is Ylfa Einarsdóttir and I think we need to talk. Would it be okay if I were to come inside for a few minutes?'

That managed to get her to raise one of her eyebrows slightly at least.

'Would you mind telling me first what it is that you think we need to talk about, Ylfa?'

I nodded vigorously as if I thoroughly understood her need for an explanation before I launched into my diatribe. All the same, what I really understood was that she should have been sitting down before I told her about what her husband had been getting up to with my sister and why I very much wanted to see him go to prison.

'Okay,' I said, a little background information was needed here to put her in the picture but not so much that it would scare her off. 'My sister Elín went missing recently and as it turns out, she knows your husband.'

The eyebrow raised itself a little higher. She suspected already that she was not going to enjoy where this was going. She couldn't possibly have had any idea just how much she wasn't going to like it, though.

'Your husband called me yesterday to tell me that he doesn't know where she is but I think he's lying. He threatened me and told me to leave him alone otherwise something might happen to me too. When I got home last night someone had broken into my flat and stolen my computer. There's something on that computer that he doesn't want you to see. He was having an affair with my sister and she made a tape of them together.'

I stopped there to see if the implication would sink in. Róshildur crossed her arms and stared at me. Still she wouldn't say anything so I had no choice but to continue.

'I know he knows where Elín is and isn't telling me. All I want is to see her again and to know that she's all right. She's not the best person in the world but she doesn't deserve anything terrible to happen to her either. She's made some bad decisions, plenty, in fact, but nothing good is going to come of him harming her in any way.'

'Young lady, you are obviously out of your mind. I want you to leave now and if I see you again anywhere near our house I shall have no hesitation in calling the police. Do you understand me?'

I looked at her imploring her to see the sense in what I was saying but there was no hope of that occurring, not in the short term at least.

Once again I probably sounded like a crazy woman and the only way that she was going to believe me was if she saw it with her own eyes. Hopefully in tomorrow's morning paper.

'If he doesn't want to talk to me about where she is I will send a copy of that tape to every newspaper and television station in the country one by one until your husband is ruined. Do you understand me?'

'Get away from me, you vile creature,' she hissed. And with that she got back into the Volvo and drove it into the garage, closing the door behind her.

I had tried being reasonable and it hadn't worked. I wasn't going to be ignored again. This family was going to have to listen to me one way or another. As the electric gates closed behind me, I strode up to the front door and started pounding on it as hard as I could. I started screaming at the top of my lungs that she had better come and open the door. Of course she didn't. Only a truly mad woman would have.

I told her that her husband was a fraud and that I had seen him having sex with my sister with my own eyes. I said it nice and loud so that the neighbours would have no problem hearing me. I told her that unless she let me in they would be on the front page of the papers tomorrow and that I wouldn't stop until either I had my sister back or they were both the laughing stock of Reykjavík.

It took a lot less time than I had anticipated for the police to show up. I guess if you're rich then you get things to happen for you much more quickly than other people do. Two officers got out of their car and walked towards the driveway gate, which opened miraculously before them much as the sea once parted for Moses. As they walked up the driveway I tried hard to find a smile but I seemed to be all out of them and the expressions on the faces of the two police officers seemed to say that it was not a smiling matter that they were here for anyway.

They told me that they had received a complaint from several members of the public about my early-morning behaviour and that they would like me to come with them. I told them that I seemed to have got all the yelling out of my system but they assured me it would still be a good idea if I went with them. Nothing about their demeanour suggested that they were kidding so I decided that I should probably do as they said. The option of running for my car and making an improbable getaway was likely to be yet another poor choice in a morning already full of them.

When I got into the back of their car I told them that all they had to do was talk to Detective Grímur Karlsson and he would tell them who I was and that I was all right. I was just under a great deal of pressure at the moment but it would pass and then I would be okay again. The one driving started to laugh and I asked him what was so funny.

'It was Grímur who told us to take you back to the station and that we shouldn't listen to a thing you said.'

As they turned the car around and pointed it back towards the downtown area I could see the figure of Róshildur standing at one of the upstairs windows. She didn't look as relieved as I thought she might to see me leaving. It was possible that I had given her something to think about after all. I had certainly given it my best shot.

CHAPTER 13

Grímur looked spectacularly unhappy to see me, just about as unhappy as a man could look. He walked into the interview room I had been waiting in for what felt like an hour but was, according to my phone no more than twenty minutes, and took a seat opposite me. He drummed his fingers on the table while staring at me. I was determined to play the aggrieved victim for as long as possible so I just stared back and waited for him to talk.

'I thought that you were a little bit smarter than that, Ylfa. That crap you pulled this morning isn't going to achieve anything, you know.'

'He had someone break into my flat and steal my laptop. He's kidnapped my sister and you aren't doing anything about it. What do you expect me to do?'

'What I expect you to do is let us do our jobs and not make a nuisance of yourself in the meantime. I don't think that's too much to ask, is it?'

'You've seen the tape Elín made. You're well aware of just how much Aron has to lose by her making life difficult for him and yet you're not doing anything about it. It doesn't take a genius to figure out what's happened to her. Why is it me in here answering your questions and not him? Just because he's rich doesn't mean he's not a criminal.'

Grímur held up one of his hands as if to signal that he'd heard enough. He was shaking his head too and looking at me as if I were a silly young girl.

'What we don't need here is you trying to tell us how to do our jobs or you telling Aron and his family, or anybody else for that matter, what they've done with your sister. There is no evidence whatsoever that Aron or anybody associated with him is responsible for Elín going missing.

'We know that she had planned to leave the country and that she failed to make her flight but that doesn't mean that she was prevented from doing so. On the evidence of her recent behaviour it would be safe to say that she has been acting in an unpredictable manner of late and that her actions have been the result of some seriously questionable judgements.

'You yourself have seen clear evidence that she intended to blackmail a prominent member of Icelandic society and it is entirely possible that this is not the only stupid idea that she has come up with lately. For an intelligent young woman she appears, to the untrained eye at least, to be extraordinarily stupid.

'What we don't want is you following in her footsteps. Standing on someone's driveway accusing them of being complicit in a major crime is not the path you want to be taking, Ylfa. You've got to use your common sense.'

I fidgeted in my seat as I forced myself to keep quiet and let him finish talking. I wanted to scream at him too but that would only reinforce his idea that Elín and I were cut from the same cloth. I didn't want to give him any reason to feel satisfied with himself. If he thought he had me or my sister all figured out then he was in for a shock.

'I know it was him who broke into my flat. If not him, then his hairy biker friend. He took my laptop so that I wouldn't be able to send that email to anyone else but I can do that using any computer I want. I could do it with my phone. Maybe he just wanted to see it so he could calculate the risk that Elín represents to him for himself.

'Either way you don't seem to care about anything except the consequences for yourself of ruffling the feathers of one of the city's biggest birds. Until now I had never thought of the Reykjavík Police as spineless but that is obviously the case. It's sad to know that you're more concerned with your reputation among rich businessmen than you are with solving crimes. My sister could well wind up dead before I can get anyone to take me seriously. Hopefully, though, that's something that you'll be able to live with.'

I took a deep breath and tried pretty unsuccessfully to calm myself down.

'I think you're overreacting, Ylfa. We don't know that anything untoward has happened to your sister, we just suspect that this is the case. We do know that Aron Steingrímsson has a very good reason to be angry with her but that is not the same thing as him bearing any responsibility for her disappearance. We know from her laptop that she demanded money from him but there is no indication that any money changed hands; in fact Aron has denied that any exchange took place. He says that a demand was made but that he steadfastly refused to bow to her threats.

'We know she was planning to fly to London but never boarded the plane. Apart from that we have no idea where she has got to or what has happened to her. So far, the only crime that has been committed has been by her and as soon as we find her she will be charged with the attempted extortion of ten million krónur from Aron Steingrímsson.

'You are not very far behind her there, either. If you insist on continuing with your campaign against Aron Steingrímsson and his family you will find yourself being arrested also. You cannot attempt to do the work of the police yourself, Ylfa. If you continue to do so, you will find yourself in all sorts of trouble. Do you understand me?'

'I do. I can see now that I was wasting my time hoping we would get any help from the police. You're only seeing what you want to see here and nothing else.

'Anything more would be too uncomfortable for all concerned, wouldn't it? If anything happens to her I will never be able to forgive you. Not ever, do you understand? I made a mistake expecting you to help. It won't happen again.'

I stood up and walked out of the interview room and out of the station. The wind was biting cold outside so I walked to the taxi rank next to the Hlemmur Bus Station and took a taxi back to Túngata to fetch my car. I wasn't in the mood for rearranging my flat yet so I chose to visit Dad instead. I was desperately in need of talking to someone who might just take me seriously.

When I walked into the living room in Hafnarfjörður, Dad was sitting in his favourite chair as he always did. He looked tired around the eyes like he hadn't been sleeping well. I wouldn't have been surprised if he hadn't been sleeping at all since Jóhannes was killed. I know I wouldn't have been. On the table in front of him was a small pile of legal documents. He motioned towards it with his eyes and told me to sign them once I'd read them. It was the deed to the property. He had told the lawyers to send them out to him since I hadn't made any attempt to visit them. He said he wanted me to take legal ownership of the place sooner rather than later. I no longer felt even the slightest bit like arguing with him about why he wanted me to do so, he would tell me in his own good time, but I told him that there was something I needed to tell him first. He nodded and got up to make us some coffee. He was moving gingerly as though really feeling his age.

'Your story can wait five minutes while you read the papers and sign them, my girl. I didn't get them sent over to lie about on the table.'

He busied himself in the kitchen preparing the coffee but what he was really doing was waiting for me to look at the documents. He looked pleased with himself when he came back with the cups and saw that I had done as he'd wanted. I guess I wanted to please him more than I wanted an explanation as to why this was happening now. He passed me a coffee and put the papers away after checking that I hadn't missed anything out.

'Now what was it you wanted to tell me?'

'It's Elín, Dad.'

'Why do you start spending time with her again after all these months? She doesn't change, you know. What's she done now? '

'She's gone.'

'Gone where?'

'I think she's been kidnapped; in fact I'm positive.'

He looked at me as though he expected me to start laughing and he would suddenly get the joke. When I didn't, he realised that I was serious and that we might just have a problem.

'Start from when you saw her last, and take it slowly.'

I told him about the concert the evening before and how she was meant to have met me at Harpa, but didn't. I told him about finding her office empty and the strange note on the wall. I told him all about her stupid plan to blackmail Aron Steingrímsson with a naughty recording on her laptop and the tickets to London and northern Spain that she never used. He listened carefully as I told him about the money changing hands and Aron telling me to stay the hell away from him or else he'd make me disappear too.

He didn't ask any questions; he just sat there and listened to me describe the map that his eldest daughter had used to get herself so very, very lost. He looked as though something inside was breaking slowly, the way that things do when you shake them too hard.

She had never been his favourite child; I sometimes suspected that he didn't really like her at all. She represented everything that he thought had gone wrong with the country and in many ways it was hard to argue with the man on that count. A lot of people had sold their souls for money while many others had merely traded them in for shiny new ones.

It was hard to tell what he thought of it all. I wasn't sure what sort of response I had anticipated but I barely got one at all.

Elín had finally been listed as a missing person on the evening news and people were being asked to look out for her and contact the police if they saw her. There was no mention of the fact that she was wanted for questioning regarding her extortion attempt, which I was pleasantly surprised at. Whether that was to protect her or Aron I wasn't at all sure. The photo they used was from her driver's licence but she still looked great. If she was around she would be spotted soon enough – no one misses a pretty girl like that.

Jóhannes was still in the news as the police admitted that they were no closer to finding his killer. Suspicions that it had been gang related were rife. No one really had any idea why he had been murdered but everyone seemed to agree that the country was a more dangerous place than it ever had been before.

This seemed to be an opinion shared by my father. He had taken to keeping a loaded shotgun in his room. The one he had used to shoot ptarmigan up until about five years ago. In years gone by I would have been dismayed by such irresponsible behaviour but now the weapon didn't seem so out of place in the house. Even so, it made me more than a little nervous.

I went to bed praying that he wouldn't shoot his foot or anything else off in the middle of the night by mistake. The last thing I wanted was him hunting imaginary prey around the house in the dark. He would be just as likely to blow my head off as I got myself a glass of water as catch an intruder.

Dad had always risen early so I wasn't overly surprised to see him missing from his room by the time I got up the next morning. I did wonder why he'd taken the gun with him, though. That was until I heard the shouting.

I hurried outside in nothing more than a t-shirt and knickers to find my father standing in the near darkness pointing the shotgun at head height, straight at a man standing at the top of our driveway. He had either been instructed to hold his hands well above his head or he had simply chosen to do so himself when confronted by an angry old man in the mid-morning gloom with a loaded gun in his hands.

I called out to Dad to lower the weapon but he wasn't in the mood for listening; he was in the mood for shouting, which he seemed to be doing plenty of. I looked at the terrified man and asked him what he thought he was doing on our property unannounced at such an hour. He really did look terrified so I yelled at Dad to point the gun somewhere else. When he didn't comply, I walked over and shoved the end of the barrel towards the ground and finally he stopped yelling. I looked at the stranger again and told him that he could put his hands down. He lowered them slowly, thanking me for my intervention as he did so. After taking a deep breath he said, 'My name is Stefán Jón Tryggvason, please don't shoot me.'

CHAPTER 14

I told Stefán Jón that he could put his hands down and that we weren't going to shoot him. Probably. I asked him again what he thought he was doing on our property. He told us that he was worked for Fréttablaðið and that he just wanted to talk. When Dad heard that he worked for a newspaper I actually had to pull the gun from his hands and take it away from him. I told Dad to make himself scarce and that if he did then Stefán Jón and I would get out of his hair. He begrudgingly agreed and stomped off to the stables doing his best to keep an eye on Stefán Jón.

'I'm sorry about all that. We've been a bit on edge of late,' I apologised. From the look on his face he was trying really hard to understand but not quite getting there.

'That's what I came here to talk to you about. I've seen the email you sent to the paper and I was wondering if I could ask you a few questions for an article I'm going to write.'

'Wait here.'

I took the shotgun inside and put it back next to the bed in Dad's room. I was starting to have my doubts about the wisdom of keeping it in the house. The way we were going, we would all be in jail by the end of the week. I quickly threw some more clothes on and headed back outside.

I guided Stefán Jón away from the house and back down the drive to where he had his car waiting. As we walked side by side I noticed that his hands were still shaking a little.

By the time we were nearing the Fréttablaðið offices on Skaftahlið I was starving so I suggested we stop off at the Kringlan Mall for coffee and pastries first.

We had already covered a lot of what Stefán Jón wanted to know on the drive into town so he decided to give the office a miss and take breakfast somewhere a little more comfortable. He lived on Skipholt near the Hlemmur Bus Station, which was much closer than my place so we decided to head there with breakfast.

His apartment was small but clean, well, in that bachelor kind of a way. He apologised quietly as he slid about the place tidying up papers and takeaway food containers but he soon had the place looking fairly shipshape. His actions were those of a man with some considerable practice at the last minute neaten. The amount of mess in the room was still exactly the same, he had just organised it so it looked a whole lot better. I was already thinking that there might be things I could learn from this man. I also saw him as someone I could bounce a few ideas off so once we'd polished off the pastries and coffee we decided to get down to business.

'What I really want to ask you is this: do you think there's a connection between what happened at your father's place and your sister's disappearance?'

'I'm not too sure,' I replied.

I had assumed that he was going to start off by asking me about the email that I had sent to the paper but obviously he wanted to approach it from another direction. I wanted to hear his opinions first. Was he planning to expose Aron or was that something that the paper wouldn't want to do quite yet?

I also needed to know how much he knew about the circumstances surrounding Jóhannes's death and just what, if anything, he might have managed to find out about that. I assumed he got a lot of his leads from sources within the police force and wasn't too sure what they may or may not have told him.

'You want to hear what I know first, right? Or at least what I think might have happened?'

He got the idea much quicker than I thought he would. Smart boy.

'Of course. You don't think I agreed to come here to just help you out, do you?'

'Of course not. I assumed it was because you were struggling to resist my undeniable charms,' he teased. 'And losing.'

'Oh, is that how most people usually wind up here? Maybe I should have shot you while I still had the chance.'

There was something about this man that was hard to resist. He was very comfortable in his own skin, I think is the saying. Either that or he was ever so slightly full of himself. Whichever it was, it worked.

'I've been told that despite the police not mentioning anything yet there was a link of some sort between the two crime scenes. They won't tell me what, though. At this time they're not prepared to describe your sister's disappearance as a crime. As far as they're concerned she is a missing person. Is that right?'

'I'm not sure what she is. All I know is she's gone.'

'She was planning to leave, though, wasn't she? They found plane tickets amongst her belongings?'

'Yes, but she never used them. They even waited for her at the airport. Their main concern seems to be that she might have done something wrong rather than the fact that she's missing.'

'Okay, okay, go on. I haven't heard anything about this. What is it that they think she's done?'

I told him that the email I had sent to the paper was part of her failed attempt to finance her escape from the country and that she had tried to get Aron to pay for it. I said that I was convinced that because of the threat their affair now presented him with that Aron was responsible for whatever fate had befallen her. Even if he didn't have anything to do with her disappearing, he had broken the trust between himself and his wife and could suffer the consequences of his actions when the truth came out. He was no different from the rest of us.

Everything in this world comes at a price and he would just have to pay up like everybody else. He had been involved in some sort of pay-off with my sister and then his muscle for hire had somehow got the cash back for him. In the meantime my sister had vanished. I struggled to believe that he was innocent of any wrongdoing.

When I told him about Aron ringing me and denying any knowledge of Elín's whereabouts he looked a little incredulous but he did suggest that he might have actually been telling the truth. It could be possible, he mooted, that the hired goon had been given some kind of no-questions-asked assignment to get the cash back and then after that, the less anyone knew the better. I shuddered to think of her at the mercy of the drunken, leather-clad biker. I had to admit that I hadn't thought of that and wondered if the argument I'd witnessed between the two of them might have been about the finer points of just such a deal.

Maybe I had been focusing on the wrong man after all and it was the biker who I should have confronted. I had no idea how I would go about tracking him down but it looked as though it would have to be the next job on my list.

Stefán Jón had been scribbling down notes as I talked but hadn't taken his eyes off me for more than a few seconds at a time. He was listening intently but it seemed to be leading to something that we weren't talking about yet.

Eventually, I stopped thinking aloud and waited for him to make the next move. Although I felt completely comfortable in his presence I wasn't too sure why I should trust him apart from the fact that I didn't really have anyone else to talk to and without someone's help I didn't stand any chance of finding my sister.

'There's one other thing I had hoped you would be able to help me out with. I've been told about some notes that have been found in some odd places. The rumours have been quite unspecific. Do you have any idea what I'm talking about?'

I nodded slowly, I had been wondering when he would get around to those. For me they were the most troubling ingredient of all my woes. Simply because they were the most difficult to explain.

'Why don't you tell me what you've heard first? I've been doing far too much talking as it is,' I said.

Stefán Jón put down his pen and pad and arranged his thoughts. At least that was what he looked like he was doing. He definitely seemed to be concentrating rather intently on something.

'I've heard from some unsupported sources that there have been notes found by the police, although they still deny this. Messages of some sort from the criminals. At the scene of Jóhannes's murder, on his body, even, and at your sister's office. I've been told that there was one found before the young man was even killed; in Mosfellsbær.

'If any of this is true then it would suggest to me that there's something else at play here, not just a case of extortion gone wrong. To be perfectly honest with you, I think your theory about Aron Steingrímsson is just a little bit too simple to be right. It would seem to me that there is something much more sinister at play here.'

'What you've heard is right,' I said. 'There was a note found in Jóhannes's mouth, which the police haven't told anyone about. The text of it I found written down in Jóhannes's flat in his own handwriting after he was killed. I don't know how, but he had come across it before he was murdered. It was similar to the one found in Mosfellsbær, and the one left in my sister's office the night she disappeared. They are all quotes from the Book of Daniel about King Nebuchadnezzar and his bad dreams.'

I had finally made an impression on Stefán Jón. The look of shock on his face wasn't faked. I pulled my mobile out and went through my photos until I'd found the picture that I'd taken of Elín's office wall.

*Suddenly the fingers of a human hand appeared
and wrote on the plaster of the wall.*

Stefán Jón jotted it down in his pad nodding to himself intently as he did so. As he busied himself making his notes I wondered how many of his interviewees he brought home with him. I would have asked him but I didn't really want to know the answer.

'If I found a Bible online do you think that you could find the other two messages for me?'

Stefán Jón pulled his laptop out of a satchel and waited for it to power up and connect to the Internet. When he had an online copy of the Book of Daníel ready for me to peruse I found the part that had made up the note that Inga Björk had showed me.

*I had a dream that made me afraid.
As I was lying in my bed,
images and visions that passed
through my mind terrified me.*

'There's one more,' I told him and found the passage that I had seen in amongst the chaotic mess of Jóhannes's belongings. The very same one that Björn had told me about; the one that had been left in his mouth as he lay dying.

*Let him be drenched with the dew of heaven,
and let him live with the animals.*

'I have no idea what these mean but there has to be something linking each one to the next, don't you think?' I asked hoping that Stefán Jón, who was still writing furiously in his pad, might be able to see something in them that I couldn't.

When he'd finished writing he looked at me again with that intense air of concentration that he seemed to carry about with him.

'I'm not big on coincidences,' he began. 'With these, though, now that I look at them all laid out in front of me like this, there's more to them than coincidence. They're a message of some sort. Someone is trying to say something in a rather passive way. The notes are saying something but it's the actions that they accompany that are telling us the real story.'

'Go on,' I said. Since Elín disappeared I had entertained so many conflicting theories that I had been getting myself confused. I was ready for someone else to point the way.

'The first note that appears does so at a veterinary clinic that your father deals with. The note is left in place of drugs that are taken and then used in the commission of a terrible crime.

'We cannot be completely sure that the very same drugs were used in the killing of Jóhannes and the horse, but let's assume for the time being that they were. At the scene of this crime the second note is left. You find the same note in the dead boy's room and then yet another when your sister simply vanishes into thin air.'

'Now that you put it like that... ' I began, not really knowing what I made of it all. The way he had laid it all out made it sound simpler and yet more complicated than ever before.

'What the hell do you make of it all?' I asked. 'Because I'm more confused now than before we started talking.'

He smiled a gentle, slightly self-conscious smile suggesting that perhaps I wasn't the only one.

'If we look at all these things together there has to be one thing that connects them all. A common denominator. Whatever it is has to hold the key to what's going on. The key to what we don't as yet understand.'

'And that common denominator is?' I really wanted to know.

He looked at me in a way that left me feeling a little colder than it should have. He had a theory somewhere behind those dark brown eyes of his and it was slowly but surely working its way out to meet me.

'I think it's your father.'

'You sure about that?'

'No, I'm not sure about anything. It's just a theory but he's the only common thread running between all three events.'

'It's not just because he wanted to shoot you this morning, is it?'

It was the first time I'd heard him laugh.

'I would like to think that I'm beyond such petty reasoning.'

'And to think you were saved by a girl in her underwear.'

'It wouldn't be the first time.'

It was my turn to laugh then, the first time I had laughed in quite a while and it did the trick. I don't know whether he had planned the whole thing or not but I never made it back to Hafnarfjörður and Stefán Jón never made it back to work.

CHAPTER 15

Really rather early the next morning I sneaked out of Stefán Jón's bed and looked about the room for my clothes. He slept right through my clumsy dressing and I had to steal the exact fare for the bus out of his change bowl next to the front door, thereby doubling my feeling of helplessness. I wasn't at all used to getting around without my car but I wasn't going to wake him just to demand a lift home. So before shuffling down to the bus station I left him an IOU and a brief note explaining that I had left, but not why.

A few short blocks of struggling through the wind brought me to the Hlemmur Bus Station from where I would be able to find my way home to Hafnarfjörður and my car. During the twenty minutes that I had to wait for the next bus to arrive I contemplated going into the Central Police Station next door. I figured that if Grímur had anything to tell me he would have done so already and I was hardly the flavour of the month with him any more as it was. I decided not to aggravate the situation any further and just head back to Dad's place. I suspected Grímur's silence only hid the fact that they were getting nowhere fast. If Elín was going to surface of her own accord she would have done so by now. The fact that she hadn't filled me with a sickening fear that I wouldn't see her again.

When I got home I found Dad asleep in his bed. Not wanting to disturb him I showered and then took the horses out for a ride one by one even though it was still dark. It was almost nine by the time he made himself visible, which in itself was rather odd. He wasn't prone to lying in or unnecessary resting but he looked fine and happy enough to see me when I came back.

'This is a pleasant surprise, my girl. What has you up so early this morning? Someone kick you out of their bed?' he chuckled to himself.

Although his witticism was remarkably close to the mark, I didn't want to let on about my night with someone who was, after all, a reporter for a major national newspaper. The last thing he needed was any further encouragement. It was better to let him think whatever he liked and leave it at that.

'Never mind that, what has you sleeping in all day like this? You would almost think you had been feeling a little under the weather lately.'

He turned and looked at me as if he suspected there were something wrong with me instead.

'That's enough of your cheek, young lady. There's nothing wrong with me. I just fancied a lie-in this morning. Aren't I entitled to one every now and then? It's not as if I lead a life of leisure like yourself.'

'I've just been wondering, that's all.'

'Wondering what?'

'Why you really wanted to sign the farm over to me now instead of waiting until further down the line. It's the timing of it that's got me thinking. Why now? Why not in a year's time or five years, for that matter? What's the rush?'

He looked at me long and hard before replying, the machinery of his mind clearly ticking over furiously.

'What is it you suspect, Ylfa?'

'I'm afraid there's something wrong with you you're not telling me about.'

The turmoil began to surface in his eyes once again and then just as it reached the surface, it was gone. Back down to the depths from which it had risen as if it had never been there at all. Someone could almost mistake it for a trick of the light. If you didn't know him better than that.

'I'm fine, my girl. It's just as I said before. I want to make sure that it's you who gets to decide what to do with all this when the time comes. Whenever that may be. There's no need to worry about that yet, though. I'm not planning on going anywhere anytime soon, I can assure you.'

I didn't really have any choice but to leave it at that. I didn't believe him entirely but whatever it was that was bothering him he wasn't about to tell me.

'Okay then, but if something was wrong you'd tell me, right?'

'Not everything in life has a hidden meaning, you know, Ylfa. Sometimes things are just what they appear to be and nothing more. I just don't want any nasty surprises down the track, that's all.'

'Okay, Dad. If you say so.'

I had never been less convinced of anything in my life.

It was time to talk to Kristjana and see what she made of it all. If necessary we would come back together and demand he tell us. If he was sick or even worse then we deserved to know. I knew that once I told Kristjana about my suspicions she wouldn't let up until she had received a satisfactory answer from the stubborn old fool. In that respect they were definitely cut from the same cloth.

'You know,' I said, 'if you're lying to me, I'll never forgive you.'

Something in his eyes told me that he knew that already. Whether he cared or not was another thing altogether. You can try to scare people into doing the right thing but it didn't mean they would. Not in my experience, anyway.

CHAPTER 16

Sometimes it's easy to get a bad feeling about things. Far too easy. You get an idea in your head that something's wrong or that something's going to happen and the next thing you know it is, or it has. This was one of those times.

By the time I'd arrived at Stýrimannastígur I had convinced myself that Dad was dying and just wouldn't tell me. I had left Hafnarfjörður with something of a suspicion and had arrived back in town with the cold hard certainty stuck hard and fast behind my eyes.

When Kristjana didn't answer the doorbell I decided to let myself in with my own set of keys. If it was all right for her to do it, then it was all right for me. She was probably just out at the shops picking up a few things and would be back soon. I certainly didn't feel like standing around in the cold waiting for her.

Her flat was tiny like mine but was insanely tidy. The girl was a neat fetishist of the worst type. Every time I visited her it hit me just how traumatising my apartment's constant state of upheaval must be for her. She was as uptight about the place's appearance as I wasn't about mine. And it showed.

One thing I couldn't place amongst the delicate arrangement of her living room was her beloved cello. It was possible she hadn't picked it up from Harpa yet but it was unlike her to go very long without it. She stayed closer to it than most mothers did to their children. I took my shoes off at the door, took a seat on her couch and put my feet up.

She wasn't answering her phone either, which was slightly odd in itself. She usually only ignored it when she was practising and as far as I knew she always practised at home.

She had a chair positioned next to the front window expressly for that purpose from which she could watch the world go by on Stýrimannastígur as she played Haydn, Bach or Mozart as her whims took her. Sitting atop her specially appointed chair was a small stack of sheet music. Presumably whatever it was that she wanted to learn next or had just finished learning.

Boredom must have overtaken my more rational side as I decided to have a look at what it was she had been practising. In hindsight I wish I had never got up from that sofa.

The top sheet of music was not Haydn or Bach, nor was it Mozart. It wasn't even music. It was a proclamation. An announcement. A warning that no matter how worried you were about one thing or another, there would always be something else waiting just around the corner to completely take your breath away and drain you of all hope. It wasn't Dad's health I was worried about any more.

His face turned pale
and he was so frightened
that his knees knocked together
and his legs gave way.

I read the typed page over and over again until I screamed and tore it in half. I ripped it again and again and again as if by destroying its message I could erase what it was trying to say to me. I dialled Stefán Jón's number and waited for his voice.

'Hello, Ylfa. Where did you disappear to?'

'I'm sorry about that but it's happened again. She's gone too, Kristjana's gone. She's been taken from her flat and they've left a note behind again. It's Stýrimannastígur 16,

Apartment 2. You've got to get over here as soon as you can.'

The rest of the words stuck in my throat and he told me that he'd be there as soon as he could. I hung up wondering what anyone could have possibly done to deserve this. I saw the terror forming in my father's eyes again. From the dark pools to the surface and back again. A man who had never been afraid of anything in his life. What had he seen with those eyes that had filled him with such dread? Something evil on its way into our life?

I could hear the window panes straining against the force of the wind. From somewhere out there I heard someone curse as they were blown off their feet. The storm from the west had finally arrived just as they said it would. What could Kristjana possibly have done to bring this upon herself? Up until now I hadn't figured her as part of all this. My sweet, naive sister had never done anything in her life to threaten anyone else. I sat down on her sofa, put my head in my hands and waited for help to arrive.

It seemed to take forever but eventually they showed. Stefán Jón was the first to arrive and assured me that the police were on their way as well. One by one I watched them enter and walk around the flat, taking notes and talking to each other but it felt like another world they were operating in, one as distant from mine as another planet.

Grímur looked at the pile of shredded paper in his hands and grimaced yet again as if by facial expressions alone he would be able to turn back the clock and reconstruct what I had so effectively destroyed.

'I really wish you hadn't done that, Ylfa.'

Stefán Jón had appointed himself as go-between for me and Grímur and seemed determined to stand up for me now that I was unable to or simply no longer cared. The bottom line was that I just couldn't be bothered with the police any more.

'I'm sure she didn't mean to do it. Try to imagine the strain she's under right now,' he said. 'You wouldn't be thinking rationally either.'

The wind was now blowing so hard outside it sounded as if it was trying to get in through the walls and windows at us. As I sat and stared out of the window I could see men in safety harnesses and hard hats get out of a 4-wheel drive across the street. Someone's roof had come loose and the corrugated iron was dangling from the building like a flap of skin that needed to be trimmed off or stitched back where it belonged. The 4-wheel drive belonged to a search and rescue team from Hveragerði, some twenty-eight miles to the east of Reykjavík. I could hear one of the men yelling to one of his companions on the other side of the glass. I could hear people talking behind me as well but I didn't want to turn around. I no longer wanted to know what they had to say. As soon as I possibly could, I would leave. I had to get out of there before I lost my mind.

'She's destroyed what could potentially be important evidence,' Grímur continued. 'I know you don't see it as a particularly serious matter but I can assure you that it is.'

'The poor girl's upset, can't you see that? She's not in any sort of a state of mind to be held responsible for her actions. She's in shock,' Stefán Jon continued in my defence.

I loved the fact that he was sticking up for me but I was sick and tired of listening to them argue with each other.

'When she's ready to talk she can explain herself. Until then I suggest you mind your own business. If she doesn't start talking soon, I may be left with no alternative but to arrest her.'

Grímur was getting angrier by the minute.

'You can't do that, she's done nothing wrong. Can't you see that she's just very upset? It's only natural. All she needs is a little more time to collect herself and she'll be fine.'

'She looks fine to me. She's not helping anyone like this, least of all herself.'

There were arms placed around me from behind. Comforting is probably what they were supposed to be but all they did was make me feel more trapped than I already did.

The men across the street got a ladder off the roof of the 4-wheel drive and leant it up against the building with the injured roof. They had bandannas tied around their faces to protect themselves from the freezing wind. I finally turned around and looked at the men behind me. Grímur was the first of them to address me.

'Can you tell me why you tore up this piece of paper, Ylfa? You must have known that wouldn't be a good idea.'

'Take your time,' Stefán Jón added as if by thinking about it I would be able to satisfactorily explain myself when all I wanted was my family back.

'It's really cold out there, can't you see that? She's not here and she's not coming back here. She's freezing to death out there somewhere. I tore that piece of paper up because they've got my sister and I want her back. These notes are mocking you and your inability to help me. My sisters are missing and some crazy bastard wants you to know that he's smarter than you all are. So why can't you do anything apart from prove him right?'

I had finally had enough. I couldn't understand all the fuss over one torn note. They had three others I knew of and not one of them had done a damn bit of good. Both my sisters were gone and no amount of standing around talking about it was going to bring them back.

I excused myself and stepped outside for some fresh air. Grímur told me not to take too long and Stefán Jón may have argued with him about that as well. The noise in the flat faded as I closed the door behind me and immersed myself in the tempest that was baring its teeth outside. I felt safer in the freezing wind than I had indoors.

One of the mountain rescue men had made it onto the roof and was fastening himself to it with some sort of rope and harness. I watched him as he methodically made himself fast to the roof and then slowly, carefully went about dragging the corrugated iron back to safety in spite of the gale blowing around him.

Stefán Jón came outside to see how I was doing. I told him I was feeling a little off colour and that I would stay out in the fresh air until I was feeling better. Grímur apparently still wanted to talk to me but was okay with me taking a little time to compose myself. The urge to flee was rising inside me the way bile rises in your throat. I told him that I'd be back inside in a few minutes knowing full well that there was no way I'd be stepping back into that flat. They'd been in there, whoever they were, and that meant that the place had been poisoned.

I was going to be next, surely. I looked up and down the street to see if there was anyone watching me. The only people around were the mountain rescue team, who were too busy to be paying any attention to me. The atrocious weather had cleared the street of all other forms of life.

As I stood there studying the street warily another police car arrived and the officers in it began the task of knocking on all the neighbours' doors one by one to ask if anyone had seen anything unusual recently. Could someone possibly have seen my sister being dragged from her home? I told Stefán Jón that I would be back in the flat in a minute or two and he disappeared back into the warmth.

Eventually Grímur appeared outside to seek me out as well. It must have sunk in that I wasn't returning to answer his questions so he had come to me instead. I apologised for having destroyed the note and told him that I was slowly going out of my mind. He now seemed more concerned for my wellbeing than he had before, when it appeared that all he cared about was the note. He suggested that some officers keep an eye on me in case I was the next target. Grímur had a more paternal look about him now but he did have a warning for me.

'Ylfa, I don't want to scare you but whatever is going on here now unquestionably has a pattern to it. I would be very wary of staying anywhere on your own. If you have to go home to get a few things, do so. But I would recommend staying somewhere else until we know what is going on.'

I nodded and told him that I would go home briefly but then I would be going to see Dad.

'I don't think he should be alone now either. If we're together it will be more difficult for anything else to happen.'

I didn't wait for a response and launched myself headlong into the windstorm. Apologising yet again to Stefán Jón for leaving in such a hurry was going to have to wait for another time. It was the second time in a day I had run out on him but I just had to get away, and I had to see Dad. I could feel something circling our family. Something as wild and as dangerous as the storm sweeping through the city.

The men across the street were making good progress repairing the roof. They were used to searching their part of the countryside for lost walkers and tourists but were just as capable in the city when they were needed. My own street had become a wind tunnel and the force of the storm almost kept me from crossing the road and making my way the short distance down the hill to my flat. I very quickly grabbed a few things and threw them in the car.

As I made my way out of the city there was no mistaking just how much work the mountain rescue boys had on their hands. The police were out in serious numbers as well, taping off dangerous buildings and closing off streets wherever necessary. I turned on the radio to listen to what was happening elsewhere. In the centre of town, the main shopping street, Laugavegur, had been closed by the police to park a giant crane next to a building. It also had lost its roof, which was hanging so far off the building that it had become a danger to pedestrians and traffic alike. The crane was being used to hold the roof in place as it dangled above the street until such time that workers could safely get onto the roof. The height of the building meant that the wind speed at the top was too dangerous to make the ascent just yet.

Down at the cargo terminal a shipping container had been blown from the top of the stack it was perched on and onto the wharf below – a height of about ten metres.

People were being told to take great care if they had to go out anywhere in the storm and to stay indoors if they didn't have to be anywhere important. The winds would be around for at least another twenty-four hours until they had made their way across the country and towards the Faroe Islands.

In the south east of the country drivers were being told to stay off the roads as the wind was whipping up giant ash clouds, which would reduce visibility to practically nothing in some places. Meanwhile, out in the middle of all that chaos and pandemonium both my sisters had gone, perhaps never to return.

CHAPTER 17

Our property appeared to have escaped any serious damage from the weather, possibly as it was far less exposed than a lot of the city. I was going to tell him about Kristjana as soon as I walked in the door but he already knew. He had been watching the news on television and had seen a short bulletin regarding her disappearance and the possible link to what had happened to Elín. Stefán Jón and his journalist friends had obviously wasted no time alerting the various stations to the breaking story.

Dad said that Aron Steingrímsson had been mentioned on the programme. They said he had been questioned by police about his possible knowledge of Elín's whereabouts and stated only that he knew Elín but not how. After his questioning he had been released with no further action by the police expected.

I marvelled at the treatment money could buy you. If it hadn't been Aron Steingrímsson with his army of lawyers, the real story would have been plastered all over the tabloid publications by now. A man such as him had to protect his reputation; the public couldn't be allowed to find out what the people running our country were really like. I imagined the questions he'd faced at home could well have been more uncomfortable than the ones that had been posed by the police.

I hugged my father and asked him what was going on. He held me tighter than I had expected and told me he didn't know either.

'It's as if our whole world is coming apart,' he whispered.

I let go of him and tried to read what emotions if any might be passing across his face. It wasn't a complicated face, he just looked miserable.

I thought about what Stefán Jón had said to me about how everything that had happened so far, in one way or another, revolved around the man standing in front of me right now. It was hard to imagine why anyone would pick such a fight with a cantankerous old sod like him but you never knew. He had been known to rub people up the wrong way.

I met with little in the way of an argument when I told him I would be staying at the house for the foreseeable future. In many ways, it was what he'd always wanted.

Later that evening, after we'd spent as much time tending to the horses as we could manage in the conditions, we decided to call it a day and retreat once more to the living room. As the dutiful daughter I cooked dinner for the two of us while Dad watched television. At my behest we were to avoid all news programmes while I was in the house, a stipulation that my father didn't seem to mind meeting. By the time I had the food ready I found him watching a documentary set mainly in the Westfjords. I had expected a wildlife programme of some sort but it couldn't have been more different.

The documentary was about something that had very rarely been talked about in Iceland until quite recently. The boys in it were all grown men now but they all had one thing in common: they had all been removed from their families, sometimes just single parents, in the 1950s and taken to a home for wayward boys in Breiðavík at the very western tip of the country. Breiðavík was out on the furthest tip of the Westfjords, far removed from any towns or cities. In the 1950s there hadn't even been a road to the place. Everything had been transported in by boats and offloaded onto dinghies before being rowed ashore. They had been as isolated as anyone could possibly be. It had proved to be a recipe for disaster.

Many of them had been abused while in care there and had struggled to deal with the remainder of their lives after the place was shut down in the 1970s. They found adapting to what we would call normal life again all too difficult and soon turned to lives of crime.

Some even found life in prison preferable to having to look after themselves on the streets. At least in there they didn't have to worry about looking after themselves. It was better than sleeping rough and begging for money on the streets. I found their stories extremely sad and thought it was inexcusable that such things could happened in a seemingly modern society, albeit many years ago.

I was just about to ask Dad what if anything he had heard of these homes when I noticed he was crying.

'Dad, Are you okay?'

He didn't answer me but he did look as though he was about to say something.

'What is it?' I asked. 'Did you know some of those boys?'

He would have been just the right age but as far as I knew he had been raised on the other side of the country.

'You're looking at one of those boys. Not from Breiðavík but somewhere just like it. A long time ago now but sometimes it feels as if I'm still there after all these years.'

He shook his head and wiped the tears from his face. I didn't know what to say; I had never seen him look so vulnerable, so utterly human.

'Why have you never told us about this? How come Mum never mentioned anything?'

'I never said a word to your mother. It was a part of my life that existed long before I met her. I thought I'd just leave it where it belonged. In the past. It wouldn't have helped anything if she'd known. Quite the opposite, in fact. People always say they want to know everything about you but they never do. Not really. It was easier to carry that with me in silence than it would have been to speak of it.'

'Those places, like Breiðavík, I mean, were they as bad as this programme makes them out to be?'

He put his plate down on the coffee table and pulled himself up from his chair with what looked like considerable effort. He turned without a word and headed towards his room.

'Dad?'

That stopped him in his tracks but he still wouldn't turn around. He couldn't or simply wouldn't face me.

'No, Ylfa, they were worse than you could ever imagine. They were places filled with a certain kind of horror that destroyed young boys' lives.'

I watched him slowly disappear down the corridor to his room. How could anyone keep something like that to himself for what must have been at least sixty years? It made me wonder what else there might be in his past that he hadn't deigned to share with any of us. Not telling us children was one thing but the fact that Mum had never known was something else altogether. Maybe I was just naive but I couldn't imagine being married to someone all that time and not telling them something like that. He had said he thought that she wouldn't really want to know but how could he be sure? He simply hadn't had the necessary faith to share an enormous part of his life with her. He hadn't trusted her and that was the saddest thing of all.

A troubled night's sleep ensued and wasn't helped by my phone ringing at some ungodly hour. I fumbled around blindly in the dark for it but only succeeding in knocking it to the floor where it continued to bleat relentlessly for attention. I reached down under the bed and found it with the tips of my fingers but by the time I'd pulled it to my face the caller had given up. Almost as an afterthought I checked the caller ID.

What I saw on the screen made me gasp and I dropped the phone again and once more it bounced under the bed. This time, on my hands and knees, I made sure I got a good grip on it before returning the call. It rang and rang as I cursed it for not being answered. The call had been from Kristjana's phone and I had missed it.

I so badly wanted to believe she was all right that for the time being I was willing to put all other alternatives out of my mind. Some little part of my brain told me I was better off having not answered the call. I checked the time, it was 4.45 a.m. Whoever it had been, they must have known I would be asleep. That's why they had chosen to ring at that hour. To build my hopes up so they could be destroyed once again.

I dialled Grímur's number and waited impatiently for him to answer. It took some time as I expected it might. And he sounded none too pleased when he finally did so. He had probably taken a moment to check the time and the tone of his voice suggested he was none too impressed.

'She's just tried to call me. I just got a missed call from Kristjana's phone. She hung up before I could answer it and when I rang back there was no answer. We've got to do something, haven't we?'

'I can try to find out where the call was made from. Try to call the phone again and if anyone answers try to find out who it is. Give me some time and I'll have someone trace the mast that the phone was connected to when the call was made. Just be aware that if someone does answer that phone it's quite possible it won't be your sister. Don't get your hopes up too high. The fact that someone called you is a good sign but it may not necessarily be good news. If anyone besides her answers, find out who they are and what they want. I'll be in touch as soon as I can.'

He hung up leaving me wondering exactly who it might have been on the other end of the phone. If it had been Kristjana she would have answered straight away when I called back. Whoever it had been was toying with me. I called her number again but the phone had been switched off.

I considered waking Dad up but decided it could wait. Finally telling me the truth about what sort of a place he had grown up in should have brought us closer together. After all, being honest with the people you love is what it is all about. This time, though, it had driven tiny doubts into my mind and made me worry that there might be something else in store for us. Something else hidden away that I was yet to discover. I wasn't sure if I was ready for any more surprises just yet. The best thing to do was to put my head back down on the pillow and wait for morning. Either I would get another call or I would ring Grímur again as soon as I woke. If I could back to sleep, that was.

When I did wake after what might have been an hour or so of very light sleep I crept out of the house leaving Dad a note on the kitchen bench.

Dad, someone called me in the middle of the night using Kristjana's phone. I've gone into town to see the police. If I get any news I'll let you know. We need to talk more later. Y.

The wind was still blowing mightily but it seemed to have lost some of its intensity. Hopefully we had been through the worst of it. I was stopped at a set of traffic lights on Suðurlandsbraut when Grímur called. He sounded as if he'd had even less sleep than me, possibly even none. He did, however, sound as though he had been putting his time to good use.

'We've traced the location of the phone when it was used to call you last night. We can't be precise about where it was but we have an area to focus on that it was used in. It was only switched on for a very short period of time and has been off again ever since. The masts it was connected to at the time suggest it was very close to this station.

We'll continue to monitor the number just in case the phone is switched back on again. I would suggest to you again that you not spend any more time on your own than is absolutely necessary. If you would like me to send an officer back to your father's place I will.'

I could still picture the last poor officer who had been on the receiving end of my father's early morning tirade and decided against that idea. Things were tense enough at home as it was without a stranger becoming a permanent addition to the household even if it was to be just in the driveway.

'No thanks, Grímur, that won't be necessary.'

There was a slightly uncomfortable silence on the other end of the line.

'We're doing all we can, Ylfa. The main problem we have is that we don't know what we're dealing with here. If we could find out why this is happening then I'm sure we'd be able to figure out who it is pretty quickly. Until then I can't stress strongly enough that you need to take care. Have someone with you whenever possible. That will make you a much more difficult target for anyone wanting to do anything stupid.'

It was an interesting choice of words. Not dangerous, or deadly or completely life altering, but... stupid. In his world people only did clever things or stupid things. If they only ever did clever things he would be out of a job.

Day after day he was obliged to track down and arrest the ones who were stupid and from what I had heard, he was good at it.

I thanked him for the call and headed into the city centre to find a coffee. If I was going to get through this day in one piece I was going to need one, and soon. After parking outside my flat I walked back down the hill to Austurstræti and got a double cappuccino and the latest edition of Fréttablaðið in my favourite bookshop. It didn't take me long to find what I was looking for. I wanted to see what Stefán Jón had been doing with himself.

Another Religious Note Left Behind At Crime Scene

Reykjavík CID are now investigating a fourth crime scene at which a quotation from The Book of Daniel has been left. Another woman is thought to have been taken, this time from her apartment on Stýrimannastígur. She is the sister of a woman who also disappeared recently from an office building on Borgartún, where another of the notes was found.

The first note was found at a veterinary clinic in Mosfellsbær; the second at the scene of a murder in Hafnarfjörður at the farm belonging to the father of the two women who have recently disappeared, Einar Dagsson.

It would appear that all four crimes are related but Detective Grímur Karlsson, who is in charge of the case, declined to comment on what the connection might be.

Despite every effort to contact the women, their whereabouts are still not known. Fears are held for their safety and anyone with any information regarding either Elín or Kristjana Einarsdóttir is asked to contact the police immediately.

Underneath the article were photos of my two sisters. Seeing their smiling faces looking back at me from the newsprint, I was overcome by an indescribable dread that I would never see either of them again. In this torment there would be an abyss that I would either see in time and avoid, or be consumed by. There was no way of knowing yet which it would be.

CHAPTER 18

Not wanting my melancholy to overwhelm me I set my newspaper down and went back to the counter for another coffee. The seat I had chosen was at the front window on the first floor of the shop and afforded me a great view of the street below. The position gave me the feeling that I was the one doing the watching and not the other way around. It was hard not to think that if I was to be the next target of these madmen then it was entirely plausible I was already being watched.

I decided on a single shot of espresso the second time around. I didn't need a caffeine overdose adding to my already rampant state of paranoia. Upon returning to my seat overlooking the windswept pedestrians on Austurstræti I noticed something had changed. My newspaper was no longer sitting on the page I had left it opened to. There wasn't a soul in sight anywhere near my seat or on the whole floor, for that matter. Apart from the coffee shop the place was deserted.

The obituaries column in the classifieds had been left staring back up at me. Not the cheeriest of pages in the paper but after a quick check I realised I didn't know anyone unfortunate enough to have made the grade that particular day. I assumed that some nosy person had decided to have a read of my paper while I was getting my coffee and left it at that.

It wasn't until I turned back to the article I had been reading that I realised what had really happened in my absence. If the man in front of me in line for coffee hadn't argued about where his Americano was in the barista's list of coffees to make then I very well may have got a look at whoever had left me the note. This time it didn't aspire to any sort of contrived references; it had a much more direct approach.

Next to the church in Hella you will find Inga Rós and her daughter. If you heed what they have to say, they will tell you all you need to know about your sisters.

The way I saw it there were two routes clearly open to me at this point. I could do the sensible thing, pick up the phone and call Grímur to tell him what I had just found, or I could do what he would most probably refer to as the stupid thing.

In the end I decided on the obvious course of action for someone who had never been particularly good at heeding advice. I picked up the phone and called Stefán Jón to tell him we were going for a drive, to Hella.

CHAPTER 19

By the time the dark gravel cliffs of Hveragerði loomed up on our left, the rain had started to come down like some sort of warning from above. We had just passed a small church, upon the cross of which a single raven had been perched despite the power of the torrential downpour. The stubborn refusal of the bird to seek shelter from the storm gave me the distinct impression that it had been waiting especially for us to pass, for as soon as I remarked on its presence and turned to point it out to Stefán Jón it had taken flight and disappeared from sight.

I had been trying to justify my somewhat hasty decision to myself by talking Stefán Jón through it as he drove.

'It could be nothing, right? We're just checking it out to make sure it's not some sort of hoax. After all, it could be nothing more than an elaborate ruse.'

I looked across at him waiting impatiently for the moral support that didn't appear to be forthcoming.

'Well?' I demanded. A response of any sort, even a non-committal grunt would have sufficed.

'Either that or we both wind up in jail,' he joked but we both knew what Grímur would say if he knew what we were doing.

The town of Selfoss came and went as we continued our journey east through the ever-intensifying rain. The wind had mercifully dropped in strength as the storm moved its way across the country but it had done precious little to ease the conditions outside.

The biting wind had simply been replaced by a ceaseless downpour that threatened to be even more unpleasant to be exposed to. Conversation was in short supply as Stefán Jón concentrated on the road and I fixated on what our quest actually meant in the grand scheme of things.

If I'd stopped long enough to examine whatever it was we were doing I would have come to the conclusion any reasonable person would. I should have simply passed the information on to Grímur and let the police do their job. The only thing was that from what I had seen so far, that wasn't going to bring my sisters back to me and I had simply run out of patience.

Eventually, we crossed the bridge over the Ytri-Rangá River and arrived in the tiny town of Hella. Some caves nearby had once been home to Irish monks around the time of the settlement of the country by the Vikings, but that was all I knew about the place.

The small wooden church with its distinctive red roof wasn't hard to find and as we pulled up in front of it I wondered what it was exactly we were supposed to be looking for. The note had said to look for Inga Rós and her daughter next to the church.

As far as I could see there wasn't anything next to the church. Apart for the graveyard.

Now that I looked around the place I realised why we had been sent there. It hadn't been to talk to anybody at all; it had been to find a story that lay somewhere beneath the cold hard soil of that little church's graveyard. We were looking for the kind of truths that only the dead can hold on to. I swore quietly under my breath as I let this sink in.

Stefán Jón and I looked at each other and without swapping a word he pulled his woollen hat tightly over his head and opened his door.

'I'll be back soon, I expect,' he said quietly and with that he stepped out of the car leaving me in the relative luxury of the vehicle's shelter.

With his shoulders hunched against the downpour he wandered in and out of the rows of old and not so old gravestones. Eventually, he seemed to have found what he was looking for as he bent over at the waist and appeared to start talking to one of the headstones. Maybe all that rain had begun to leak through his hat. I assumed the peculiarity of the situation had got the better of him and he had taken to conversing with himself. Or even worse, with the dead. Either way I held concerns for his sanity, not to mention his general health as he was sure to be soaked through to the skin by now. Eventually, he came jogging back to the car with rain bouncing off his shoulders.

He threw himself back into his seat and slammed the door behind him.

'Good Lord, it's wet out there,' he said as he shook his hat out and wiped his face with his hand.

'Another minute and I'd have ended up halfway down to the sea.'

'What were you saying to yourself over there? As far as conversations go for you it seemed quite involved.'

He smiled his charming, slightly cocky smile at me and laughed.

'I wasn't talking to myself. There's an old man over there tending to one of the graves.'

'In this weather?'

'I know, you'd think he would have picked a better day for it.'

'Well, what did he have to say?'

'The two graves he was looking after belong to Inga Rós Gylfadóttir and Erla Diðriksdóttir.'

'Inga Rós and her daughter?'

'Yes, this old man was none other than Diðrik himself. They were his wife and daughter.'

'Ouch.'

'Yeah, they're buried right next to each other.'

'Did you tell him why we were here?'

'Of course. When I started telling him the story about your sisters he said he'd also heard something about it on the news but as it was all happening in Reykjavík he hadn't paid too much attention. He was at a loss to say what the connection might be between his family and yours. Frankly, I think he thought we had wasted a trip coming all the way down here.'

As I looked about the rain-swept fields surrounding Hella I thought he might just be right. We must have been out of our minds.

'There has to have been some reason why the note brought us all the way down here. It couldn't have been just to waste all this time, could it?'

Or get us out of Reykjavík... but I couldn't even bring myself to voice that concern aloud.

'I don't know. He seemed pretty sure there wasn't any way his wife or daughter could have had anything to do with what has been going on in Reykjavík. I just can't really imagine how they might be connected.'

There was nothing for it but to go find the old man myself and ask him questions until something fell into place.

There simply had to be a connection and I was going to find it. There was no way we were heading back to the city empty handed.

'Wait here, I'm going to talk to him,' I said and hopped out of the car into the pouring rain.

For some reason I hadn't even brought a hat with me. Of all the days we could have chosen to go chasing ghosts in the rain. As soon as we got back home I was going to get my head examined. It was going to be a very long trip home for both of us in soaking wet clothes and nothing to show for our efforts.

I made my way over to where I thought I'd seen Stefán Jón talking to himself. I soon found myself rubbing the water from my eyes wondering what the hell was wrong with me. Either I had lost my bearings on the sodden trek through the headstones or my eyes were playing tricks on me. I was convinced I was in the right spot but there was no old man to be seen no matter where I looked. It was as if he'd crawled into one of the graves and disappeared.

I bent over to make sure that I was standing in the right place. Right in front of me, side by side, stood the headstones of Inga Rós Gylfadóttir and Erla Diðriksdóttir, no doubt about it. I could feel the rain starting to run down the inside of the back of my jacket and the futile nature of what we were doing started to incense me.

I found myself wanting to kick the headstones and demand they tell me what I was doing there. From what I could see at my feet, Diðrik had done a lovely job of tidying around the headstones. Not a weed had been left to prosper anywhere near the graves of his loved ones. The story that the headstones told was somewhat more disturbing, however. Erla had died at the rather tender age of fifteen in November of 1991, surely the result of some sort of accident.

It would seem this early departure from her parents' life had led in some way to her mother's passing. Inga Rós had been buried just a few short months later in February of 1992. There had to be a story of some kind there. Perhaps that was what we had been sent to investigate. It pretty much had to be.

I hurried through the rain to the church itself. Even if it proved to be deserted, as I imagined it might, it would provide me with some much needed respite from the rain, which was proving to be unyielding in its onslaught.

I opened the front door and stepped inside. The first thing I saw was an old lady cleaning down the side of a row of pews. She appeared to be the building's only occupant so I made my way over to her trying in vain not to drip everywhere as I went. She turned slowly to greet me as I approached.

'Hello there.'

'Hello. I was wondering if you could help me. My friend was just talking to an old man outside who was tending to a couple of graves.'

She laughed as if I'd just told her a joke.

'In this weather, are you sure?'

'Yes. His name was Diðrik. He was at the graves of his wife and daughter. Maybe you know him.'

The old lady looked at me with what might have easily been mistaken for suspicion.

'I know who you're talking about but he hasn't been seen here in a while. If you were talking to him out at those graves it would be the first time he's visited them in almost a year. He comes down on the anniversary of their deaths but apart from that we don't see much of him any more.'

'Really? My friend was definitely just talking to him. It would seem that he left before I could ask him a couple of questions. I'm curious about how Erla and Inga Rós died. You wouldn't be able to tell me, would you?'

'I would, but I'm not sure that it's any of your business. What is it exactly that brings you out here on such a day as this?'

I told her who I was and who my sisters were and that Stefán Jón and I had ventured out into the countryside looking for an answer to what had happened to them.

She also had heard about the 'goings on in the big city' as she put it. I told her about the note that had been left for me in the bookshop and she looked at me with what might only be described as sheer disbelief. I was forced to retrieve it from my jeans pocket where I had forgotten all about it. It had survived being out in the rain with me but only just. It would not be presented to Grímur as forensic evidence anytime in the near future.

I unfolded it ever so carefully in front of the old dear as she looked on as if awaiting some kind of divine proclamation. By the time I had it open and she'd read it her opinion of me had been swayed to the good and it seemed that I was to be humoured after all.

'Young Erla died just over twenty years ago now. She was only young at the time.'

'Fifteen years old.'

'Yes, that'd be about right. There was an accident out at the family farm one night. One of the barns caught alight and the girl got herself trapped in that barn somehow. She was burned alive in there, the poor thing. Her mother took it hard and she took her own life a handful of months later. Sad tale, but I don't see what it could have to do with you and your troubles. It seems that no matter which family you belong to there is always trouble of one sort or another to look out for.'

She suggested I visit Diðrik at his farmhouse if I wanted to know anything more. She suggested that I show him the note, too, as it would be my only chance of getting him to talk about it. Otherwise he would consider me to be a city-dwelling lunatic, much as she had.

There was no hint of humour in her voice when she told me this. She gave me directions to the old farmhouse where he still lived, albeit on his own now. I thanked her for her time and made my way back outside to see Stefán Jón, who was doing his best to get out of some of his damper clothes without leaving the car again.

'So, what did he have to tell you?'

'That's the weird thing. He was gone by the time I got over there. He must have got sick of getting soaked out there and decided to go home.'

Stefán Jón looked a little surprised.

'Must have, I guess. Was there anyone in the church?'

'A little old lady who told me how they died and where Diðrik lives.'

'I guess that's where we're off to now then.'

'It's not far from here and it seems a waste to come all this way and not talk to him properly.'

'And this time we can do it inside. How did they die? Is there an obvious connection?'

'Not that I can see. Erla was killed in a barn fire and her mother killed herself out of grief. You tell me if there's a connection there.'

Stefán Jón just shrugged and shook his head. It was obviously no clearer to him than it was to me.

'I still think it's an odd day for doing a spot of gardening at the local graveyard,' Stefán Jón said as we pulled away from the church. 'No matter how little else you have to do all day.'

'Maybe he likes a bit of peace and quiet. The lady in the church said that he usually only comes down once a year. It could be that he only likes coming out here when he knows there'll be no one else around.'

'Well, if that's the case, he couldn't have picked a better day for it.'

CHAPTER 20

Following the instructions I'd received from the old lady it didn't take long at all to find Diðrik's farm. The whole area was dotted with numerous colourfully corrugated iron barns all along the banks of the Ytri-Rangá River. Our journey took us out of town some way, towards the foothills of the local volcanoes.

By the time we'd reached old Diðrik's place both Stefán Jón and I were feeling rather sorry for ourselves. The cold had begun to seep into our clothing in a way that threatened to never leave. The occasional looks that we shared were silent pleas for one of us to just say what the both of us wanted to hear. That it was time to call an end to our wild goose chase and head home to our warm flats and hot showers. But neither of us had the inclination to say it. For what were probably our own reasons, we were both determined to forge ahead with our quest to find the old man and thereby discover why exactly it was we were there.

Diðrik's farm had a certain air of dilapidation about it. The term rundown could be used to describe many rural homesteads but with this farm it really fitted the bill. It looked as though he had probably held on to the place out of fear of moving away rather than anything else.

Any pretence of the place being run as an actual farm had been given up long ago. I could only imagine that after he lost his daughter and wife in quick succession he had also, to some extent, lost the will to go on. I know I would have.

Someone probably would have had to stop me finding a good solid piece of farmhouse and stringing myself up by the neck from it for good measure. The fact that he hadn't and still took the time to tend to their graves in the pouring rain said a great deal about the man and made me want to meet him all the more.

'You want me to go check that he's home first?'

Under the present circumstances, I had to offer.

Stefán Jón was looking somewhat forlorn but pulled a stoic expression together for my benefit and shook his head.

'I want to hear this too,' he said. 'If I had asked all the right questions the first time around we could be on our way home by now. And who knows, maybe it'll be warm and dry in there.'

I had to admit, he had a good point. Even if this old man had nothing of any use to add to our trip, he could at least offer us the opportunity to dry out for a while.

'All right, off we go, then. You never know, he might even have some coffee in there to offer us.'

After what seemed like an awful lot of banging on the front door we looked at each other, ready to admit defeat. I no longer needed to be convinced that it was time to head back home; that time had come and gone as far as I was now concerned. I flicked my head back in the direction of the car and was just about to grab Stefán Jón's arm and pull him away from the door when it finally opened.

Diðrik had obviously perfected the art of moving about his house silently. He had also somehow perfected the art of rendering Stefán Jón speechless. As I waited in vain for the words to come out of him I realised something was wrong. I just didn't know what yet.

Stefán Jón stumbled over his words the way a drunk might exit a bar at 5a.m. Diðrik looked up at him wondering who had appeared at his door and what the problem with them might be. I felt forced to say something just to break the increasingly awkward silence.

'We were wondering if we could have a word with you. My friend was just talking to you at the graveyard not far from here but I was wondering if I could ask you a few more questions myself.'

'Ylfa, there's something... ' Stefán Jón began but again he seemed unable to finish his sentence. He tried once more to tell me something when Diðrik himself spoke up.

'I'm afraid I don't have any idea what you're talking about, young lady. Maybe you'd like to explain yourself a little better,' he said.

I looked at Stefán Jón, who looked back at me and just shook his head.

'Who are you exactly, if you don't mind me asking?' he asked the old man.

It didn't feel as if the conversation was going the way any of us thought it would. I suspected that all that rainwater had indeed got into Stefán Jón's brain. The old man looked us up and down and then up and down some more while letting the silence hang in the air between us. God only knows what he was thinking. Whatever it was, he wasn't in any hurry to let on.

'My name is Diðrik Guðmundsson. And who might you two be, if you also don't mind me asking?'

I looked at Stefán Jón waiting for some sort of explanation as to why they didn't recognise each other. Then it hit me. Given my sudden understanding of the confused faces in front of me I had expected to feel better about things, but I felt worse.

Much worse, in fact I felt pretty ill. I didn't understand anything any more, except maybe that I should listen to Grímur a little more carefully from now on. Possibly even a lot more carefully if I was to remain alive much longer.

Stefán Jón fumbled around in one of his jacket pockets for something and eventually pulled out a business card. Diðrik looked at it suspiciously and then handed it back.

'I still don't see what it is that that you want from me.'

'I was, that is, we were, just up at the local cemetery and I was talking with you. At least I thought it was you at the time. Obviously it wasn't, I can see that now, but I really thought it was. There was a man there tending two of the graves. The ones belonging to Inga Rós and her daughter. Your daughter. That was why I assumed it was you I was speaking with. That and he told me his name was Diðrik.'

Stefán Jón smiled in a slightly uncomfortable fashion and paused, hoping that he would understand how this misunderstanding had come about. From the look he gave my mildly idiotic sidekick, he didn't.

'And this man. He said he was me?'

'Yes. I told him who we were and why we had come and he didn't seem to think that he could be of any help but Ylfa here, she's sure that you can be, for some reason.'

He turned to me as if to signal that it was now my turn.

'That's right. You see, when I went back to look for him, he'd gone but there were some more questions I wanted to ask.

'So we tracked you down with a little help from the nice old lady who was cleaning the church. The question that now needs to be asked, though, is, if that wasn't you, then who was it?'

Diðrik sighed as though we were an intrusion upon his calm that he didn't really require.

'I think that you will probably not leave me alone until this has somehow been explained to your satisfaction. So you'd better come in and I'll make us all some coffee. You're going to have to start from the very beginning if I'm to have even a tiny chance of understanding you people. I used to have sheep that made more sense than you, and they were stupid animals.'

He turned and walked into the house leaving the door open for us. We kicked off our sodden shoes at the door and gratefully followed him inside. He motioned without saying anything to the sofa so we both took a seat and waited for him to make the coffee. By the time it was ready neither of us could hide our excitement at the prospect of something hot to drink. He could see it in our faces when he returned and almost smiled as he handed the steaming mugs over. He took his own seat opposite us without a word and looked at the two of us and waited.

I ran through the story from the very first note that I had been shown on Inga Björk's phone to the present day. He didn't really need to know everything but I thought that it might help when I eventually pulled out the note I had with me.

I told him about Jóhannes and my father's horse. I told him about my two sisters and my fears of what had befallen them. I left out a lot of the stupid stuff that Elín had done. I figured he already thought we were idiots so why overdo it? I pulled out the note that had been left for me to find, the one that had led us to the graveyard in the rain. He took it from me to read it for himself. He was still suspicious but, as I'd hoped it would be, the note was the turning point. After reading it his face softened and I could tell that he believed me and was going to help us if he could.

'So those two girls on the television are your sisters?'

I nodded.

'And this note was left for you by the man who took them?'

I nodded again but with a lesser degree of certainty.

'And this old man you talked to in the graveyard, the one who was tending the graves of my Inga and Erla, you suspect him of something?'

He directed that comment at Stefán Jón, who shrugged a little sheepishly.

'At the time I assumed it was you, but now I just don't know. He could have been the man who killed Jóhannes and has taken her sisters. Or he could have been some old crank doing the rounds in the graveyard for a laugh.'

'What exactly did he say to you?'

'He said he had heard about the case but he thought we were probably wasting our time coming all the way down here on a hunch.'

'He just might have been on to something there, you know,' Diðrik offered with a grin.

There were a few things that weren't quite right in my mind that I needed to address.

'What did this old man look like?' I asked.

'I didn't get that good a look at him, to be honest. It was really raining and he had a lot on.'

'What do you mean by a lot on?'

'You know: gloves, raincoat, hat and he had glasses and a big ratty-looking old beard.'

'Did you get to see his face at all, then?'

'Not really, you couldn't see much behind the beard and the glasses. They were all fogged up and wet from the downpour. It could have been anybody, really, now I think of it.

He seemed to know what he was talking about, though, so I had no reason to doubt he was who he said he was. He looked just like a little old man tending a couple of graves,' Stefán Jón shrugged as if to say there was no way to know we were being fooled.

'That was him waiting for me to show up so he could get his hands on me too and complete the set,' I whispered.

Diðrik had been sitting quietly listening to the two of us and he finally decided that he had something to add.

'It sounds as if you've done something to really piss someone off,' he said looking straight at me.

'I don't generally go around doing such horrible things to people that they want to kidnap everyone in my family. If Stefán Jón hadn't volunteered to go out into the rain for me...'

I couldn't even finish the sentence. I could feel my voice beginning to break and I didn't want them to know just how scared and upset I really was.

'If it was a trap, why did he use your family to lure me down here? What could your wife and daughter have to do with my family? There has to be something here that we're not seeing. The old lady in the church told me that your daughter died in an accident.'

I wasn't at all sure that he would want to talk about what had happened to his family and if he didn't, then our time in Hella was at an end and our trip had indeed been a wasted effort. I decided not to push him, so I just sat there watching him sip his coffee and mull things over in his head.

'It's been just over twenty years since I buried my two darlings. Erla died in 1991 in a fire in one of our barns. It was late in the year, very cold outside. Colder than now, even.

We were never really sure what she was doing out there but we suspected she had gone looking for her new puppy and may have followed it into the barn. We never found out how the fire started but it seemed that some fuel cans had been spilt and the fumes had ignited somehow. By the time the alarm was raised the barn was too hot to get anywhere near. My wife and I just stood there and watched it burn. As far as we knew, all there was in there were a few sheep we had put indoors to safeguard from the cold. We had no idea that Erla had got herself trapped in there until we realised that she was nowhere else to be found.'

He paused and had some more of his coffee. I could tell that these were not easy memories for him to be reliving.

'That little dog of hers escaped the blaze somehow and that was when we began to panic. Inga Rós ran through the house looking everywhere for her but she wasn't about. Standing in front of that barn as it burnt to the ground broke our hearts. The iron walls got so hot they glowed in the darkness. By the time the firemen arrived there was nothing to be done. They found our little girl when they went through the wreckage the next morning. There wasn't very much left of her when they pulled her out. There was even less of us left after that.

Inga Rós never recovered and could never come to terms with what had happened. Three months later she used the tranquilisers the doctor prescribed for her to take her own life. Just before she killed herself, she became very quiet to be around. It was like having a ghost in the house. Now I have two ghosts to keep me company and precious little else.'

I looked at Stefán Jón. He had stopped taking notes and just stared at me. I could feel a tear running down my cheek. I still didn't know what this poor man's story could possibly have to do with my own but I felt as if we had trodden upon ground on which we had no right to be standing.

Stefán Jón was the first to break the silence that had descended over the room. 'Was there anyone your daughter was close to at the time? A school friend, perhaps?'

Diðrik seemed to think this over carefully before answering.

'There was her cousin, Halldóra. She lived in Selfoss in those days but they used to spend their holidays and a great deal of time together. If you can track her down she might just be able to help answer any more questions you might have.'

I gave Stefán Jón the look that said we were done. I thanked Diðrik for letting us into his home and his life. I decided that I had been feeling way too sorry for myself of late. I could do something about what was going on with my sisters, or I could not. That was still my choice.

Sitting around wondering why it was happening to us and not someone else wasn't going to achieve a thing. I had to get them back before they were gone for good. I had seen the end result of not doing anything, and I didn't like the way it looked.

CHAPTER 21

When I rolled over and felt the other side of the bed it was already cold. He must have left early to work on whatever piece he was going to write next without the distraction of having me around. One thing I liked about staying at his place was that no one knew to look for me there. I was out of reach of even the most determined of pursuers. It was starting to concern me a little that our spending the night together was beginning to constitute something of a pattern. I guess I was just reluctant to admit that I really liked him. I didn't feel the instant need to keep him at arm's length, which was my tried and true approach to most men in my life. Baldvin hadn't bothered keeping in touch either so maybe that was a sign that I should just let things turn out the way that they were going to turn out.

The trip to Hella had instilled in me an appreciation for just how vulnerable I was if someone wanted to get at me. If Stefán Jón had made me get out of the car first into that pouring rain it would have only taken a moment for him to straighten his hair or find himself distracted in some other manner, and I would have been gone. That's how fine the line had become between escaping and being swallowed whole. If I wasn't more careful in future, I would only find darkness.

The link between the story of Erla's death and that of my own family still eluded me but I imagined that there was one there somewhere, waiting for me to dig far enough and in the right direction.

As I made myself some coffee I toyed briefly with the idea of getting in touch with Grímur and letting him know what we had been up to.

Every time I ran the conversation through in my head, though, I sounded more and more like the crazy woman he had specifically told me not to become. I really should have thought harder about who had left the note for me in the bookshop and why before embarking on a cross-country expedition after a dead girl and her dead mother.

The sorrow in Diðrik's voice had left me worrying about what would become of us and how I would deal with never seeing my sisters again should it come to that. It wasn't something I had allowed myself to think about too much but now, now it was all I could think about. A harrowing unease that I was about to be abandoned had permanently set in and it was an existence I wanted no part of.

After a quick shower I made my way back to Vesturgata and picked up the car without even going inside. I wanted to see Dad as soon as possible. It was time to find out if he'd ever had anything to do with Hella or that part of the country in general and it couldn't wait. I had the feeling that time might just be running out for us all.

As soon as I pulled up the driveway in Hafnarfjörður I could see he had company. The two of them were standing near the entrance to the stables chatting away to each other and hadn't even noticed me arrive. The man Dad was standing next to had a certain rustic quality to him. A little frayed around the edges but not yet quite falling apart. None too concerned with the way he looked or the way others perceived him was the impression I got. My first guess was that he might be a farmer friend of some kind. Definitely not a city dweller. Possibly even the help that I had been quietly suggesting he get for the horses.

Although if that were the case I had pictured him finding someone a little younger. Quite a lot younger, in fact. This man was Dad's age at least, possibly even a little older. They seemed very relaxed around each other as though they may have known each other for some time.

So as not to disturb their conversation I made my way into the house and put some coffee on. Sooner or later Dad would have to bring his friend indoors and introduce him. There was a travel bag sitting on one of the living room chairs. Perhaps a sign this new arrival was planning something of a stay. It was possible that Dad had simply grown tired of having no one his own age around. Even though he was a stubbornly independent man he had to find himself getting a little lonely sometimes. I might have been his daughter but I wasn't a peer.

I rather quickly became sick of waiting for an introduction to our mystery guest so I went looking for one instead. I loaded myself up with coffee cups and made my way out to the stables. They were nowhere to be seen but I could hear their voices from within.

'I thought you two might like some coffee while you're catching up.'

The two men smiled as they accepted their cups.

'This is my daughter, Ylfa. Ylfa, this is an old friend of mine, Ólafur from back east. We haven't seen each other in an awfully long time.'

Ólafur shook my hand and looked me up and down in an effort to appraise his friend's prodigy.

'Pleased to meet you,' Ólafur said. 'I'm sorry to hear about all the trouble you've have been having. These are indeed terrible times for your family.'

'How do you two know each other? I don't remember Dad telling me he was expecting a visitor.'

'He wouldn't have told you because he had no idea I was coming. I've made a completely unannounced visit, I'm afraid. I saw your father's name in the newspaper and thought it was time I paid a very old friend a visit before neither of us are up to it any more.'

I looked from one man to the other trying to comprehend what the relationship between the two of them might be.

'How long exactly have you two known each other?'

Dad and Ólafur looked at each other as though it would take the two of them thinking about it to figure it out. Either that or they weren't completely sure they wanted to let on. I had never heard of any Ólafur in my father's past. It was Dad who eventually broke the silence.

'It would be sixty years now give or take. We grew up together in Höfn back in the day but we haven't seen each other since. Life conspired to separate the two of us and then did its very best to keep us apart. It's been our own fault we haven't kept in touch but I guess friends you make at that age are for life.'

The look he gave me suggested that as explanations go that was going to have to do for now. I would wait till later until I could get Ólafur alone and then get the rest of the answers I wanted. It seemed odd they had never tracked one another down and yet I could see there was a real bond between the two of them.

Obviously a phone call would not have sufficed or Ólafur wouldn't have bothered travelling the length of the country to see Dad. Maybe it was just concern at his wellbeing after what he had read in the papers or seen on the news, as he had said, but I felt there might just be more to this reunion than met the eye. I was sure that with a little patience and a little investigating I would soon know. I would bide my time and wait for their story to unfold.

'It will be nice for Dad to have someone to keep him company when I'm not around, anyway,' I said to Ólafur. 'Do any of the horses need a run out while I'm free?'

'The two of us have already taken Farfús and Leppatuska out so you could take Alvari if you like. That way he won't end up feeling left out.'

I took my cue to leave them alone and led Alvari out of his stall, much to the stallion's delight. The fresh air was just what the doctor ordered for both of us. Now that it had finally stopped raining it was actually pleasant to be outdoors even though it was still bitterly cold. The ride would clear my head if nothing else and give me some time to think. Some alone time was just what I needed. Even though we had been sent to Hella to meet Diðrik and hear his story I still felt that Stefán Jón just might have been right all along. A little voice inside me was telling me that Dad held the answer to all this whether he knew it or not.

When the three of us – Elín, Kristjana and myself, that is – had been little girls I had once asked Dad why he got so very angry at things which seemed to me to be at most slightly annoying. Either I hadn't been old enough to understand what had been frustrating him or my youthful intuition had been right and he became furious at things that simply weren't that infuriating.

He had taken his time answering the question. So long in fact that I thought he had chosen to ignore me. Eventually, he told me it was because of where he had grown up. He had been, in his own words, the best of a very bad bunch. I didn't really understand what he was getting at at the time and had let the subject of his childhood drop without becoming any wiser.

Even now in his old age he would become angry at things unnecessarily. His outbursts had never really bothered me very much because I had always felt they were a healthy release for him. What worried me much more, and always had, in fact, were the things he never actually said. There had always been a suspicion between us girls that Dad kept way too much to himself. He used silence as a tool to keep people at bay, his own family most of all.

I had asked my mother, Margrét, on numerous occasions why he was that way and she patiently told me time and time again that people were the way they were and that was that. She told me I would understand what she meant better when I grew up.

By the time I had finished letting Alvari lead me in a big circle back to the stables, the hours had slipped away and I had completely lost track of time. I gave him a quick wash and a scrub before heading back to the warmth of the house. My father was nowhere to be seen but Ólafur was standing at the sink washing some dishes. I had to suppress a smile at the sight of him concentrating so hard over the dirty plates; he looked somewhat out of place in the kitchen as some men his age do. He eventually looked up and noticed I had returned.

'Your father's having a rest in his room so I thought that I'd help out a little with the cleaning up,' he smiled. 'Not that it's much help, of course.'

I picked up a tea towel to dry the dishes he had just washed.

'Did you two have a good catch up, then?'

'Your father's not the boy I remember from those long ago days but it was a very long time ago, wasn't it? It would be silly to expect that nothing's changed since then.'

'I can't believe it's been sixty years since you've seen each other. I can't imagine going that long without seeing someone I knew. Something must have happened for the two of you to lose touch like that. Dad's never mentioned you before, either. In fact he's never even mentioned Höfn before. He's always been a bit mysterious about his past and now I think it's time I found out why.'

'The last time I saw your father was in 1952. It's a whole lifetime ago now. We were eleven years old and we behaved the way most children of that age do. It was a difficult time for our families and things could have turned out a lot better than they did, I suppose.'

He rinsed off another plate and put it onto the drying rack beside the sink before continuing.

'One stupid mistake too many all those years ago and our lives changed. Irreversibly, as it turned out. One thing leads to another and before too long you no longer remember what your life was like before the mistake was made and you've lost all control of how it's going to turn out for you.'

Ólafur finally looked up at me, having avoided my eyes so far. Now that I looked more closely at his face he looked like a man with a burden of some sort. Maybe that was what he had come to town for. To release himself from something that had been bothering him all this time. He looked back down at the sink again as he fiddled about in the suds, searching under the water for something else to wash.

'Einar told me you saw the programme about the boys' home. That was the inspiration behind my visit. I, like others, have decided it is time the truth was told about those places. There's not many of us left now and if we don't say something then the others will have been lost for nothing.'

'And what does Dad think of all this? If he's never said anything to his own family in all this time then what makes you think he'll want to talk about it now?'

'Because we have a duty, Ylfa. Neither of us are young men any more and there are things that need to be said while we are still around to say them. I for one feel a great responsibility. One that, in my opinion, can no longer be ignored.'

'What about in Dad's opinion? Not everyone will want to relive those times, for some there may be no need.'

'I'm the reason your father wound up in Lönguhólar. It was a terrible place and very few of us who were forced to live there deserved to be there. We were all just children and many had their youth taken from them. Nothing can ever undo the things that were done there.

It never leaves you and it never lets you forget. We can't hide forever from what happened even if we might want to.'

His eyes had filled with tears. Despite his age he looked like a terrified child all over again. He was the second extremely sad old man I'd talked to in a short space of time. I wanted to delve further into what Ólafur had told me but it would have to wait. He was in no shape to continue and I was feeling worn out as well. I put the tea towel down and walked away. Maybe he was right but what if he was wrong. What then?

CHAPTER 22

My phone rang early the next morning – too early. It was Stefán Jón letting me know that Diðrik's niece had called the newspaper and wanted to see me. Diðrik had said she was from Selfoss or had used to live there at any rate, so I told Stefán Jón that I wasn't sure if I was up for another road trip just yet.

'Don't worry, she's in Reykjavík at the moment. Diðrik managed to track her down through some relatives and told her who I worked for. He related our little get-together to her and now she wants to see you.'

'Did she say why?'

'No. All she said was that she wants to talk to you in person and while she has nothing in particular against me, she wants to see you alone.'

I wrote down the number he gave me and wondered what exactly it was she wanted to talk about. My head was still racing from the conversation I'd had with Ólafur the night before. There were dozens of questions I wanted to ask Dad but I was well aware that if he didn't want to talk about it, and there was a very good chance that would be the case, then he simply wouldn't. All communication would simply shut down.

If he had kept that part of his life quiet all this time it was unlikely to be a simple task to get him to open up about it now. I would probably just have to let him come to me in his own good time. No matter how long that might take.

Like it or not, and I didn't, I was going to have to be patient. Ólafur may well have come to see him with the notion of reliving old times but I knew from experience that my father would not be swayed in his thinking by a journey that he would undoubtedly view as sentimental nonsense.

I decided to phone Halldóra instead. I couldn't imagine that she would have anything much to add to the story that Diðrik had told us but it would be rude not to meet up with her if she wanted to talk. As it turned out she was just in town staying with friends while the music festival had been on. The last shows had been the night before and she was due to head home as soon as she could get the energy together to do so.

She chose one of the city's older cafés on Hverfisgata and told me to meet her there in an hour for coffee. I agreed and rolled out of bed into the shower. By the time I'd arrived to meet her she was on her second coffee, a necessary pick-me-up after the nocturnal exertions of the five previous nights, apparently.

Halldóra was somewhere in her thirties, but it was hard to tell exactly where. She was a bit overweight but with a very pleasant smile and beautiful dark brown hair. She looked tired but as though she'd just been enjoying herself too much.

I ordered myself a double cappuccino and took a seat next to her at the front window, which looked up onto the footpath outside. The café was at basement level and you got a great view of everyone's ankles as they walked by.

'I was worried that we might have given your uncle a bit of a shock showing up like that out of the blue. We were given a lead suggesting that we look in Hella for clues about what might have happened to my sisters.'

I pulled out the now rather tatty note and handed it to her to read. She took her time doing so before handing it back.

'He must have thought we were quite mad,' I continued.

'He still does, I'm afraid. At first he thought it was some sort of practical joke. In very bad taste, I might add. He hasn't made it to the graveyard as often as he would have liked to and he thought you were winding him up.'

My coffee arrived and I stirred some sugar into it not knowing what to say next. I felt bad for dragging Diðrik through his past with our visit. He didn't need reminding of everything he had lost. He had to deal with it every day in his own quiet way without us bouncing into town to make him relive the whole nightmare.

'I can assure you that wasn't our intention. We were simply curious as to what our stories might have in common.'

'The summer before Erla died I spent a lot of time with her. I would head across from Selfoss and stay with them on the farm. We were best friends as well as cousins. Pretty much inseparable when we were teenagers. Erla was a lovely girl but she had something of a mischievous streak to her. Being an only child, and a very attractive one at that, she used to get away with murder. Figuratively speaking, of course. She had a real soft spot for people she liked but she could also be cruel to those she wasn't so fond of.'

'Cruel? In what way?'

'The summer before she died she befriended this orphan boy who had just moved to Hella. He didn't know anybody and was terribly shy about making friends. He just wasn't very good around other children and they all gave him a bit of a hard time because of it.'

'Who was this boy?'

'He was the only one who wasn't from Hella or Hvolsvöllur, from out east somewhere. He was just awkward and you know what children are like at that age, they can be mean.

'At first I couldn't understand why she wanted to befriend him. I thought maybe she felt sorry for him but that wasn't really her style. All the other boys at school fell over themselves trying to get her attention so when she started hanging out with this other boy, it just made them hate him all the more.

'One day, though, I found out what she was all about. It was my birthday. She told me she had a special present for me and that I was to head out to the old barn on their property and wait for her at a certain time. She wouldn't tell me why but she said that I had to hide at the back of the barn behind some old machinery that was stored there. I didn't have a clue what she was up to but I played along with it and hid in the barn and waited for her to show.'

'How old were you then?' I asked.

'I turned fifteen that day but it almost seems like a lifetime ago. She was way too young to die the way she did.'

I didn't think any age would be ideal to be burned alive but I didn't say so. I didn't mention anything but I was getting a little impatient for Halldóra to get to the point.

'So what happened?'

'The barn stank of sheep and I really didn't want to be there any longer than was absolutely necessary but she had assured me that it would be worth my while so I held my jumper over my nose and mouth and waited. And waited. When she finally showed she had this boy with her, the odd one with no friends. I could hear them talking but I couldn't see them very well without giving myself away. That would have ruined everything, she'd said.

'There was lots of giggling and whispering but I couldn't tell what they were talking about, either. A couple of times I tried to get a look at what was going on but it was too risky so I just stayed hidden like I'd been told. I was so worried they were going to see me and spoil it all.

'Eventually, I heard Erla call out my name, really loud so I knew it was time to come out of hiding. She said my birthday surprise was ready and I should come and get it. When I came out of my hiding place I was a little shocked at first but then just really amused. Erla was good at getting boys to do exactly what she wanted them to. She could wrap them around her finger, as they say. Not like me, I had no luck with the boys. Not then, not now.

'She knew I had never seen a boy naked before so she had lured him into the barn and convinced him to let her tie him to one of the posts. She had tied his hands behind him and then stripped him, right down to his underpants. Probably with promises of what she was going to do for him.

'She had her shirt off and was standing there in her bra so he probably thought he was about to get really lucky. He looked pretty relaxed at first considering his predicament but when he saw me appear out of nowhere he looked a little more tense. He hadn't been expecting company I don't think. He got a little annoyed with Erla and told her to untie him. She just laughed and told him not to be silly.

'When he realised she had no intention of letting him off the hook he tried to wriggle free from his bonds but she had done a good job with the knots. She had grown up on a farm so she knew what she was doing. The more he thrashed about trying to get free the more upset he got and the more she laughed.

'She tried to warn him that if he made too much noise someone might come to investigate what all the fuss was about. She told him that if that happened we'd run off and leave him where he was. That calmed him down a bit; he realised that he had got himself into something of a pickle and was just going to have to deal with the consequences. He was pretty annoyed by this point but probably with himself as much as anything else.'

I had to smile at the image of the poor boy, one minute thinking he was about to pop his cherry and the next trussed up in front of two girls. Boys would do pretty much anything to get laid. Didn't matter if they were fifteen or fifty.

'Then she pulled out a knife and told him that if he behaved himself she would cut him free and let him get dressed again. He said that was all he wanted to do, his expectations had dropped to the point where he was happy to just go home.

'She walked up to him and kissed him. At first he didn't know what she was up to but then he started to enjoy himself. She told him he had been a good boy and soon we could all go home.

'She told him that I had never seen a boy naked before and that he was going to be my first. She ran the knife gently over the ties that held him to the pole as a tease but then cut off his underpants instead and wished me happy birthday.

'All their kissing had definitely had the desired effect on him and he was really embarrassed, as I'm sure you can imagine. He went bright red and started yelling at her to let him go. Well, she was right about someone hearing all that noise. Diðrik had been wandering the farm as he tended to do all day long and he came to investigate what he thought should have been an empty barn. When he reached the door, he called out to see who was there and we did exactly what she'd said we would. We ran for our lives.

'We disappeared out of a door that had been left half open at the back of the barn and didn't look back. I know we should have untied him before we escaped but there just wasn't time.

'Diðrik walked in on this boy standing naked in his barn and screaming his head off in a state of adolescent arousal and freaked out. He took off his belt and whipped him ferociously. He eventually let him go but not before he had given him a real hiding. He probably thought he'd been trying to deflower his little girl and wouldn't have been too wide of the mark. We shouldn't have left him there but we were afraid of getting caught too. After that he never talked to anyone again and became silent, like a stone.'

I still didn't understand what her story had to do with me, or anything for that matter. I was starting to fear that she was just some kind of crazy lonely person who had found someone to listen to her stories that could quite easily have been completely made up.

'Why are you telling me this story, Halldóra? What does it have to do with me and my family?'

I tried not to sound too put out but I really couldn't see what she was getting at. She looked a little exasperated herself but it could have just been the hangover or the look on my face that had done it. I probably shouldn't have interrupted her and just let her finish.

'Well, when I saw the story in the newspaper about what had happened to your sisters and the boy on your father's farm I started thinking about those notes that had been left behind for the police. When Diðrik rang to tell me you had been asking all those weird questions it suddenly came to me. The note that led you to Hella was pointing you in a specific direction but it isn't a where, it's a who.

'That boy we played the trick on, he became a very angry person after what Diðrik did to him and it was all our fault. You know that Erla died less than a year after that. In that same barn. I know he set that fire. I don't know how he arranged it but I know it was him.

'I saw him once after she died when I was back in Hella to see Diðrik and Inga Rós not long before she killed herself and when he looked at me he smiled. It was the most evil smile I've ever seen in my life. He was telling me with that smile that he had finally got even with us and that he had won what we had started.

'That boy's name was Daníel. Just like the book in the Bible those notes were taken from. He lived around Hella somewhere with his foster parents. His name was Daníel Bergsson.'

CHAPTER 23

Halldóra had decided she was ready to drive back to Selfoss and left me sitting in the café to finish my coffee and ponder what, if any, significance Daníel Bergsson might have to my sisters' dilemma. The connection seemed tenuous but there was no denying we had been led to Hella for some sort of reason. Maybe I had uncovered nothing more than a disparate collection of facts and the actual link between them and who had taken my sisters was still to be uncovered.

The boy she'd described was certainly capable of great cruelty if her suspicions were correct but I would have to find out more about Daníel Bergsson before I could tell if I was on the right path this time around.

I called Stefán Jón and filled him in on what Halldóra had told me and asked him to do as much digging as he could on anyone called Daníel Bergsson who would be in his mid-thirties by now and get back to me. He said he'd contact the Selfoss police as well to see if they had any information on the death of Erla Diðriksdóttir that might be of use to us.

I told him I'd see him later when we could compare notes on what might be going on. Once again I toyed with the idea of getting in touch with Grímur but once again decided against it. Until I knew exactly what was going on, he could wait.

By the time Stefán Jón had finished work I'd decided that we were wasting our time thinking that Daníel Bergsson might have anything to do with Elín and Kristjana. The fact that the boy had the same first name as one of the books of the Bible and used to live in Hella was not enough to make me think we'd cracked the case.

I'd made a respectable effort to tidy the flat before Stefán Jón's arrival and although he hadn't said anything when he'd walked in I could tell from the look on his face that he was used to more organised surroundings. He was perched on one of my chairs trying to get comfortable when I came back in from the kitchen with a glass of wine for each of us.

I tossed a cushion on the floor next to him and suggested that he might be more comfortable on it. I stretched out on the sofa and waited for him to tell me what he'd managed to find out about our friend Daníel. After weighing up the pros and cons of the cushion he decided to sit on it and stretch his legs out in front of him. It was going to take him a little while to get used to my cramped little flat.

'I talked to a contact at Selfoss CID who has been there so long he actually remembered the case. He said they found Erla's body propped up against the remains of a pole in the barn. She was horribly disfigured from the fire, burned beyond recognition. The strange thing was that she was still almost exactly in the middle of the barn. Not at one of the doors trying to get out but slumped in the centre of the inferno. Not only that but she was naked. What was left of her clothes was found in a pile not far from where she died. The fire had started from some cans of fuel that weren't even supposed to be kept in that barn and Diðrik couldn't remember at the time how they had got there.'

'They didn't think any of that was suspicious at the time?'

'They thought it was odd, but they weren't really looking at it as a murder scene. No one had any motive to kill the girl and it looked for all intents and purposes like a terrible accident.'

I went over the story Halldóra had told me once again, mainly for my own good. It sounded as unlikely, as I listened to myself repeat it, as it had the first time. Nevertheless, there was something about it that rang true.

The look on Halldóra's face and the nervousness in her voice as she had told me about her friend's death. She had been completely serious about the fact that a boy of fifteen had been responsible for such a terrible act of vengeance.

'Even if the boy had something to do with her death it would be impossible to prove anything after all this time,' Stefán Jón said, thinking out loud. 'Giving him a motive after all this time isn't going to give the police anything new to work with.'

'Maybe that's the point,' I added.

'What do you mean?'

'Whoever has taken Elín and Kristjana left that note for me to find, right?'

Stefán Jón just nodded as he tried to get his long legs comfortable once more and took another sip of wine.

'So... ' I continued. 'Maybe he was pointing us towards a crime he knows we could never prove or maybe he's just trying to scare us. Even if we knew beyond a shadow of a doubt that it was him, he figures he's safe after all these years. He's showing us what he's capable of just to scare us even more.'

'You think the same boy is responsible for slashing Jóhannes's throat and kidnapping your sisters? The same guy who may or may not have killed this girl all these years ago? If you don't mind me saying so, that seems pretty far-fetched.'

'Of course it does. That's why he's done it. He's convinced that if we were to tell anyone, they'd think we were crazy. He leaves me a note directing us to the scene of a crime that he committed all those years ago knowing that there's no way he will ever be held responsible for it. He's telling us that there's no way he'll ever be caught for these ones, either. He's trying to tell us he's just too smart to get caught.'

'But what on earth would be the point of that?'

'Everything he's done so far has been to instil as much fear as he possibly could. Tying Dad up and making him watch; leaving those notes everywhere so that we knew it was the same person responsible each and every time; the phone call from Kristjana's phone in the middle of the night with no one on the other end, knowing that I'd be sound asleep when it rang; waiting in a graveyard in the rain in the middle of nowhere for me to show up. If he had wanted to kill Dad, he would have done it the same night he killed Jóhannes. If he had wanted to kill me I'm pretty sure he would have done it already. We're still alive because he wants it that way. He wants us alive and he wants us scared.'

I finished my glass of wine in one go and went to find the rest of the bottle. Stefán Jón had stopped fidgeting around and was staring at the wall behind the sofa as though trying to burn a hole in it with his mind. I noticed he had finished his glass as well so I filled them both up.

'So, what do you think? Am I crazy or am I making sense?'

'I'd say there's a good chance that you're both.'

'There's a man, Ólafur, staying at Dad's place at the moment who arrived out of the blue to see him. Apparently, they knew each other when they were kids in Höfn. I never even knew Dad grew up there. They haven't seen each other in something like sixty years. Can you believe it?'

'So why show up now?'

'According to Ólafur, he saw something on the news about Kristjana and Elín going missing and decided to pay a visit.'

'Do you believe him?'

'I'm not sure. Apparently they were in a state-run home for boys all those years ago and now that the home at Breiðavík has made the news Ólafur thought he'd try to reconcile with some of his old buddies before it's too late.'

'I've heard stories about what went on in those places. What does your dad have to say about it all?'

'I'm pretty sure he doesn't want to relive those days all over again. He never told any of us about them, not even Mum. Let's finish this wine and go to bed early. I want you to stay here tonight if that's okay,' I said, pleading with my eyes as I did so.

'Of course it is,' he nodded.

'So what do we do about this guy next, then?'

'We find out who Daníel Bergsson is and what he's up to these days.'

CHAPTER 24

The next morning Stefán Jón set off for work after promising he would be in touch as soon as he found out anything about Daníel Bergsson. I'd got used to having him around in what felt like a very short period of time and didn't want to contemplate him not being around, which it would be fair to say was totally unlike me. The circumstances that had brought us together had been far from ideal but that aside, there was definitely something about his relaxed manner that made him very appealing. I hoped that if I spent enough time around him a little of whatever it was that kept him so relaxed might rub off on me.

As if to jolt me back from these thoughts, my phone rang. It was Baldvin. I had been meaning to call him to tell him that we wouldn't be seeing each other any more but had decided that if he had been at all interested then he would have called. Before now, that is.

I tried to sound as pleased as I could to hear from him but wasn't entirely sure I'd pulled it off. At first I thought he might want to carry on where we'd left off. He wouldn't have been the first man to cool things off a bit before resuscitating them on an even more casual basis. One that suited his needs, if you know what I mean.

For some reason, men always shied away from telling you what they actually wanted. They were often too scared to tell you the truth in case they might sound bad. They preferred to lie first, then when things turned out the way they had expected them to and not the way they'd hoped, well, then it was time to tell you the truth. And then leave.

As such, my expectations of the phone call were not great, pretty much from moment I saw his caller ID. Before I had even heard his voice I was planning some cunning way to get rid of him. Politely, of course.

It wasn't that I no longer liked him, it was just that I had found something else to be getting on with. Someone I could see a future with, even in what were undoubtedly uncertain times. Maybe that was what I liked about Stefán Jón. The worse things got, the more I saw of him. Not the exact opposite, as was so often the case.

'Ylfa?'

'Baldvin, what a surprise.'

'I was just wondering if I left my watch at your place the other day. I've looked everywhere for it and it hasn't turned up. The last time I remember wearing it was the day I posed for you. I think I must have taken it off then and forgotten to put it back on again. Would you mind having a look around the flat for me?'

'Not at all, Baldvin,' I said, shaking my head in desperation.

I should have known it would be too much to expect for him to ask me how things were going. It really wasn't worth the hassle of saying anything so I simply said I'd have a quick look around the living room for his watch. I hadn't noticed it when I'd been tidying prior to Stefán Jón's arrival but I hadn't really been paying that much attention to what I'd been doing. I'd been frantically doing my best to rationalise the place from disaster zone to what I hoped was something more like bohemian clutter. Of course, to Stefán Jón, a mess looked like a mess. And that's what it still was, no matter what name I chose to give it.

After roughly thirty seconds or so of fruitless searching I started to lose what little patience I had left. He could have left his stupid watch pretty much anywhere.

'Do you remember where you might have put it after you took it off?' I asked him, no longer caring if it was found or not.

If it had taken him this long to ring up about it then surely he could have been mistaken about wearing it that day.

'Now that I think about it, I might have accidentally kicked it under your couch when I grabbed my clothes to get dressed again. Could you just check there for me?'

Muttering obscenities under my breath I got down on my hands and knees and peered under the couch. It was something I had avoided doing for quite some time now and as soon as I stuck my head under it I knew why that was.

Underneath it I found a collection of dirty cutlery, paintbrushes and chocolate wrappers, even an empty pizza box. I cursed again as I realised that from his vantage point the night before Stefán Jón must have had a perfect view of my poor housekeeping habits.

Baldvin heard me swearing and asked if everything was all right. I ignored him and rolled my eyes in further frustration as I came across his watch underneath the far end of the sofa. I brushed aside an empty container of fruit-flavoured skyr, with the foldable plastic spoon still protruding through its crumpled foil top, and plucked it out. The watch was a nice one, chunky and expensive-looking.

'I've got it. It was under the couch just like you said.'

'Fantastic. I was worried sick about it. Do you mind if I pop over tonight and pick it up?'

That was not something I wanted so I had to quickly come up with an alternative plan that didn't sound too much like he was no longer welcome to just pop over whenever he felt like it. Even though he most definitely wasn't.

I realised that I'd never known where he lived, which hinted at a total lack of interest on my part. I could find out and then pretend I had other business to attend to and drop it off on my way. Just as long as he didn't live somewhere ridiculously out of the way, that would work fine.

'I don't know about that, Baldvin. I've made other plans for tonight. How about I drop it off to you while I'm out and about this afternoon? That might be easier.'

The silence on the other end of the phone suggested that he understood what I was getting at. His little plan to weasel his way back into my bed wasn't going to work. It probably wouldn't stop him trying another angle, though. They always did.

'Okay,' he said rather reluctantly. I could almost hear his brain ticking over as he tried to find another excuse to drop over to Vesturgata.

'Baldvin,' I was losing patience with him and wanted the conversation brought to an end.

'How about...' he tried once more.

'Listen, why don't you just tell me where you live and I'll drop it off this afternoon? I'm seeing someone else now and don't want you dropping by any more. I hadn't heard from you and just assumed you weren't interested.'

I had no idea why I was trying to justify myself to him. If he had wanted anything more than just a casual screw then he would have put way more effort into it. Once again his silence loomed over the phone like heavy cloud cover. I really hoped that he wasn't going to make this difficult.

'It's Álftamýri 26, apartment 18. I'll be home all day if you want to swing by. I hope you're not mad, Ylfa. I thought we were just having a bit of fun together.'

I didn't really want to get into what we had been doing together. Whatever it had been, it was no more; that was all too clear now.

'I've got some errands to run but I should be over sometime in the next two hours.'

I didn't want to sound too keen to get rid of the watch but I would have quite happily driven straight over there and dropped it through his letter box if I thought I could have got away with it.

'No problem, I'll see you then. And thanks, Ylfa. I really appreciate this.'

You'd bloody well better, I thought and hung up. It was going to be an unnecessary distraction that I hadn't bargained for in my day, but when I stopped to think about it, I didn't have that much else to be getting on with. It was more the thought of having to go out of my way for him when I'd hoped that things between us were done and dusted. Realistically though, I was always going to have to make some time to see him again. He wasn't to know I'd met Stefán Jón and had moved on in such a short space of time. I was in danger of making a big deal out of nothing if I wasn't careful.

Álftamýri was on the way to Dad's place so I decided to use him as an excuse to get out of any plans that Baldvin may have dreamt up in the two hours I had conveniently given him. Hopefully the knowledge that I was seeing someone else would have removed any such ideas from his head but you could never be too sure. He'd been on to a pretty good thing when it came to no-strings-attached sex with me over the last few weeks and chances were that he'd become a little accustomed to it. I was fully expecting him to make a one-for-the-road play of some sort for some more.

His flat was in one of three identical concrete apartment blocks opposite a primary school. The only distinction between the rows of buildings was their colour schemes. One block was yellow, one was red and one was blue. Baldvin's was the blue one. His 4-wheel drive was parked outside looking as though it could do with a good wash. I found the front door and made my way inside and up the stairs towards apartment 18.

On the way up I came across an elderly lady struggling with her heavy shopping bags. I offered to help and after a quick visual appraisal of me she readily accepted. She told me that she had just seen a young man collapse in the car park outside the Kringlan shopping mall. She had waited there until the ambulance and a police officer had arrived to see if he was going to be okay. The man had been disorientated and had needed help to get into the ambulance.

She said that he had been young enough to be one of her grandchildren and had looked like one of those 'silly young drug-users', as she put it. She grumbled that life was so easy for young people these days that they had to go out of their way to make it as difficult as they could. In her day there would have had been better things for them to worry about. I didn't doubt her for a second. My father, too, was of the opinion that most young folk had far too much time on their hands, as were most people of their generation, I suspected.

When we reached her door she thanked me and asked me when I had moved into the flats and which number I was. I think she thought she had found a new friend in the building, or at least a useful neighbour. I told her that I was just dropping something off for a friend. She smiled and told me again that she was very grateful for my help. One day she would move into a building that had a lift but until then she would have to rely on the kindness of people like myself.

Baldvin answered the door almost as soon as I'd knocked on it. He looked unsure as to whether he should give me a hug or not and in the end just stepped aside and let me in. To describe his flat as sparsely furnished would have been something of an understatement. He had taken the Icelandic concept of minimalism to new heights. The place had the bare necessities required for existence and no more. I couldn't decide if he hadn't lived in the place long or just preferred it empty.

There were a few dirty coffee mugs and plates on the kitchen bench and a television and sofa in the space that passed for a living room. Next to the television were a computer and a collection of DVDs. The place was impeccably clean, which made me feel even more out of place. It really couldn't have been any more different from my own apartment. While he busied himself in the kitchen making some coffee, I took a seat on the sofa and put his watch down on the coffee table. His head turned slightly when he heard the noise.

'Thanks for bringing that over. I must have kicked it under there when I was grabbing my clothes after your sister burst in on us.'

'No problem. I'm heading out to see my father so it was on the way.'

He brought my coffee over and put his watch back on before taking a seat next to me and fixing me with a slightly quizzical look.

'So you're seeing someone else?'

It didn't sound as though he was really expecting an answer so I just nodded.

'I suppose I've only got myself to blame,' he said.

'I thought because I hadn't heard from you that, you know, it had just been a bit of fun and nothing more.'

This time it was his turn to nod his head slowly and sip his coffee.

'I guess you're right. I should have known better than to ignore a pretty girl like you for too long.'

He smiled when he said that but it was an unnatural smile that made me feel uncomfortable. I didn't know whether to be complimented or not so I just kept my mouth shut. If he was waiting for a reply he wasn't going to get one. I didn't feel like making unnecessary conversation. It would only prolong my visit and now that I was on the way towards Hafnarfjörður I thought I may as well keep going and see Dad and Ólafur while I had some free time.

'What are those plans that you have for today? I don't suppose you'll be able to stay very long.'

'No. I'm on way out to the farm to see my father. He's got an old friend staying with him who he wants me to meet.'

Another smile. This time it was more confident but it made me feel just as uncomfortable as the first one.

'An old friend?'

'Yeah, an old school friend, I suppose. Someone he hasn't seen for quite some time, anyway.'

The way he looked at me, it felt as though he knew I was lying, or at least not being completely honest with him. Either way, his smile was one of over-confidence now and I couldn't quite figure out why. He had his watch back and I had made it clear that we weren't going to be seeing each other any more. What could he possibly be feeling so smug about? Not wanting to sit and ponder that question too long I finished my coffee, put my mug down on the table and stood up to leave.

'I've got to get going. It was good to see you again but I've got loads to do.'

I needed to use the toilet before I set off so I asked him where it was. He said it was just off the bedroom and pointed me in the right direction. His bedroom was just as frugally furnished as the rest of the flat. I couldn't imagine living somewhere with no artwork and nothing to look at on the walls. The place felt clinical, like an office or a workplace, not somewhere you might call home.

Just as I closed the bathroom door behind me my vision started to fade in and out of focus. When I looked at myself in the mirror I saw a confused woman who looked considerably paler than she should have. I ran some cold water and splashed it over my face just before I threw up violently into the hand basin. I stood there gripping the sides of the basin with both hands, wondering what I was doing. I had no idea what was wrong with me but I felt as weak as a child, and a rather poorly child at that. I threw up again and then washed my mouth out with water.

I didn't fancy spending any more time in his overly clean little flat than I had to. I didn't fancy that at all but the bottom line was that I didn't feel up to going anywhere just yet. I used the toilet and then made my way into the bedroom. My phone started to ring as I stood next to the bed trying to collect my befuddled thoughts. I sat down gingerly on the edge of the bed and tried to get my phone out of my jeans pocket. Such a simple everyday task had somehow become unmanageable and I was forced to lie right back to get my hand into my pocket. By the time I had extricated the mobile, the call had gone to voicemail. What felt like several minutes of fumbling with the buttons ensued before I was able to listen to the message. I think Baldvin may have called out to see if I was all right but I just ignored him.

The message was from Stefán Jón. He had done some digging on Daníel Bergsson and had come up with some news. Apparently, he had, until very recently, worked part-time at a law firm on Borgartún. Elín's law firm, the one that belonged to Elias and Bjarki. He said that would explain how he would have been able to take her from her place of work so easily. If in fact it was him. He probably still had access to the building and knew her well enough for her to feel completely comfortable around him.

Finally it all made sense.

He had weaselled his way into Elín's workplace and then I had invited him into my bed before introducing him to my other sister. I couldn't believe how stupid I'd been. I managed to roll over onto an elbow before I dropped the phone and vomited again. This time all over the bed and onto the parquet floor.

Baldvin, or Daníel as he was really known, stuck his head into the bedroom and asked how I was getting on. He picked my phone up off the floor and smiled at me again. Finally, I understood why he had been smiling so much. I couldn't move my legs anymore. Whatever he had put in my coffee had done the trick. My head and my stomach had traded places and brilliant colours spiralled across the walls.

Before I fell away into an invisible hole that had opened up below me in what was beginning to feel like a really bad dream I tried to call out to Stefán Jón and tell him that I needed his help. I wanted to tell him that I knew what Daníel Bergsson was up to these days, and it was no good.

Daníel stood at the end of the bed and lent over me. I wanted so badly to kill him and tried to tell him just that before the world around me became very small and very cold and then very, very dark. It was going to have to wait.

CHAPTER 25

By the time I had regained a vague semblance of consciousness I found my hands and feet were tied and there was some sort of vile-tasting gag in my mouth. Luckily, though, the urge to throw up had passed, which didn't appeal one bit with a mouth full of what tasted suspiciously like an oily rag. I was lying on my side in the back of Baldvin's 4-wheel drive with something hard and painful sticking into my ribs. It felt like I was lying on a selection of tools, which may have been exactly what I was lying on.

I could hear the rain beating down relentlessly on the roof as we turned sharply at speed onto much rougher ground. I had no idea how long I had been out of it but my instincts told me that we had travelled quite a distance. We were definitely no longer on the smooth streets of Reykjavík. Every turn we took sent me rolling from one side to the other and without my arms free to protect myself I banged my head over and over again until I was swollen and sore all down both sides.

When I managed to get myself into something akin to a sitting position by pushing my legs against one side of the vehicle I could glimpse a small amount of the outside world through the darkened windows of the vehicle. We were already in Hella and moving towards the volcanic hills to the north.

Another twist in the road and I was thrown back down onto my side. I decided to stay where I was rather than risk injuring myself any further. Saving whatever strength I had left was more important than ascertaining my exact whereabouts. I was in trouble; that was all I needed to know for the time being.

I soon saw the world go dark again but this time it was as we came to a shuddering, stomach-churning halt. I heard Daníel get out of the vehicle and slam the door shut. The sound that followed was the unmistakeable high-pitched scream of corrugated iron rubbing against itself. He had driven us into a barn and was closing the doors on the world behind us.

The rear of the 4-wheel drive was thrown open and his hands felt around in the dark for my feet. When he had a good and firm grip on them I was pulled out of the back of the vehicle so hard my head bounced off the dirt below like a ball. He rolled me onto my stomach and with a knee on my back he pressed all the air out of me and held me down until I was deflated and broken.

He took one of my arms and drove a needle into the vein. The cool liquid that ran up my arm almost felt nice for a moment before sending me diving back into that jet-black pool that I had just pulled myself out of. Once again I fell, once more down into that deep, cold hole from which I feared I would never return.

Next thing I knew, I was cold. Not merely a bit chilly or uncomfortably frosty, but frozen to the bone. I was pretty sure that I was well along the road to hypothermia and then inevitably freezing to death. I was as wet as if I'd just stepped out of a bath and I could feel the wind coming in through one of the walls of wherever I was. It was very dark. Black, like the middle of the night. I noticed I had been tied up again, only in a slightly different fashion this time, and I had been stripped of all my clothes. He had left the oily gag where it was, tied in place by a piece of string, but even if it hadn't been there I doubted there would have been anyone close enough to hear my screams. It was small and outdoors somewhere. It was old and falling apart. The front of it appeared to be wooden with an old bent out-of-shape door in it. The rest of it smelled as if it had been dug out of the side of a hill.

It was probably an old sod hut that had once been used to shelter sheep during foul weather but had been left to fall apart long ago. Abandoned and left to decay much the same way as I was going to fade from this life. I was going to die there, I could see no other way for it to end.

I heard him somewhere behind me. He cleared his throat as he grabbed me under my arms and pulled me up so that I was sitting with my back against his legs.

He was on a chair behind me and had a fistful of my hair. He ran his fingers across my throat and made me flinch as they dropped further down my chest. As my eyes slowly adjusted to the dark I could see shapes beginning to form around the two of us. The floor was dirt. Three walls were a combination of wooden supports and dirt; the other had the broken down old door, which didn't shut properly, and a tiny window somewhere near the top of it. I was hidden away from the world and alone with his voice.

When he started talking it was slow and methodical as if what he wanted to say he had thought about for some time, such was the deliberate manner of his delivery.

'We used to share a room together in his house. My mother, Lauga and I. Surrounded at all times by the fury that we had learned to endure and cower from, the way beaten dogs hide from their masters. How my mother came to be with him I was never told. I could never imagine how she could ever have made such a mistake. She had wound up in a poor situation from which she had never been able to recover. One thing she did tell me, though, over and over again in fact, was that he was not my father. It made the circumstances even more difficult for me to understand but she insisted that it had been someone else even though she never told me exactly who it was who had left us both in such a lurch. Whoever it had been, he had fled like a coward and sentenced us to a nightmare of a life.

'Men used to sleep over in the house, often in the living room. I used to sneak out of our room in the middle of the night once they had fallen asleep and go through their pockets for loose change. Once I had been successful with my thieving I would return to our room and hide whatever I had found inside the old torn mattress we slept on. Most of the time they wouldn't even notice it was gone. They had come to spend their money on sleeping with her and drinking. By the time they had passed out they had probably had so much to drink that they had lost count of what he had charged them for the privilege of indulging their sins. Sometimes they would pay with something for us to burn to keep from freezing, coal, perhaps, if we were lucky or dung from their animals. Sometimes they would bring home-grown food or homemade liquor from their illegal stills. Mostly, they drank from the one that bubbled and gurgled away in our shed. The one I was never allowed into.

'All forms of payment were considered. He would accept almost anything for her services that he could use for himself. If he could burn it, eat it or drink himself stupid with it then she would have to let them defile her or risk yet another beating.

'Even if they discovered that they had been stolen from, very few of them would ever say a word. To incur his wrath over a few coins was foolish. His fuse was short and his temper volatile.

'There were times when he looked for a fight just to see if they would stand up to him. Most of them thought better of it but there would always be one or two who fancied themselves after an afternoon or evening of heavy drinking. Normally, he would win these drunken stupidity contests but occasionally not. Sometimes, when a particularly determined adversary would get the better of him, a beating would come his way to even things up for a while. I used to love seeing his face bruised and bloodied but I soon learned that it would be a fleeting pleasure.

Once he had recovered his bearings and readjusted his damaged pride, the way a clown hitches up its fallen pants, he would seek revenge on the softest targets he had available to him. My mother and me.

'I was no more than five years old so the majority of his anger was vented on my sweet but tormented mother. He would avoid hitting her in the face but would instead take his frustration out on her with a leather strap that he used to thrash her legs and backside until they were red and raw.

'If I was stupid enough to try to protect her he would just whip me instead. So I would hide in that room of ours and listen through the door to him behaving like a monster. At least the other men never hit her. They degraded her in many other ways but the violence was his and his alone.

'When she made her way back to our bedroom I would hold her and let the tears she had been holding in finally flow.

'She would read to me from her Bible. It was the only book we ever had, the only one I ever knew and how I learned to read. The stories were supposed to help me get through what was happening to us. They were meant to make me believe. Believe that there was another way for us to live. A better way for me to hope for, a brighter tomorrow somewhere for us both.

'The Book of Daniel was her favourite and has always been mine as well. When anyone has such terrible dreams all they want is for someone to explain what it is that they have been seeing. I'm sure you must agree.

'Every time I hear her voice, I hear those words about Daniel and how his faith preserved him in the face of such ungodliness. Every time I see her face, it is the face that convinced me to run away from him. Even though she never made it further than the front of the house.

'You see, he knew we were going to run and he set a trap for her. By the time she attempted to smuggle me through the front door late one night he had attached a bell to it so he would hear us as we left. As soon as we heard the bell ring she picked me up and ran but only managed a few steps before she fell. He had dug a hole in front of the house right in front of the door. He had covered it with branches and leaves and filled it with spikes. The same way they trap wolves in some countries. She fell through the cover and got caught on those spikes like an animal.

'She told me to run, to get away but I couldn't leave her. So I cried and I watched him work her loose from those horrific lances. He said he was going to take her to someone who would make her better and I wanted to believe it so badly that I did. But the look on her face told me that as a team we were done and from then on it would be just me and him until I got away.

'At first I pleaded with him to take me to see her but there was always some reason why I couldn't go. He would make up such ridiculous stories to keep me quiet and to make sure I would wait for her to return. He used hope as a means of keeping me there until he could use me to fill the one void she had left that he couldn't fill himself.

'It wasn't until he raped me in the bath that I finally found the courage to run away. Why he would have wanted to do that to such a young child I still don't know. Something must have made him evil before we came along. What that was, I will never know.

'I was found and eventually taken in by another couple while he just moved on with his life without us. Years went by as I tried and failed to forget the evil that had been handed down to us like an old pair of shoes that were worse than no shoes at all. Eventually, it became clear that I would never forget and so I could never forgive. My life had nothing of any worth left in it so I decided to take what was left of his. That's where you came into it.

'You never asked to be part of my world, but then, I never asked to be part of his. I guess we both got what we were given, not what we asked for.'

Somewhere behind me a small lamp flickered into life filling the black void around us. Its flame searched across the walls to illuminate his next message for me. As he tossed me to the ground I could see what he had painted on the wall, just for me.

*God has numbered the days of your reign
and brought it to an end.*

My eyes raced about the tiny hut trying to find anything that might lead me to an unlikely salvation. What I saw not only gave me nothing in the way of hope but filled me with a certain knowledge that I was about to die. It was a map to the other side.

In one corner there rose two elongated sections of dirt. I knew instantly what lay beneath them the same way I knew what would shortly lie in the third and as yet empty grave. He let me stare for some time at what was surely to be my fate before he spoke again. He let the impact of what I was witnessing sink in and break my spirit just like he knew it would.

'I sent Stefán Jón a text for you, telling him that you were heading to Hella and that he should join you as soon as he could. If your new lover left as soon as he received it then he should be here anytime now.'

He dropped my phone in front of me in its various broken bits and pieces. He then picked up a syringe and slid it once more into my arm.

I had to wonder if that was to be my last participation in this life or if more awaited me; and if there was to be more, then what hell would it be?

Back into the void I headed. The sickening sensation of falling rapidly backwards while going nowhere at all. Freefalling into hell.

When I came to again there was light somewhere just beyond me and this time I was tied to a chair. The gag was still in place in my mouth and I was still tied hand and foot but this time there was something new to experience: a rope curled around my neck, which then rose straight up into the darkness above me. If I struggled to get off the chair or tip it over I would hang myself. Clever.

Between myself and the light was a slatted wooden door of some sort. I was in a cupboard or what may have been a pantry at some point. It was pitch black in my prison and with the downward-facing slats on the door I could see out into the room but I would be completely invisible to anyone even if they were standing only a few feet in front of me.

Behind me on the floor somewhere I heard something scurry from its hiding place to investigate my presence. I tried hard not to think about what it might be and what it might want – and failed.

A radio played soft, dreamy music as if from another world. Voices rose and fell from yet another room further beyond my vision. I thought back to what he had said to me in the hut and shuddered at what was to come if that was Stefán Jón I could hear. He had simply picked the very worst of times to meet me. The qualities he possessed that drew me so strongly to him would wind up costing him dearly. I wished he had never come to visit us in Hafnarfjörður. If only my father had succeeded in scaring him off. He would have been better off staying away from me. Far, far away.

I tried to cry out as they walked into the room in front of me side by side but I was barely able to breathe let alone alert him to the danger he was in. It looked like a kitchen from what I could make out, old and in need of repair as well. Wherever he had brought us, it hadn't been used to live in for some time. His foster parents had lived out this way somewhere; perhaps it had once been the house where they had raised him as their own.

Stefán Jón took a seat at the table in the middle of the room and sat with his back to me as Daníel made them some coffee on an old stove. The smell made my stomach knot into a ball. As he did so, he turned the radio up just a little and glanced in my direction. I tried once again to move or loosen my restraints but every time I moved they seemed to tighten around my limbs and the rope around my neck threatened to cut off my supply of air altogether.

Every now and then Daníel would glance over towards me. No matter what precautions he had taken he was still a little nervous that I would be discovered before he had played his endgame. As he looked in my direction I flinched involuntarily, almost suffocating myself without even trying. I had to stretch my chin upwards and put all my concentration into just breathing to stay alive. What I really needed to do was relax but nothing so simple to conceive of had ever been so impossible to achieve.

Daníel took a seat as well after placing the cups of coffee on the table. He glanced once more in my direction, this time almost imperceptibly.

'So tell me. I'm curious as to who this person is who thinks I could be connected with what has been going on in Reykjavík. You must understand that their theory sounds completely outrageous. Such accusations can be quite dangerous. You do see, that don't you?'

'I do, but there are some questions I would like to ask.'

'Of course, ask away.'

'How long have you lived in Hella?'

'I only spend some of my time here, otherwise I'm in Reykjavík. This house once belonged to my foster parents. They've both passed on now but the two of them saved my life I think it would be fair to say.'

'How so?'

'Anna and Bergur took me in when I was very young and had lost my way in life.'

'So that is why you are called Bergsson?'

'My legal name is still Lauguson, after my mother. I never knew my father.'

'What is it you do in Reykjavík?'

'This and that. I'm not working anywhere at the moment.'

'But you were working at a law firm on Borgartún?'

'You have done your homework. Yes I was but that's finished now.'

'During your time there, did you meet a woman called Elín Einarsdóttir?'

'Briefly, yes.'

'Are you aware that she is missing at the moment and hasn't been seen for some time?'

'Yes.'

'Do you have any knowledge of her whereabouts?'

'No.'

There was a silence as Stefán Jón made some notes.

'My source, a woman from Selfoss, said you knew a friend of hers many years ago here in Hella. A young girl you went to school with, in fact. She died in a barn fire not far from here on the property of a man called Diðrik Guðmundsson. There were rumours at the time that you may have been involved but nothing was ever proved as far as I know. The dead girl's name was Erla Diðriksdóttir. Do you know who I'm talking about?'

'How many years ago are we talking here?'

'It was 1991. You would have been fifteen at the time. You had just moved to the area and were living with your adoptive parents.'

'Twenty-two years ago, that's quite some time. I'm not sure that I remember this girl. What did you say her name was?'

'Erla Diðriksdóttir. She lived on a farm not far from here with her parents Diðrik and Inga Rós. She was found dead in a barn on their property after it burned down one night with her trapped inside. No one was ever sure what she was doing in the barn when it caught fire or why she couldn't get out. There were rumours at the time that the two of you had some kind of falling out and that you were looking for revenge.'

'And so you think I killed her? I really don't know where you get your information from. I don't understand what connection there could be between a poor girl dying here twenty odd years ago and those women going missing in Reykjavík.'

'The truth is that we don't know either. That's why we wanted to come and see you today. I thought that you might be able to remember this girl. Maybe the two things have nothing to do with each other, maybe they do. I wanted to hear your side of the story.'

'You say "we" but I see that you have come here all alone.'

'I was really hoping that my friend would be here as well. I was supposed to meet her in Hella but I don't know where she's got to and her phone's switched off.'

'So you're just going to believe some crazy notion based on hearsay, is that right? It seems a rather odd reason to drive all the way down here to make such bizarre accusations. Maybe your friend, if she were here, could help make more sense of it. When did you say she was going to arrive?'

'I'm not really sure. I thought I was supposed to meet her here but I could have got it wrong.'

'That's too bad. Without her here to make some sense of this I don't really know how I can help. I don't remember this girl that you're referring to or her family for that matter. It was such a long time ago and I was rather new to the place. I didn't really know anyone all that well back then so I don't see how I will be able to help you out. It seems that you may have wasted your precious time coming all the way down here.'

There was a brief pause as one of the chairs groaned against the old wooden floor.

'I'm not feeling terribly well. Would you mind if I used your bathroom?' Stefán Jón said.

'Not at all. It's just down the hall, the last door on the left. You don't look that well, either, if I may say so. Maybe all this fresh air doesn't agree with you.'

I could hear Stefán Jón get up out of his chair rather awkwardly and walk slowly out of the room. From the other side of the table I could see Daníel look straight across at me. Even though there was no way that he could tell exactly where I was in my darkened cell he looked straight into my eyes. The way a fox looks at a rabbit just before the end.

CHAPTER 26

Even though I had a pretty good idea of what was in store for Stefán Jón, it didn't make it any less traumatic when it finally came. Not that it happened quickly; just the opposite, in fact. It was in unbearably slow motion and all the more painful because there was no way he would understand what was going on. Then again, maybe that was for the best.

One minute he had been conversing normally with Daníel, the next he was struggling to make it to the toilet without throwing up all over himself. I could hear him vomiting down the corridor somewhere as Daníel turned the music off to give the two of us a chance to hear his discomfort. Through it all he just sat there staring in my direction and chuckling to himself as though it was the funniest thing he had ever heard.

When Stefán Jón reappeared, he was in bad shape. On the way back to his chair he stumbled, tripped and then fell against it, tumbling to the floor in a marionette's clumsy dance. As he lay there somewhere just in front of me trying to hold on to whatever was left of his self-control, Daníel began to speak again. This time he had to know that whatever he said would be primarily for my benefit. I couldn't tell if Stefán Jón was still conscious but I doubted it.

'Now that I've had a little time to think about it, I do remember the girl you were referring to earlier. The one who died in the fire you mentioned. There were two of them if I remember correctly. Erla and Halldóra. I was, as you recalled correctly, very new in town. It was difficult to make friends being the only child who wasn't from around here. We were all rather young at the time and anyone who didn't fit in was treated badly. It's the same everywhere, I guess, and I would have behaved no differently had I been in their shoes. Nobody ever wants anything to do with an outsider.

'I should have known better when Erla took an interest in me. If something feels as if it's too good to be true, then it usually is. Her having any kind of interest in me definitely felt too good to be true but I was desperately lonely and I just couldn't help myself. When she asked me to meet her in that barn I agreed straight away even though I had no idea what she had in mind. The two of them just wanted to have themselves a little fun but then her father showed up out of nowhere and beat the hell out of me after they'd run off and left me there. That was something I would certainly never forget.

'There was no way I was ever going to be accepted after that so I decided to bide my time and wait for an opportunity to get even. Luckily, I had learnt to be very patient from a very early age. There's no point in fighting back if you're just going to get beaten every time, so you wait and you come up with a way to get back at them that they'll never forget.

'The dog was the key. She loved that stupid little thing more than anything else in her life. It was almost too easy. A love like that can only provide a person with a weakness that's all too simple for others to exploit. The moment she discovered it was missing she just had to go look for it. She was so worried about what her parents might say to her for losing it that she didn't even mention it to them. I had it tied up in the barn. The same one she'd used to play her little trick on me.

'Once she was inside I hit her over the head and knocked her senseless. I undressed her and tied her to the same pole she had tied me to. When she woke up I made sure she couldn't raise the alarm by using the very same thing that you have in your mouth now, and then I made sure she realised why it was that she had to die. The only time I pulled that rag out of her mouth was to wipe my hands on it after I had poured the petrol around her feet. She tried to scream but it wouldn't come out of her for some reason. By that point she had pissed all over herself so maybe she was just a little bit too scared to scream.'

Daníel stood up and walked towards me. He stepped over Stefán Jón's prone figure and stood briefly on the other side of the slatted doors before pulling them open in an unwelcome blaze of light. He grabbed the gag from my mouth, taking the string that held it in place along with it. I gasped for fresh air in deep frantic breaths and tried in vain to swallow but there was nothing left for me to get down my throat.

The taste of twenty-year-old petrol had left me praying for water and wishing that it would all just end. One way or another. The look in Daníel's eyes told me that any such dream of a speedy conclusion was as futile a wish as I could possibly have. Nothing about this man was about haste. He was about waiting and scheming and flawless execution. No one puts as much effort into his hatred as he had over the years to not enjoy it to its fullest. He wasn't about to hurry through his final work.

'He had begun to take such a shine to you, too. It's almost a shame he has to leave us now, but as long as you're not too far behind then I don't really see the harm. It hurts to have something you've become accustomed to taken from you, doesn't it? A little like losing a finger perhaps. Or was he something more like an arm?'

Daníel turned Stefán Jón's prostrate form over so we could both see his face. He certainly looked unaware of what was going on around him. For that I will always be grateful. Before I knew what was happening, Daníel had pulled a knife from somewhere beneath his clothing and slit Stefán Jón's throat wide open. His blood sprayed delicately across the floor leaving a feather-like pattern across his face. It then began to ooze in a mechanical fashion out of the wound and into an ever-increasing pool beneath him.

I looked at the strange expression on Daníel's face. Something inside him was reliving a moment from another time. For the briefest of moments he looked like that little boy he must have once been. And then, just like that, it was gone.

Standing in front of me once more was a killer, blood dripping from his knife and pooling around his boots.

'Someone else will have to write my story now.'

He cut the rope that was tied around my neck and the ones holding me to the chair. The effort required to remain upright suddenly became too much to ask of my body and I rolled down onto the floor. Stefán Jón's blood stuck to my cheek and the cloying metallic odour filled my nostrils. I closed one of my eyes so as not to get blood in it and stared up at Daníel with the other. He tucked the blade back into his waistband and picked me up like a bag of dirty laundry. Even though there was a little light left in the day he carried me across the fields not seeming to care if we were seen or not. Somehow I doubted there was anyone else around us for miles.

Finally, my voice returned, although I sounded weak and lamentable when I spoke.

'Why go to all this trouble? Why don't you just put me down and kill me here?'

'There's someone I want you to get to know a little better yet before we're done. I want you to know why this had to happen and I want him to know that you knew.'

I tried to cry out into the cold night air but my throat gave in to the pain and failed me. As we approached the decrepit sod hut he laid me down on the damp grass almost tenderly. He ran his fingers down the side of my face and sighed. The door complained noisily as he wrenched it open. He smiled uncomfortably before grabbing hold of me under my arms and pulling me back into the hut where I had first awoken to his exhibition of atrocities. This time around the stench was unmistakable. Once he had lit the small lamp again I could see the interior more clearly than I had been able to before. Protruding from one of the shallow graves was a pair of hands tied together at the wrists.

Their owner had been buried face down in the dank, volcanic soil. From the lack of nail polish on the fingertips I could tell they belonged to Kristjana. He hadn't even bothered to bury her properly. For some reason, that hurt more than I thought anything possibly could. He propped me up against the wall and sat down against the opposite wall underneath his hand-painted sign.

'Once he had finished with me he let go of my hair and let me slip back down into the barely tepid bathwater. I curled myself up into a little ball and waited for him to get out of the bath and leave me alone. I never wanted anyone to ever touch me again. I wanted nothing more than to wash away the filth he had left inside me but he didn't get out of that bath and he wouldn't leave me be.

'He stood over me as I huddled beneath him and asked me what was wrong. I closed my eyes and waited for it to all go away. All I heard was him swallowing from his bottle and chuckling to himself. Then the disgusting, warm sensation on my back as he relieved himself all over me. It sprayed through my hair and ran between my fingers as I tried to cover my face with my hands.

'He told me that I would have to toughen up if I was to survive in this world. I was five years old, a little boy whose mother had just been taken from him. In his mind he thought that raping me and humiliating me would make me a better person. Perhaps he just wanted me to be more like him. I don't suppose he ever told you about me, did he?'

Nothing I could say was going to change anything. This was an unstoppable journey that had started three decades earlier. I was so cold I could barely feel my fingers or toes any longer. My suffering didn't appear to concern him in the slightest. He wasn't going to continue until he had a response of some sort so finally I just shook my head in despair. It was about all I could manage but it seemed to do the trick.

'I know he never took her to a hospital. He said she was being looked after and that we would be able to visit her when she was feeling better. Of course we never did. I never saw her again. He drove her away that night and killed her somewhere in the hills. She was in so much pain anyway that it was probably kinder to just finish her off.

'He couldn't have taken her anywhere for help without having to explain to someone how she'd become so badly hurt in the first place. She would have finally been able to ruin him and there was no way he could allow that to happen. As soon as he got back home he filled that pit in again as if it had never been there. Then he went back to his drinking as if nothing out of the ordinary had happened. After that he had to find new ways to bring in money now his golden goose was dead and buried but he found ways to scrape by and still managed to keep himself drunk every day of the week. Eventually, though, his sick and twisted mind decided he could use me to satisfy his sexual needs now that his whore was no longer around. He wasn't about to let that stop him having his fun.

'After I ran away I tried for years to forget about those days but there were always times when I couldn't help but wonder what had become of him. I guess he just got on with his life before eventually finding himself a wife. He must have straightened himself out before he met her, don't you think? Margrét had no idea who she was really married to. If she had been told, she would never have believed that her beloved Einar was capable of such things and would have laughed at the foolishness of it all.

'In some ways it's a shame she wasn't around long enough to see what became of her family. I would have liked to hear him try to explain all this to her. I would have liked to see him tell her all about what he once was. To tell all of you about the monster you were never allowed to know.

That would have been some day for your family and some day for me. That I never got to see him do that is one of the few regrets I have left.'

CHAPTER 27

I wasn't really ready to die, no matter what I had told him about killing me. Not by any stretch of the imagination. I thought I had prepared myself for the possibility of it happening as much as anyone actually can, but I was not ready for the finality it would bring. I wasn't willing to become just another of his victims and I didn't want to give him the pleasure of completing his heinous jigsaw puzzle. There were, however, some very serious problems that stood between my desire to carry on with my life and the fulfilment of that desire. I was totally drained of heat and energy, to the point where I could no longer feel my extremities and the drugs in my system were making me want to be sick all the time even though there was clearly no longer anything left in my stomach to expel.

Worse than all those things, I was terrified. More terrified than I had ever thought possible; consumed by the relentless, funereal pace of the procession I was following to my death. As I sat staring at my captor's feet, no longer wishing to look into the eyes of the man who was going to kill me, I realised that the game was most definitely up. I couldn't be sure if I had hours to live or merely minutes. Whichever it was I knew it couldn't be long before he let me join my sisters one last time.

As I sat there listening to him explain his life and its consequences, to himself as much as anybody else, I decided that if the opportunity arose I would attempt to give him one last thorn in his side. Even if it cost me my life, which I figured was all but forfeit by now, anyway.

'At some point it finally hit me. When he filled in the pit outside the front door, the spade he used to throw the earth into that hole he'd taken from the back of his car.

'At the time it didn't strike me as terribly strange but it should have. He didn't keep his spade in the car and I had never once seen him put it in there. He had pulled it from the car because he'd just finished using it to bury her. Up in the hills somewhere, or down by the beach. Where he hid her away, I guess I'll never know.

'There were beaches nearby where I would walk along the black sand while dreaming of getting away and starting my life again. I would steal out of the house at night when I could get away unnoticed. Somewhere beyond those vicious breakers were other families much happier than my own in other countries, which may as well have been other worlds they were so far away.

'Eventually, I did get away but not to some far-off land where I could start afresh and not before your father had ruined me. Where he grew up they didn't have any girls to play with so they were forced to experiment with each other. I was five years old when he did that to me. He would have been at least twice that age before the same fate befell him. It builds such anger within you that it either destroys you or you pass it on, like a disease, so that it may ruin someone else's life. Either way you're never the same again. The only choice you have is between keeping it to yourself and letting it infect everything and everyone around you. It eats away at all that is good and leaves nothing of any use behind in its wake.

'You're only now discovering what it is capable of. Until recently the worst things you'd had to contend with had been your mother's death, the fact that your father never talked to you as much as you might have liked and the fact that you think that your sisters were both a little bit strange.

'I first tracked down your father over a year ago. I told him who I was and why I had come to see him. Of course, at first he didn't believe me and pretended not to recognise me but it didn't take long to jog his memory.

'The funny thing is, I gave him a choice. I told him that he could tell all of you what he had done to me and my mother or I would take all of you from him and kill you. One by one. When I killed Jóhannes and that horse I thought the warning might cause him to change his mind, but I was wrong.

'When I found Elín working late one night all on her own I acted again thinking he might change his mind and save you two, but again I was wrong. When Kristjana needed a lift to pick up her cello I acted again but that failed to change his mind as well. I'm not sure if I'm impressed by his determination to save his own hide or disgusted by his contempt for you all. I actually thought you meant more to him than his foolish pride.

'There is no way he could ever be proud of what he did to us all those years ago but to do nothing now when he knew the consequences of his inaction, I found that fascinating. Even after both your sisters were dead I was still convinced that he would tell you and let you live.

'Now, once you're dead, he won't have to worry about telling the truth ever again.'

He smiled when he said that last bit. I guess he found humour in the darkest of places.

'I've got to bring him up here, too, so I can bury you both together.' He grinned again and disappeared back out through the old creaking door. The blast of freezing wind made me shiver so hard I thought I'd never stop.

I pulled my knees towards my chest and rolled slowly onto them until I had balanced myself in an upright position. I leant forward and rested my head against the wall. If I could have made the choice to end my own life there and then I think I would have. Not just to deny him the pleasure of killing me but because I could genuinely see no point in continuing.

On my knees, with my face pressed hard against the cold wall I was in just the right pose to do some praying. So, that is exactly what I did.

There weren't many things left I wanted any more. Nothing for myself, anyway. I had given up on getting out of that hut in one piece. What I wanted now was for my father to not be the man that was being described to me. I wanted all the things that Daníel had said about him not to be true. I wanted it to be a lie that Dad knew about this. I wanted it to all be lies, nothing more than the product of a diseased mind.

I could die knowing that my father had survived a hard childhood and that he had made some very poor choices in his life early on. Before we came along. I could handle knowing that he hadn't always been the man I knew and loved. I could handle all that. People mess up, they make mistakes. It's how you recover from them that makes you who you are.

What I wanted most of all, what I prayed for more than anything, was that he never had the opportunity to do anything about what had happened to us now. I didn't want him to be so weak that he would keep something like that to himself. I wanted him to be better than that so I could die knowing that a decent part of our family would live on.

I didn't want all the good bits to be gone and only the wreckage to remain. That's all I asked for as I waited for Daníel to return.

I rolled back to my original position as Daníel entered backwards through the door. He was dragging Stefán Jón's body behind him as he did so. When he had him inside the door he let go of his shoulders with a tired-sounding grunt.

I looked over at my friend, hoping that the uncomprehending look he had acquired in death had left his face. It had not.

Daníel looked across at me as he wiped the sweat from his brow. He seemed to be searching my eyes for something. Exactly what that might have been I couldn't tell.

When he'd caught his breath he completed Stefán Jón's journey by dropping him unceremoniously into the last open grave. As he did so I got a glimpse of the knife he had killed him with, still stuck into the waistband of his jeans. My legs twitched involuntarily when I saw it and I noticed for the first time that my ankles weren't tied nearly as tightly as I had thought they were. If only I could muster the energy to work them a little looser, I would give myself a fighting chance of getting out of them. If only I had the energy required to do that. If only I had the energy to do anything apart from pitifully wait for the end to come at the end of that knife. I pulled my feet slowly up towards my hands and started work on getting the knot loosened further.

It had been tied well as far as the knot went; it just hadn't been tied when my ankles had been pressed tight together and so I had a little leeway to work with.

Daníel's attention was taken completely with his struggle to get Stefán Jón's rather lanky body into the hole. As the grave had been dug with me in mind it was short by a good six inches or so.

I let him curse and work up more of a sweat despite the chilling air as I fumbled about in the gloom trying to somehow unravel my bonds and take a small step towards my freedom. As he continued to fret I finally got one side of the knot to loosen slightly for me. It wasn't much, but it was a start. Slowly, the knot loosened its grip on me as I fed one end of it carefully back through itself.

As I unwound the rope from around my ankles, I strained to see if I could tell exactly what Daníel was up to. He still hadn't turned to face me, so I rolled carefully onto my knees and very slowly and carefully inched my way across the floor until I was directly behind him. He let out another groan as he finally positioned Stefán Jón's body to his satisfaction.

Just as he was about to stand up again and come for me, I snatched the knife from his exposed waistband. He felt the movement on his buttock and one of his hands felt around his backside for the missing knife.

Thinking that he must have let it fall to the floor, he turned and ran his fingers over the dirt in an attempt to locate his missing weapon. He had no idea where it was and what it was about to be used for. If he had, he would have put a lot more effort into finding it.

Even though my hands were still tied at the wrists, I was able to get a good grip on the knife with both hands. As the realisation that all was not as it should be began to sink in for Daníel, he lifted his gaze from the floor up towards where I now stood. I used my whole weight to fall forward onto him and drive the blade as far as I could into whatever I hit. Even though it meant possibly saving my life, the thought of stabbing him made me close my eyes so that I would not have the sight of the knife disappearing into his flesh come back to haunt me at a later date.

Despite my squeamishness, I managed to force the knife into him, all the way up to the handle. It entered him somewhere just in front of his collarbone on his left side. The metal of the blade slid into his body with disturbing ease at first but then hit bone and more solid connective tissue.

I immediately let go of it as he began to scream in what had to be excruciating pain. I pulled away from him but not fast enough to stop him grabbing my ankles and pulling me back down to his level. Once he had me on the floor with him he tried to pull the blade from its gruesome new home. The first tug he gave it had him recoiling in desperate agony and that was when I pushed myself away from him and used my hands in the dirt to press myself upward to a standing position and stumble toward the door.

It was still open from when Daníel had dragged Stefán Jon through it and I unsteadily put one foot after another towards the old broken frame, not wanting to trip and fall, only to seal my fate once and for all. Somewhere behind me

Daniel was still trying to extricate the knife from his body. His screams growing in anger as he did so, like a wounded animal intent on taking its foe with it into the afterlife.

As I felt the freezing air hit my face like a wave, I dared to dream that I was free. I don't know what overcame me, but I was sure I had escaped. As soon as I thought that, though, I felt the sharp, unmistakeable pain of metal slicing into my body. My hip exploded in white-hot pain and I staggered no more than another foot like a drunkard rising too quickly from his barstool, only to stop dead in his tracks.

The joy I had felt at the thought of escaping his clutches was quickly replaced with the feeling that I had only delayed the inevitable, perhaps even worsening what was already undoubtedly to be a terrible fate. This time, though, there would be no delay in his vengeance. He had seen chances come and go, and wasted them in his obsession to get everything just right and now he would not hesitate to take hold of me like a disobedient dog and drag me back to my hole in the ground. I instinctively kicked out as I was pulled backwards and connected with his head as we both tumbled to the ground. His knife slid home again, this time entering my calf.

I pulled my leg free and squirmed out of his grasp. He had the desire to kill me but the injury I had inflicted on him was considerably lessening his ability to do so.

I stood up once more, slipped on the wet ground and screamed as my right leg failed to fulfil its prime objective. If I wasn't able to stand, how was I going to get away from him? Again, I pulled myself up and fought against the pain in order to force myself forward and away from him. A few steps and I fell once more, but the beginnings were there.

Each time I rose again from the grass, to my knees and then to my feet, I could feel I was making progress. The pain wasn't lessening any but I was forcing it away into a place where it was capable of doing less and less harm. I was too afraid of dying to let it win. If anything was going to save me, it was going to be fear. The greatest motivator I would ever find.

Even once I was up and moving it seemed that every three or so steps I took, I fell down again. But each time I picked myself up and tried to run some more. At first it was little more than a hobble and I kept waiting for that crunching tackle from behind that was going to get me down and keep me down. As I ran I could hear my heart straining to keep up with the demand that was being placed on it. The pounding of it swelled in my ears until it had achieved a deafening roar.

I could feel my pulse swelling again and again in my head as it beat in time with every step I took.

By now, I reasoned, I had to have put enough distance between the two of us. I slowed momentarily to turn and see how far behind I had left him, the pounding in my head not lessening for a second. As it banged, again and again and again I saw to my horror that the noise I thought was all in my head was the footfalls of Daníel running behind me. He had risen and given chase, almost catching me in the process before I had even noticed, such was my terror.

Suddenly the ground fell away from under my feet as Daníel crashed into me, knocking the air from my lungs and the wind from my sails. As I stared down into the black void into which we were falling, I wondered how I hadn't noticed earlier where I was headed. I guess between the fear and the adrenaline and the dark night all around me I just hadn't noticed the river.

We flew as one through the air before hitting the water. It was so unbelievably cold, glacial melt kind of cold, that it knocked the air right out of me all over again.

We had fallen into the river that runs from the north of Hella all the way down to the sea, the Ytri-Rangá. In the dark, I hadn't seen its banks approaching and had simply tumbled into its freezing maw.

Freed from the hold of one assailant, I was now in the frozen arms of another even deadlier foe. Once I had resurfaced, I tried to pick out the bank closest to where I had fallen but quickly realised that I was hopelessly disorientated. We had turned as we had fallen and I could no longer tell from which direction we had come. To confuse matters further, I couldn't see where Daniel was, if he had even resurfaced. I was so pathetically weak that my only option was to try to keep my head above the waterline and let the current take me away as far as it would. As far away from him as I could get.

After what was probably only a few minutes but what felt like hours, I found myself being able to just make out the lights of an approaching car. I could barely keep air in my lungs long enough to draw breath though I cried out all the same as it passed by, but my voice was whisked away by the wind and the car disappeared into the night.

Another eternity passed before I felt my knees being scraped against the gravel on the side of the river. I fought for purchase with what little strength I had left and eventually found my feet touching the bottom. The first two times I tried to stand I fell and was forced back into the current. The third time I scrambled towards the shore and grabbed a hold of something fibrous in the dark. Even once I was free of the freezing water the fear that I was going to die still wouldn't leave me. I was so cold that I could hardly move and any adrenaline that had sustained me earlier was long gone.

I knew that if I didn't keep moving I would die where I lay so I struggled through the dark and followed the riverbank south until I came upon the Ring Road.

I forced myself to stand there in the dark waiting for someone to find me. I knew that if I were to lie down and wait for help, I would die. Eventually, a driver approached and as I stood frozen and naked in his headlights I knew that I was going to survive and that soon I would be home again. No one thought had ever made me so sick with worry before in my life.

CHAPTER 28

When I first opened my eyes in the bed at the National University Hospital in Reykjavík, I had no idea how long I had been there. The motorist who had discovered me on the Ring Road had wrapped me in a blanket and driven me back towards Selfoss. At some point I had been transferred to an ambulance but where that had happened, or when, I simply had no idea. I had pleaded with him not to leave me, convinced that Daníel would still be coming after me but he had assured me over and over again that there had been no one else in sight when I had been found. Once I had decided that I was safe, my body had effectively shut down. It had been in serious need of self-repair for some time.

I still couldn't really believe that I was still alive. Unlike my beautiful sisters. It hadn't sunk in yet that I wouldn't be seeing them again. It probably never would. As soon as I awoke in the hospital I began crying, unable to understand why I had survived and they hadn't. There was nothing I could have done in Hella to prevent their deaths but I still blamed myself for what had happened to them. It would always be that way.

There was a police officer inside my room, looking down at me with a confused version of what might just have passed for concern in her eyes. She held my hand until I stopped crying and then told me she would fetch a doctor. Apparently, they were going to be thrilled that I had woken up. Thrilled about what, I wondered. She smiled in a somewhat awkward fashion and told me I was a brave and lucky woman and then disappeared to find the doctor she had mentioned. When he finally arrived, he reiterated the fact that I was lucky to still be alive. Not simply because the police had retrieved three bodies from the hut I had escaped from but because I had managed to get so cold that I could have quite easily died before being found standing in the middle of the road.

My wrists ached in a way that made me think they would never be right again and my hip and my calf, where I had been stabbed, felt as though they had sustained considerably more damage than I had originally thought. When I asked the doctor if I was going to all right, he smiled and told me that I would be but that it would be some time before I felt like my old self again.

He said that the stab wound had done some serious ligament damage in my hip but that with any luck it should cause minimum discomfort in the years ahead. When I asked him exactly what that meant he said that I would able to walk just fine but that with an injury like that, there would always be the possibility of something of a limp. It would be impossible to know straight away; it would only become apparent in time. I would have a permanent reminder of my struggle to escape. A physical one to go with the rest of the other ones Daniel had left me with.

There were, apparently, lots of people who wanted to talk to me but they had all been told that they would have to wait until I felt stronger and up to the task. My doctor gave me a mild sedative to help me sleep and kept saying over and over again that I needed my rest more than anything else. As if to prove that I was in complete agreement with him I fell asleep in the middle of our conversation and when I woke again my room was dark but I could occasionally hear soft voices just outside my door.

Every time I closed my eyes I fell back into that sod hut and instantly felt the cold and the fear all over again. He would be back to get me again. I just knew it. While there was any breath left in his body, he would return for me. If he had drowned in the Ytri-Rangá they would have found his body by now and told me. If they had found him and arrested him, they would have told me by now. He was still alive and out there somewhere, plotting to come after me again.

I wondered how badly hurt he was and how long it would be before I saw him again. I felt that we were destined to meet again; all that was left to be determined was where, and when.

For the next day, maybe longer, I faded in and out of consciousness with alarming regularity. My doctor didn't seem the slightest bit concerned that I would wake for a short while before returning to the sanctuary of sleep once again so I didn't concern myself with it much, either. The only thing that caused me any real concern was that my slumber wasn't quite as peaceful as it could have been. It was going to take some time before I could wake and not feel as though I had just been trapped in a cold, dark place waiting to die.

Grímur was my first real visitor apart from the police officer, Binna, who never left my door. She would come into my room whenever she could tell I was awake to see if I needed anything. She seemed a little in awe of me, which made me uncomfortable. I felt like a failure, I felt alone.

When Grímur arrived she took what may have been her first real break since my arrival and went to get herself something to eat. I had struggled to find anything remotely appetising since I'd woken up and told her so. She promised to bring something back that I might actually find tasty.

Grímur took a seat at my bedside and looked at me with what could only be described as fatherly concern. I felt as though I was about to get told off for not taking proper care of myself or denting the family car. His look conveyed a mixture of anxiety and disappointment with me as if his favourite child had somehow let him down, but was at least glad she was still alive.

'How are you feeling, Ylfa?'

I shrugged, 'I've been better but I'm still here so I guess that counts for something, right?'

I tried to smile but it felt phony and weak, just like the rest of me. As far as I could see, I didn't have too much to be happy about. I still remembered insisting that the man now standing in front of me do something more when Elín went missing and being told, in not so many words, that I was making it all up.

'Yes, it does. As you will have noticed, we've put a guard on your door and there are extra officers in and around the hospital as well. There's an alert out for the arrest of Daníel Lauguson and we hope to get our hands on him soon.'

The look on my face must have said it all. He had survived my attack and got away. I was sure that he would stop at nothing to complete his revenge. Once begun, he was not the kind of man to leave a game unfinished.

'With the injury you described him as having received it is unlikely he will make it on his own for very long before having to seek medical attention of some sort.'

I couldn't for the life of me remember telling anyone about what had happened during my escape but it was entirely possible that I had told anyone who would listen.

'At some point I am going to have to question you at length about what happened in Hella but I have been told to wait a while until I do that and so that's just what I intend to do.'

'There's a lot I don't remember; I was pretty out of it for most of the time,' was my way of making sure he understood he may not get all the answers he was looking for. I was in no particular mood to help the man who had refused to help me. That may have been overstating it somewhat, but that's how it felt.

'That's entirely understandable, Ylfa. You were pumped full of Ketamine for much of the time. To be honest, I'm amazed you remember anything at all. We found your sisters' bodies in the hut along with Stefán Jón's. I'm very sorry for your loss.

'We've talked to your father and he is very much looking forward to seeing you again. The doctor tells me it won't be much longer before you can go home. That will be good, won't it?'

Home? I couldn't answer that one for him, not honestly, anyway. I just stared at him wondering for a minute if by some chance he could possibly know the things about my father that Daníel had told me. I was being silly. That information, be it real or make-believe, was mine and mine alone. I lay back on my pillow as if I couldn't continue with the conversation. It wasn't far from the truth; I didn't know what to say to anyone any more.

I didn't know what I was going to do when they released me from hospital. My little flat on Vesturgata was going to feel like a cell and not the oasis that it had been for so many years. And as for going to see Dad, I wasn't sure I'd ever be ready for that. It was going to take some time to assimilate what Daníel had told me. Quite some time. What to believe, what not to believe and how to tell the difference between the two. That was the game still to come.

'It will be good to get out of here,' was as much as I could muster. 'As soon as I feel up to it, I'll come and see you but I'm not sure how much help I'll be.'

'When you're ready I'll need to hear everything you can recall. Four people are dead and the only real link we have to the murderer is you.

'We are confident of getting hold of him one way or another but you may be able to help us speed up that process. I understand that you've been through a great deal, Ylfa. God knows, I can only imagine what it must have been like for you but this won't be over for any of us until we have Daníel Lauguson in custody.

'I don't know what you're planning to do when you're released but my advice, for the time being anyway, would be to stay with your father.'

'Safety in numbers?' I suggested.

Part of me wanted to tell him everything I knew. Or at least, everything I had been told. I couldn't truly believe anything Daníel had told me until I knew it to be fact; merely suspecting it wasn't good enough. It was extremely unlikely he had made the whole thing up but I had to be absolutely certain before tearing what was left of our family apart. And there wasn't that much left of it to tear apart. If what he had told me was in fact true, then I no longer had a family.

'Exactly. You'll be safer there for now. Just until everything reaches its inevitable conclusion.'

Grímur smiled for the first time that I could remember. It made him look completely different. As he walked out of the room the female police officer walked back in, looking much happier for having had her short break. She was carrying a pizza box with her, which she dropped in my lap with a grin.

'If you tell anyone where you got that, I'll deny it all.'

When the time finally came for me to leave I actually had to dodge a reporter on the way out of the front door. I had become famous in the most disgusting way possible. They had arranged for a taxi to be waiting for me and I got the driver to drop me off at my flat on Vesturgata. I wanted to see what the place felt like first before I decided on returning to Hafnarfjörður or not. I guess I had to be sure in my mind that it was the right thing to do. At some point I was going to have to address Daníel's version of events with Dad but I was pretty sure that I wasn't ready for that yet. I stripped out of the clothes I had been given to wear home and jumped straight under the shower. It was the longest soak I had ever had under running water and by the time I was finished all I wanted to do was go to bed. Whatever else I had to take care of in the near future was just going to have to wait. The doctor had been right all along. All I needed right now was sleep, and lots of it.

CHAPTER 29

As I approached the driveway that led to what I had once thought of as our family home I was stopped by a young police officer, who had been entrusted with the job of guarding our property. He braced himself against the cold wind as he emerged from his vehicle and signalled that I should stop for him. He seemed concerned enough with the identity of anyone who might be paying the house a visit but with nearly a mile of unguarded boundary-line around the farm, I had to wonder if anyone with evil on their mind would use the front entrance. I thought not, but what did I know?

Ólafur was still staying with Dad and they were both overcome with emotion to see me again. I had become something of a celebrity in my absence; it was not something I was keen on cultivating so I decided I was going to ignore the newspapers and the television until it had all died down, no matter how long it took.

They seemed a little confused at first when I told them I wanted to take one of the horses out for a ride but when I explained that I just needed some time to myself they did their best to pretend they understood, even though they obviously didn't. What I needed was time to prepare myself for talking to Dad.

Now I was back home with him again the task suddenly appeared insurmountable. All I wanted was for someone to comfort me but he was the last person on earth I wanted touching me right now. For a while I actually toyed with the idea of not saying anything at all and just letting it be. Of course, it wasn't a realistic option but I was just so keen for the whole traumatic episode to be behind us that I was almost willing to ignore everything, no matter how unhealthy that might seem.

Nothing was going to bring Kristjana, Elín or Stefán Jón back; no apportioning of blame or regrets, no matter how sincere, would ever change the simple fact that they were all gone. I was going to have to get used to it, whether I liked it or not.

There would be no good way to go about what had to be done and the outcome was going to be a lose-lose situation no matter which path I chose to walk down. If Daníel had been right, then my father was as good as dead to me. Worse, even. If he had been making it up, then my father would never forgive the accusations I was about to make. Either way, Daníel had won. He had destroyed the part of my family that I had let him get his hands on, and he had ruined the rest. There would be no enjoying each other's company ever again; those days were gone.

When Dad voiced his concerns about me riding the property on my own I quickly suggested that Ólafur accompany me. It seemed to satisfy him even if he made no attempt to understand my choice of companion. Ólafur played the good sport and I saddled up Alvari and Leppatuska for us to ride. Dad went back to pottering about in Jóhannes's flat. He had been clearing it out and trying to decide what it would become next.

I let half a mile or so of path pass underneath us before I made any attempt at conversation. I decided to just ask Ólafur exactly what I wanted to know.

'Not so long ago you told me it was your fault that Dad wound up in that home.'

'Lönguhólar?'

'Exactly. Tell me about it. I need to know everything if I'm to understand what has happened to us.'

'You think that there's some connection with what happened at that place all those years ago?'

I looked across at Ólafur but he was well versed at playing his cards close to his chest. He wasn't about to make eye contact with me, not yet. He was waiting to see what I had first before he made any sort of move.

'I don't think you'd be here otherwise. You didn't come all this way just to pay us a social visit. If you made all this effort, it must have been for a reason.'

This time he looked over at me. He wasn't sure exactly what it was I was accusing him of but he didn't seem to like it one bit. The look he gave me confirmed my suspicions.

'It was 1952. We were very young. Neither of us was particularly stupid, but then again, neither of us was particularly smart. One night we both sneaked out of our respective houses and were prowling the streets looking for something to do. Like many children, we were simply bored.

'There was a NATO radar station near Höfn in those days. It closed some twenty-two years ago. They watched the skies with their electronics for bombers coming over the North Pole to bring destruction to the Americans in those days. It was the Cold War back then and their paranoia knew no bounds. The place is used to track civilian aircraft these days.

'Some of the staff at the base were foreigners, probably mostly American but I don't really remember. They would occasionally get up to their shenanigans after hours in town, which was what they were best remembered for. This particular night we found a car parked on an otherwise deserted street with its windows all fogged up. Being curious and a little mischievous we sneaked up to get a look at what was going on inside. All we could see was one of these servicemen with his military haircut and his hat still on with his backside going up and down like his very life depended on it.

'As amusing as that was to a couple of young lads, what we really wanted to see was more of the girl that he had underneath him. She was the daughter of one of the local fishermen and she was a fine-looking young thing. While your father was transfixed with what was going on through one of the rear windows I made my way unnoticed around to the driver's door and to my amazement, found it unlocked. They hadn't been expecting company. I carefully opened the door and looked inside. I could see their clothes piled on the front seat and the other thing that caught my eye was the handbrake. The cold air I had let into the car alerted them to my presence and the man yelled at me to get out. Of course I did just that but not before I had stolen their clothes and given that handbrake a good old twist.

'As the serviceman lunged across at me from the back seat the young lady caught a good look at your father peering in through the window at her. She screamed like someone had set her on fire and the two of us ran for our lives as the car set off of its own accord down the hill.

'As valiantly as the naked American tried to bring the car under control the odds were stacked against him. By the time he had untangled himself from Helga and got back into the front they had crashed into someone's house. Nobody was hurt in the accident but the owners of the house were fairly aggrieved, especially as it belonged to Helga's parents.

'They screamed bloody murder at the serviceman and both he and Helga had some trouble explaining where their clothes had got to. The driver hadn't got much of a look at me but she had no trouble identifying your father. She had got a very good look at him, although not as good as the view he'd had of her.

'The police visited our houses and when they saw our mothers were trying to raise us on their own they decided they weren't up to the job and they took us both away. With our fathers out at sea our mothers weren't in much of a position to stand up for themselves and the next thing we knew they had taken the two of us to the old house way out in the hills.'

'That house was Lönguhólar?'

'Yes, we thought that it would only be for a few weeks until they had accepted that we'd come to our senses and would behave ourselves again, but how wrong we were.'

'How long did you end up staying there?'

'Luckily, my parents came to an arrangement with someone in a position of authority after six months and I was released but your father was there for seven years.'

'Seven years?'

'His father had an accident on one of the boats. He caught his arm in a winch and couldn't fish any more. There wasn't any other work in Höfn so they moved to Egilsstaðir where his mother found some way of making a living. Your father was just left behind to fend for himself. He was a victim of unfortunate circumstances more than anything else. Bad luck got him in there and bad luck kept him there. Although in hindsight I could have done more to help him out. I should have taken more of the blame myself but once we were in there all I wanted to do was get out.'

'Did you see him, after you were let out?'

'No. I was never allowed back to visit and I never saw him again. By the time he got out he would have been eighteen and was probably a very different person by then.'

'What happened then? Did he find his parents again?'

'To be honest with you, Ylfa, I just don't know. I doubt it somehow. As far as I could tell at the time he just disappeared. He wasn't seen around Höfn ever again, that's for sure.'

I couldn't believe what I was hearing. I had accepted that things must have been tough for him but none of this matched my expectations of what he might have been through.

'What was it really like at Lönguhólar?'

'From the first night you arrived the other children started sizing you up. Looking you up and down as it were. Some of them were much older than we were and much bigger too. A few of them had been there for quite some time. You could tell which ones they were; they had become hardened by the walls they had built to protect themselves. It was safer not to let anyone in if you didn't want to get hurt.

'Those were the ones to watch out for, or so we thought. At the first sign of trouble we turned to the staff for help. That turned out to be a huge mistake although we wouldn't see it straight away. There was one young man in particular who seemed quite happy to take us under his wing. He gave us the impression that if we stuck with him we would be okay. And he was right, at first. Once the other children knew we were with him they left us alone. But like so many things in life, it came at a price.

'At first he would get us to run errands for him. Being eager to please, we did whatever he asked. Eventually, though, it meant spending a great deal of time with him alone. Not too long after that he began visiting us in the showers when we were by ourselves and asking us to do other things for him. He would get us to masturbate him in the showers and then pay us in cigarettes for a job well done. It made us feel ashamed and yet special at the same time. And of course, the last thing you wanted to do was tell anyone about it.

'You kept it to yourself and that was just the way he wanted it. It wasn't too long before that was no longer enough to keep him happy, though, and we were both raped repeatedly in our bedrooms. That was when I pleaded with my family to do whatever it took to get me out of there. Your father was not as lucky though. When his parents moved away he became trapped. And once it became known that he wasn't going to be let out...

'I hate to think what happened to him then. I fear that whatever it was may have changed him forever.'

CHAPTER 30

The first sign something was wrong was the sight of the frantic officer running back down the driveway to where he should have been sitting all nice and warm in his car. The panic in his movements suggested that the worst of all possible scenarios had already taken place. Ólafur and I looked at each other and urged the horses on with swift digs to their flanks. It didn't take much to shift my imagination into overdrive and conjure up the horror that I thoroughly anticipated would await us inside. We had left him alone at a time when we should have been staying as close to each other as possible. My curiosity had forced me into addressing a past I knew nothing about but one I thought I needed to understand.

But at what cost? We had left him alone and Daníel had come back to finish off his nemesis once and for all.

I've often wondered how it was that we failed to hear the final thunderclap of my father's life. Lost in conversation about his childhood, or what had passed for a childhood in the bedrooms and shower stalls of his surrogate home, we had both somehow missed it. As we raced back towards the house the noise had disappeared on the breeze. I had been so busy worrying about the demon who had been left loose in the countryside that we had forgotten about the one within.

As I ran into the house stammering my father's name I didn't know what to expect. The worst, of course – it was the only thing I had left to expect. And it was what I got. The first thing I noticed as I dropped my gaze away from his face was that he had only one shoe on.

Sitting in his favourite chair, he had curled his big toe around the trigger of his shotgun and fired it straight into his mouth. The story that he and Ólafur had started all those years ago in Höfn was finally over, really over.

I could hear Ólafur gasp noisily behind me as he finally entered the living room. I wanted to tell him not to follow me inside, not to come anywhere near what was left of my father but it was too late by the time the thought had fallen from my head to my useless tongue.

'Oh my dear Lord,' he said quietly as the vision of Dad's death almost took his voice away too.

I turned away from my father slowly and tucked my head into Ólafur's neck. I felt a lone tear fall from his face onto my ear. He held me like that until we could hear the ambulance arriving then he led me outside so they could inspect the terrible damage Dad had done to himself first-hand. It wasn't a job you would wish upon anybody. Their poor pale faces as they carried him out of the house made me shudder at what I knew could only be an accurate reflection of my own private horror.

It would be a week before we could bury Dad and my sisters. Ólafur asked if he could stay for the funerals. A request I was in no position to turn down, but after that, he was going to have to be on his way. Whatever had brought him to see us all the way from Höfn had to now be considered as finished. The end of the matter.

I had some big decisions to make and a whole new life to adjust to. There was nothing that I could have done to prepare myself for being that alone. The speed at which it had occurred had left me struggling continually to adjust from one disaster to the next.

Now that it was over, my very soul ached from the constant swivelling and realigning that my insides had been doing. I was dizzy from the pain and sick from the loss. My sisters and my father were going into the ground but it was I who wanted to lie down and never get up again.

Grímur came to visit the two of us. I was angry with him for being right all along but not being smart enough to know who it had been and how to stop him. I was angry with a lot of things I shouldn't have been angry with but if you've ever lost someone close to you, you'll understand why that was.

One of the things he asked me was what I was planning to do now. Now that everything had gone. Where was I going to live was what I think he meant. I had already decided to move into the house that was already mine and look after the horses. They meant a great deal to me and were all I had left.

Not only that, but in what could sometimes be a rather claustrophobic city I had gained the sort of notoriety that I would never be able to lose. No matter what I went on to do with my life I was always going to be 'that girl'. Even if people didn't know me I was going to think they were looking at me because they had seen me on the news and felt sorry for me. I couldn't swim through all that pity; my legs would give out and I would drown. I just knew it.

I tried to stick it out in the flat on Vesturgata for a few nights but the only memories that were left in the place were bad ones. I finally picked up Kristjana's cello from a storage cupboard at Harpa. The girl who found it for me didn't ask where its owner had been all this time. She already knew. It was those silent looks that I would never be able to deal with. Even when they were gone I would still imagine them everywhere.

It had been Kristjana's desire to get the instrument back that had led her into accepting a lift from Daníel and cost her her life. Once I had introduced them I made it so easy for him to wait for the right moment to bump into her again and offer her another lift somewhere. I was afraid the guilt would leave me bloated and useless, unable to function or to feel.

The painting I had done of Daníel the day they met was another brutal reminder of how openly I had embraced him. That, along with everything else I didn't need from my flat and Kristjana's, I simply got rid of. The painting I left on the footpath outside the backpackers' hostel across the street with a note on it saying that anyone who wanted it could have it. Eventually, it disappeared. Who knows, maybe to this day a student somewhere is still boring friends with the story of how they found the free painting of the naked man's rear end in Iceland.

Everything else I gave away to a charity for families still suffering from the economic crisis. The house already had everything I needed and I didn't want three of everything. The only thing of any real note I hung on to was my beloved coffee maker.

The night before the funeral I decided to wait for Ólafur to go to bed and then have a drink. I'd been feeling more numb than sad and I thought getting drunk might help me get upset. I wanted to get as much of it out of my system as I could before the service and having a sore head would give me something to focus on apart from the machinations of thanking people for showing up and the banal speeches about how they had all died too soon. I wasn't even sure if that were true in one case. There had been plenty of times since his death that I wondered how much suffering could have been avoided if my father had put that gun into his mouth years ago. I might have even pulled the trigger for him myself and that way he could have died with both shoes on.

In the cupboard where he hid his booze I found a nearly full bottle of vodka. I was a little surprised that he hadn't finished it off before shooting himself. It somehow betrayed his otherwise uniformly selfish principles. As I retrieved the bottle, counting my lucky stars that a trip into Hafnarfjörður wasn't required to get alcohol I noticed a pile of envelopes stashed away in a nice, neat little bundle.

My curiosity forced me to pull them free from their hiding place for a closer examination. One of them had my name on it in my father's handwriting. Some of them were in near perfect condition whereas others had been torn in two or badly crumpled up. Some had been ripped apart and disfigured almost beyond recognition. I started with the one addressed to me and removed its contents with more than a little trepidation. As soon as I had, I wished I'd never touched any of them.

It was a plain sheet of white paper. The kind that I had seen before in Elín's office and in Kristjana's flat. This one also had a message on it. In fact it had two of them.

Typed in black on it were the words:

*You have been weighed on the scales
and found wanting.*

And in my father's handwriting underneath it simply said:

Ylfa, I have become too soiled for you to take back.

Try as I might over the years to become someone good, someone better than I had once been, I failed.

I am what I always was and could never be anything more.

Always remember we can only be judged by the decisions we make. I have made many and nearly all of them have been bad. Some of them terrible.

I truly wish I could have been someone else.

As I opened the other envelopes I knew what their contents would all say but I opened them anyway. They were all there, all five of them I had seen before.

The one Inga Björk had shown me the day I had gone to help my father not knowing that it was about to cost me everything:

I had a dream that made me afraid.
As I was lying in my bed,
the images and visions that passed
through my mind terrified me.

The one I had found written in Jóhannes's flat:

Let him be drenched with the dew of heaven,
and let him live with the animals.

The one from Elín's office wall:

Suddenly the fingers of a human hand appeared
and wrote on the plaster of the wall.

And Kristjana's flat:

His face turned pale
and he was so frightened
that his knees knocked together
and his legs gave way.

And the one I'd read thinking that they might just be the last words I was ever meant to see:

God has numbered the days of your reign
and brought it to an end.

I opened the bottle of vodka and drank from it until I thought I would throw up, and then I drank some more. As I sat on the floor crying like I had many times as a little girl and I'd hurt my knees playing outside, I was finally able to let go. His betrayal of us was complete. He had known what was going on the whole time. Daníel had been telling the truth.

My father had not only known what was coming, he had even received prior notice of it in the mail. The letters I had witnessed him throwing across the living room in anger at Jóhannes had contained the blueprint to our downfall and he had just sat there and kept it all to himself. He had let it happen. All I wanted to do was bury him. And the next day, that was just what we did.

CHAPTER 31

We buried my father and both my sisters next to my mother in the plots Dad had reserved for us years ago in the Gufuneskirkjugarður Cemetery in Grafarvogur, just to the east of the city centre. The service was held at our local church in Hafnarfjörður, the Hafnarfjarðarkirkja. Despite the persistent and annoying rain, a lot more people than I had ever anticipated showed up to farewell my sisters. Everyone from Elín's work came. Bjarki and Elias had closed their legal practice for the day so that even the receptionist could attend along with several others, who I assumed were clients. It was oddly comforting listening to their commiserations and sympathetic comments. Bjarki and Elias seemed to feel responsible for letting Daníel, or Baldvin as they had also known him by, into her life and thereby ending it. Somehow the guilt they felt helped me deal with my own. It was possible that it was simply too heavy a burden to carry all alone. I tried to explain to them that he would have got to her one way or another even if he hadn't been taken on at their firm. I assured them that he had done a very good job of fooling everybody, me most of all.

Kristjana's friends from the orchestra showed up as well. Every single person she had performed with at Harpa, in fact, all fifty-six of them. She had only rehearsed with them for a relatively short time but had obviously made an impression. One by one they all came to see me and hugged me or told me how sorry they were for my loss. For someone who was supposed to be the most unsociable of the three of us she had somehow wound up knowing the most people. It heartened me to think that she had finally found her own little niche, even if it had been too late to have changed the outcome of her life. A handful of them were as socially awkward as she had been. Maybe if she had lived she would have met someone of her own to settle down with and surprised us all even more.

I knew the minister's face from the day we buried our mother. It had been a very long time since any of us children had been to his church but he had once known both my parents very well. He looked truly appalled to be presiding over the burial of the rest of the family. I guess he couldn't quite believe what had happened, either.

The only unpleasant surprise of the day was the appearance of Grímur. When I first saw him, I found I was still very angry with him for not having taken me seriously when Elín first went missing and for threatening to arrest me for sticking my nose in where it didn't belong. It was a feeling that I should have got over after everything I had been through, especially since I had been wrong about who had been responsible, but I hadn't. It wasn't that he didn't arrest Aron Steingrímsson on the spot when I had demanded that he do so, it was that he just hadn't taken me seriously enough.

I had known in my heart that something was really wrong and I had suffered the ignominy of being ignored for whatever reason. Maybe I had been acting a little irrationally, maybe I had just been too young for the old detective to take seriously, but I had been right. And that was still eating away at me. I remembered telling him when Elín first disappeared that I would never forgive him if anything ever happened to her, and I guess I hadn't.

I tried to put those feelings to one side as I made my way over to him once everyone else had begun to find their way out of the cemetery to the shelter of their cars. I wondered why he had bothered showing up at all.

The fact that Daníel still hadn't been captured wasn't lost on me and I couldn't help thinking that Grímur was probably just keeping an eye on anywhere he might show himself again. For him it would always be about the job and he probably felt as if he had failed somewhat on this case. The killer was still on the loose and that had to reflect poorly on him.

There had been plenty of questions in the media since my escape about how something like this could have possibly happened. Questions that would probably never be satisfactorily answered. He waved somewhat hesitantly as I approached him, looking a little nervous, I thought.

'Hello, Ylfa.'

'Hello, Grímur.' I really didn't have anything else I wanted to say to him, or just couldn't think of anything else.

'That was some turnout.' He looked as uncomfortable as I felt, which somehow heartened me.

'Did you think Daníel would be stupid enough to show himself today?' I had to ask the question.

'We're going to get him sooner or later, Ylfa. There's just not enough places for someone that injured to hide. You'll see.'

'I can't help thinking that most of this could have been avoided if something had been done sooner.'

I shielded my face from the rain as best I could and stared at him. If he didn't feel responsible for their deaths, he should have. I was cold from the loss of my family, but not cold enough to not burn with the injustice of it all.

'Maybe if we had known where to look in the first place we might have been able to do something. Your father didn't do any of us any favours. He must have known what was going on at some point, or had his suspicions, anyway. Maybe he didn't know exactly what was going to happen but he was the only one who could have put a stop to it all.'

I nodded. He was right, of course. I couldn't tell him about all the notes I had found in the kitchen now. For some reason, I couldn't do anything that might make him feel better about himself or what had happened.

'Of all these people here today, I've only ever met a handful of them before. I don't think we're like normal people. Elín, for all her money and toys didn't have a single friend in the world. That was what she was really running away from. Kristjana only met her friends in the orchestra recently and I don't have anyone left. No one. The last two guys I saw, one wound up dead and the other tried to kill me.

'Dad had one person he knew show up to his own funeral, and he hadn't seen him in sixty years. It's like we've been unable to get close to people or we just haven't wanted to for one reason or another. Maybe there's a danger in getting too close to others. Maybe we knew that all along. The closer they get, the more damage they can do, right?'

The look on Grímur's face made me smile but I'm sure it came out as more of a grimace. He seemed lost for words and I wanted to get in out of the cold and away from all those people. I had never been close to a single one of them and I desperately wanted to be alone more than ever before. I left him to think about exactly what I had been left to deal with on my own and headed back to the car. Ólafur followed me in silence as we made our way through the drizzle and back to what was left of our lives.

CHAPTER 32

After the funeral I decided to keep on drinking, once I had gotten rid of Ólafur, that is. I told him I needed to have the place back to myself and that he was to make tracks as soon as possible back to Höfn. We barely said a word to each other on the way home. He was coming back to the house only to pick up his things and change into something more comfortable for the long trip home.

As we were making our goodbyes and I was assuring him over and over again that I would be all right on my own, he finally got around to what he had obviously wanted to say all along. He held my hands and took on an earnest tone.

'I know you must be very confused right now, Ylfa. It's only natural. You've had everyone who ever mattered taken away from you and you need to make some sort of sense of what has happened. I can't pretend to know what went on between this man and your father but you have to try to remember him the way he was with you girls when you were growing up. I knew him before whatever happened to him happened and he was a lovely boy, just like any other child of our age.

'Whoever he became, he was still your father and he brought you up to be the woman you are today. Try to remember that. He may have been far from perfect, but from what I've seen, he tried to do his best for you.'

I wanted to hit him and tell him to get out of my house and out of my life. I had been trying hard to keep it together all day and up until that point, I had succeeded. As I started to cry, he held me tight and comforted me the way Dad once would have.

I wanted to do what he had told me to do more than anything in the world. I wanted to have a father to remember, not a monster. But it was so very hard. In order to achieve that I would have to forgive him, and I wasn't sure I could do that. Not now, and probably not ever.

I pulled away slightly from Ólafur's awkward embrace and tried to regain my composure. It was a struggle at first but what I had to say, I really had to say. I hadn't been privy to any of the conversations between Dad and Ólafur since his unexpected arrival from the southeast but I couldn't have him going home with the picture in his head of the children they had once been and nothing else. He had to hear what I had heard; it was time to share that weight with another.

I told him what Daníel had told me as he had been preparing to kill me. I told him about the house he had grown up in with my father and what Daníel, the child, had suffered at his hands. I told him about the suffering that Daníel's mother, Lauga had endured.

I told him about the tortured existence that she had endured in that house somewhere near Vík and of the horrible end that she had met.

As I was letting Daníel's story flow out of me for the first time, it struck me why he had taken the time to tell me. If he had wanted to take my life just as he had taken the lives of my sisters, there is no question that I would already have died. It struck me that maybe he had wanted nothing more than for his story to live on, and for someone to take him seriously. He had gone to great lengths to get our attention and once he had me as a captive audience, it had been imperative for him to pass on what he had been through to another soul. I couldn't help thinking that maybe I had been meant to get away from him, just for this moment.

To do a job he never would have been able to. To somehow take his place in this world as he was about to pass on to wherever it was that people like him went.

Ólafur listened in complete silence, the look of disbelief obvious on his old, tired face. When I was finished he hugged me again and told me that it would be better if I didn't listen to the advice of old fools any more.

'I was in the hands of one monster but all he wanted me to know was that I had been living with another one my whole life. He was a lie, everything he built here was just so that no one would ever know who he really was.

'We paid for this place, us girls. Elín and Kristjana paid with their lives and now I get to think about what he did every day now that they're gone.'

Ólafur kissed me on the forehead, picked up his little travel bag and made his way out to his car. I had finally got my wish. I was alone. So very, very alone.

At first the drinking was just to get to sleep when I felt there was no other way but then after a few days it was just to have a reason for getting out of bed in the morning. Not long after that I couldn't even look myself in the mirror without a few drinks first. And even then, I didn't much like what I saw.

The horses found the new smell coming off me slightly off-putting too. Leppatuska even threw me one afternoon when I was feeling especially the worse for wear. She had never thrown me from the saddle before in all the time I'd been riding her but something had caused her to fear her rider and I blamed the drink.

It was as I was sitting on the cold tightly packed soil of the riding trail that a couple of things came to me through my newly acquired fog. One: I was going to have to stop drinking, and soon.

Even I was having trouble recognising myself so it was no surprise that the horses didn't know me any more. And two: I was sure that we had only ever had four horses.

As Leppatuska ignored my obvious discomfort and helped herself to a nibble of something or other on the side of the trail I found myself with time to think.

Since Dad's death I'd had plenty of time to go over all the things I could remember him telling me, trying to pick the lies from the half-truths, as it were. He had managed to keep from lying to us by simply not telling us very much about himself. Whether it was our mother or us children, he had always kept himself to himself. A shroud of secrecy had hung over his past like a mist until we had all learned not to bother him any more. There was one thing he had said to me, however, that now stood out as nothing but a lie. We had only ever had four horses.

The day we buried our mare, Magga, he had told me of the existence of a fifth horse, which I now knew beyond any doubt to be a lie. It's always the little things that eventually catch you out. When we had been digging her grave and I'd hit something with my spade it had definitely been bone. It had, however, definitely not been a horse as Dad had said at the time.

As soon as I made a move for Leppatuska she reared away from me. It was clear that she'd had enough and I was going to have to wait to win her over again. She knew her way home, as did I, so I left her grazing on moss and lichen and set off on foot back to the house. I had some digging to do.

Even though the recent heavy rain had done much to loosen the ground again it took much longer than I expected. My ordeal in Hella and my recent drinking had left me in poor shape and I had to keep stopping every few minutes to catch my breath. On top of that I simply was terrified of what I might unearth. Eventually, though, I managed to get the hole down to roughly where we had buried Magga but I veered off to the side much as I had the first time around only this time on purpose. Dad had marked the grave well with flowers and a neat outline of stones so I soon found myself once again in the right spot.

This time, though, I knew what I was looking for. Or rather who. The connection my spade finally made with something solid made me cringe all the way down to my boots and I suddenly found myself wanting a drink, badly. A quick dash back to the house to the extensive selection of bottles I had recently acquired from three different outlets of Vínbúðin across the city and I had what I wanted. I had been visiting different shops each time I went out so as to not appear like a hopeless alcoholic but at the end of the day the only person I had managed to fool was myself.

I sat at the top of the hole I had just dug sipping from a bottle of aniseed-flavoured Opal and waited for the thick sticky drink to do its job and warm me up. It didn't take long; it never does with that stuff.

I scraped away what soil I could from the exposed piece of bone I had unearthed with the spade and then got down on my hands and knees and went about it with my hands.

Inch by inch the shape revealed itself; there could be no mistaking what it was this time around. The blackened eye sockets filled with dark volcanic soil stared up at me accusingly as though I had rudely interrupted a very private moment and that was exactly what I had done. I had to be sure it was who I thought it was so I dug further down the skeleton to where the legs had to be. As I uncovered the feet I knew I was right. One foot had been badly damaged by something that had passed right through it, snapping several bones on its way.

Once again just using my fingers, I worked my way up the leg until I found the other break. The tibia had also been fractured in what must have been a violent twisting motion. She would have been completely unable to move once her leg had been broken like that. Once again Daníel had been true to his word. Lauga had perished in exactly the fashion he had described to me. I wondered how many times she had been buried and dug up again until she'd finally come to rest where she was now.

I leaned back on the mound of dirt I'd created and took another drink. I was exhausted but I wasn't quite done yet. I pulled myself up and made my way back to the house.

I felt cold and empty even though I had the warm drink inside me. I stood in the kitchen staring at the phone and the pile of letters I'd found in the cupboard. I drank from the bottle in my hand and stared long and hard at the phone. I drank from the bottle in my hand and stared long and hard at the letters. I repeated the process over and over again until I had made up my mind.

The wind blew my hair across my eyes as I let go of the small bundle and watched the letters fall into the grave along with Magga and Lauga. Rain had begun to fall, casually at first but then hastening in its need to hit the ground. In spite of its freezing drops I took my time refilling the hole. There would be plenty of time to rest soon. For now it was enough that the cycle my father had got himself and those around him trapped in was broken.

When I was done I walked slowly back to the house with the empty bottle in my hand. It would be the last time I ever drank.

CHAPTER 33

Stefán Jón's parents finally made their way to Reykjavík from the small town in the north of the country where he had been born. They were simple people who had never understood their son's need to come to the big city to find his way in life. They were remarkably unsurprised at what had come to pass, having always seen the place as an ending and not, as he did, as a beginning.

The service was attended by a large number of people who they had never known and quite possibly never wanted to meet. I think they found the whole experience rather unpleasant. The harder everyone tried to make them feel as if they were among friends, the more they realised they weren't. They were far from home and surrounded by strangers, who had made a friend of their son only to lose him in a way none of them would ever fully understand. If anyone had ever been in the wrong place at the wrong time, it was Stefán Jón Tryggvason. He had just been trying to help and it had cost him his life.

His parents insisted on taking his body back to Húsavík with them. They wanted their son to go home. They had always wanted him to go home, just not that way. At least now he would be where they had felt all along that he belonged. They told me that Reykjavík had ruined their lives and that they would never return and I couldn't blame them.

The next day I got a letter in the post that almost made me take to the bottle again. The message inside was simple and all too familiar. The kind I had hoped I would never set eyes on ever again.

*I, Daniel, was deeply troubled by my thoughts,
and my face turned pale, but I kept the matter to myself.*

There was always going to be the possibility that he would come back to kill me but I truly felt that if he had wanted to and had been able to, then he would have done so already. I felt that in some strange way he hadn't really wanted to kill me in that hut. I have no doubt that he was planning to do just that but I also feel now that he may have just been happy for the truth to leave with me that day. Then again, I might just have been incredibly lucky to get out alive and been given a second chance to start all over again.

Two days later Grímur rang and told me that Daníel's body had been found by some children playing in an abandoned house not far from the police station. How he had made it back this far he couldn't quite understand. Daníel had died from complications from the wound I had given him that had never been treated properly. He died propped up against a wall in a decrepit house on a cold floor with an empty belly and with tears staining his cheeks. It was probably remarkably similar to the way he had started his life and it wasn't hard to imagine that at some point as a child, my father had found himself in a very similar state. Cold, scared and alone.

I had always thought life to be neither overly joyous nor unnecessarily cruel. Once upon a time, that was.

Mostly, it resembles a dimly lit trail down which we are all expected to struggle, together, yet each unmistakeably on their own. At first we carefully scan the rocky path ahead for its unpredictable obstacles, both imaginary and real.

Later, the distant hilltops are scoured with a mixture of great purpose and childlike fascination in the hope of catching a glimpse of that fabled happiness we had been promised but whose existence we had never fully believed in.

Further along the trail, our attention becomes more and more frequently caught by that which we have already passed until finally we trip and then fall upon the one last stone we have failed to kick from under our feet. Our mutual destination, our most common of bonds. The beacon we had sought and then followed from the day of our birth until the end of our days, as it falls from guiding star to darkened grave.

A lot of what I've done with my life has been at the expense of those around me. Not deliberately, perhaps, but done in the most selfish of manners nonetheless. Those who were meant to be closest to me I have constantly pushed away and given the briefest of considerations to. Doing so has made my troubles appear easier to deal with but it has made me seem elusive, insincere and uncaring to many. Of that I am now sure. I am, after all my father's daughter.

The truth of the matter is that it is not just an appearance of insincerity that has grown around me, it is the real thing. I have learned not to care genuinely for anyone.

It has taken the worst of times to befall me for that to change, and that is my tragedy.

And yet, it is my hope.

If there is any chance whatsoever of me finding any kind of forgiveness then it must come now in the choices I make from here on in, for they will stay with me for the rest of my days.

I am not a good person, but I can still be one.

I had known all along that what Elín once told me about our father was true. He did things to me too when I was a little girl that made me sick inside. Why I didn't say anything to her I can't tell you even now because I just don't know. I could have made her feel better. I could have helped her work through it, but I didn't. I let her suffer the same way that I had suffered for all these years and told myself that if I could hack it, then so could she.

I wouldn't have been able to save her but I just might have made her feel better. The problem was that it would have made me feel worse and that was something I wasn't going to allow.

Did I hate him for what he'd done to us? Of course I did, but he was my father and I had once loved him too. That's all I wanted to do from the very earliest days I can remember. Just love him.

It's very easy to say he should have said something to us but when I put myself in his place, I only see myself doing the same as he did.

Nothing.

Still, I don't know how he ever thought he would get away with it. On a small island, what goes around comes around; he should have known that. And you should too. Whatever you do in this life, be it good or be it not so good, it will chase you down through the long lonely years of your life. And it will catch you up.

THE END

Printed in Great Britain
by Amazon